MOMENT OF TRUTH

"You're not running now, Rait."

He wanted to, only his feet wouldn't move.

"I want you, Rait. And, dear heart, I know you want me, too."

He came toward her. Threw her against the wall between the windows where the moonlight shifted across his face and shadows turned his eyes black.

"Is this what you want, Katy?" He put his hands around her throat, tangled his fingers in the red ribbon and tightened his grasp until he could feel her pulse against his palm. He ran his hands down her chest, onto the curve of her breasts. And still he could feel it, the steady, solid beating of her heart against his palm.

And he kissed her. Not a gentle kiss, not a tender kiss. A hard kiss, a ravaging kiss which shook them both and made them feel like they'd been struck by lightning. He twisted his hands in the front of the lace corset and ripped it down the front. He followed the path of the tear with his hands. Softness like he'd never felt. Heat like he'd only dreamed about. Desire so strong it was like wine in his mouth.

He drank her kiss and pressed his body hard against hers. And his hands, those searching, groping hands, no matter where he moved them, no matter what unsoiled flesh they touched, always he could feel the beating of her heart against his palm.

Katy was on fire. Everything she was—everything she would ever be—she offered to him with her arms, her lips, and her heart where all her hopes and dreams waited for him to love her. And not just with his body, though Katy cried out for that. She wanted more. . . .

KATHY JONES

WILD WESTERN DESIRE

ZEBRA BOOKS
KENSINGTON PUBLISHING CORP.

ZEBRA BOOKS

are published by

Kensington Publishing Corp.
475 Park Avenue South
New York, NY 10016

First Printing: January, 1993

Printed in the United States of America

For all my heroes.

I'd like to thank my parents, family, and my husband for their support, and my friend Linda Chase for her unfailing encouragement during the writing of this book.

I owe a special debt of gratitude to the kind people in Colorado who aided my research efforts; Peggy McMahan of the Strater Hotel in Durango, Karen L'Argent of the First National Bank of Durango, Mary Marlin of the Grand Imperial Hotel in Silverton, and most of all, Alan Nossaman, Archive Director of the San Juan County Historical Society. His knowledge, friendship and assistance were invaluable.

I'd also like to acknowledge two of the characters in this book, Bat Masterson and Wyatt Earp, who stepped so easily from the pages of history into my imagination and my heart.

Chapter One

Rait Caldwell was early; the train was late. The wait gave him another opportunity to think about the reason he was here: to repay a favor. While he welcomed this chance to be finally rid of his debt of gratitude, he didn't want to think about why he owed it.

The day was warm, as the last three weeks had been. The spring weather was encouraging the mountain snowpack to begin its seasonal melt. The Animas River as it roared past Durango was close to overflowing with the milk-white waters of the runoff. The rushing and roaring sounds pounded at the air, almost succeeding in drowning out the unnatural sounds of the town.

Durango, Colorado had been founded by the Denver and Rio Grande Railroad to serve as a supply center for the narrow gauge line when it began its thrust into western Colorado two years ago. Situated at the southern end of the San Juan mountain range, Durango soon added to its roster of businesses an ore smelter to service the hundreds of mines in the mineral-rich mountains. The combination of being both a railroad and mining town caused the population to soar. As always, with people came crime, which was the reason Rait had originally come to Durango. That was something else he didn't want to think about, something else that was in the past.

"Twenty minutes," the station manager said. He shut his watch with a click and dropped it in his vest pocket. "Sorry you have to wait like this, Rait. This crew usually runs on time. Meeting someone?"

Rait leaned a shoulder against the corner of the station house. "A package."

The telegram he received yesterday had been unexpected. "Meet baggage Durango station 3:15 P.M. May 14. Stop. Keep one month. Stop. Return. Stop." Strange request, but then, Richard Halliday was a strange man the way he'd appeared out of nowhere just when Rait needed help a year ago. It wasn't his place to judge the man or his request, though. He owed Halliday. No matter how strange the favor, Rait intended to see it through.

The whistle of the overdue train split the still afternoon air with one long blast to signal its approach of the station. Rait crossed his arms over his chest and waited for the west-bound train to come into view. Seconds later the engine appeared, smoke from its stack staining the sky. A short blast of the whistle ordered the brakeman to begin applying brakes. Steam burst from the sides of the engine, obscuring from view the great steel wheels as they ground against the tracks.

There was a girl standing on the cattleguard. With one hand, she held onto her hat, which was only inches away from becoming a decoration for the span of elk antlers mounted on the engine right behind her head. Her other hand was pressed tight against her left breast, as though it was the only thing holding her heart in place. The expression on her face revealed she was experiencing absolute ecstasy.

That someone should be riding the cattleguard wasn't unusual. Train crews often gave eastern tourists a thrill by letting them play masthead on stretches of track considered safe from collisions with cattle. What caught and held Rait's attention even after the engine slid out of sight past the station house was how the girl was dressed. To be exact, the color of her dress. She was wearing yellow. From the ribbons of her high-crowned hat to the wind-whipped hem of her skirt, she was swathed in yellow as bright as a field of Kansas sunflowers.

Rait's interest in the girl wasn't because he'd never seen anyone dressed in so bold a color before. It was common to see the lower classes of mining camp whores flaunt themselves in flashy costumes. He was surprised that the girl would wear such a color while traveling. Travel anywhere, especially on trains, was a dirty business. Soot, dust, and uncontrolled streams of tobacco juice were just a few of the reasons a person should wear dark clothes while traveling, yet this girl had chosen to wear yellow.

Not that it was any of Rait's business what she wore, except for the last line of Richard Halliday's telegram, "ID baggage by yellow wrapping."

A cold suspicion began to grow in Rait; and with it, an even colder anger.

This was the most exciting moment of Katy Halliday's life. Since leaving New York City five days ago, she'd experienced a lot of most exciting moments. Boarding the train had been a most exciting moment. Leaving the city where she'd spent every moment of her entire life had been another. Then there had been the West Virginia incident.

While standing on the open platform between two of the passenger cars, Katy had tried to lean out far enough to escape the smell of the engine's smoke so she could smell the forests of the Appalachians. The train unexpectedly rounded a curve, she lost her balance, and had a *really* exciting moment. She'd barely even had a chance to enjoy it, though, before the conductor, a pudding-nosed man, had pulled her to safety.

Another exciting moment had been when Katy discovered an Indian on the train. She'd been walking back through the passenger cars hoping to find someone interesting to talk to, like a criminal being taken to trial, or even better, a convict escaping from jail. What she'd found was an Indian.

He was seated in the last car, the one where Negroes rode. He was disguised in a bowler hat and velvet-collared overcoat, but Katy recognized his true identity: a wild, savage, revenge-maddened Indian planning to go on a scalping rampage after everyone on the train was asleep that night.

The conductor had admonished her for having an overactive imagination. "It's true, miss, he is an Indian, but not a wild one and certainly not a savage one. And being as he's got more money than the Union Pacific itself, it's not very likely he'd be revenge-maddened, either. Grateful is what he should be that there are folks foolish enough to pay good cash money for the fake warbonnets he makes by sewing chicken feathers onto strips of old shoe leather."

Katy hadn't known which to be more upset about—that she wasn't about to be scalped or that the warbonnet hanging on her bedroom wall might be fake.

There had been other exciting moments on the trip, too, such as seeing the Mississippi and the Great Plains and the Rockies. Best of all had been riding the cattleguard for the last ten miles. What an incredible feeling to be so close to that much power; to be thrust forward at breathtaking speeds; to not just hear, but to feel the engine

11

roaring across the landscape.

And what a landscape it was! Mountains so big they were like continents, snow so white it had almost blinded her; and a river that was like a locomotive itself, charging along its track and roaring its power at the world. But not even riding the cattleguard could compare to what was about to happen.

With the aid of the engineer, Katy climbed down from the cattleguard and stepped to the ground.

She was here.

The West. The Wild West. The Real, Live Wild West!

It was more than a dream come true, more than a lifetime of dreams, more a universe of dreams. It was a heartful of dreams.

It had all started fifteen years ago. Katy had been four years old when her uncle Richard tried to read her to sleep with the first chapter of *The Wild West Adventures of America's Favorite Hero; or, How Davy Crockett Gave His Life for the Alamo and for Texas*.

It was the first dime novel her uncle had published. It had been a huge success that lifted his little print shop out of the bargain basement of New York businesses and into the forefront of the publishing industry. Not only had the book's exciting adventures kept Katy from falling asleep that night, they had awakened within her a dream to someday see the Wild West of fictional fame.

And now, here she was.

It was unfortunate this moment was taking place in Durango, Colorado, instead of where she really wanted it to be. But just because Durango was a mining town instead of a cowboy-populated den of iniquity didn't mean it wasn't a real Western town.

A few years ago, Durango had been called by newspapers, "the town to which, hell itself is a paradise." Recently, the town's description was changed to "the yellowpine metropolis of the San Juans." History counted for a lot in a town's standing, though, so it wasn't really too much of a tragedy that Katy's first official Western moment was happening in Durango.

Technically, she'd been in the West ever since her train crossed the Mississippi three days ago. She didn't consider traveling across a place as actually being there, though, since there wasn't time to see anything except the inside of station house restaurants during quick meals and the outside of station house privies during long waits. As a result, she considered this her first official moment in the West.

She was so excited, she could barely breathe. It felt like her chest was going to explode if she didn't do something, so she spun in a circle, trying to see everything at once and memorize it all.

She stopped in mid-circle. Her mouth fell open and her lips went numb. Standing in front of her was a man glaring at her with murderous intent.

What sent Katy into a state of paralysis wasn't the way he was looking at her. It was the way he looked. He was the perfect image of the latest dime novel rage, the badman hero. A cliche of adjectives and adverbs, Katy's uncle would say, and it was true. Blue eyes full of threatening danger, sensuous mouth hard with bitter anger, knotted fists poised for bloody action.

Even his clothes were a cliche, for he was dressed all in black from the top of his low-crowned hat to the soles of his spurless boots. And, to bring the overused look together, he had the perfect badman accessory strapped to his right leg, a Colt .45 Peacemaker, its silver handle gleaming in the sunlight like a deadly dare.

What all those adjectives and adverbs meant was that Katy was looking at a real, live gunfighter. That meant this was another most exciting moment.

Oh, happy day, she thought, and grinned up at him.

Of everything Rait had anticipated the girl might do, grinning wasn't one of them. It made him feel foolish.

"Who are you?" he asked, his voice so sharp it startled the railroad crew toiling beside the engine.

The girl didn't seem to mind, though. She just kept beaming at him, her face flushed and her eyes shining. Those eyes. They were the purest shade of blue-gray he'd ever seen. They sparkled so much there appeared to be soap bubbles dancing across them, causing them to shimmer like iridescent rainbows. And her hair. Whatever style she'd been wearing had been demolished by the wind, leaving a tangle of roughly tossed dark curls that looked as soft as a summer breeze and made a beautiful frame for her eyes.

"How many notches do you have?" Katy asked and leaned forward to see for herself, putting her nose on the same level as the buckle of his low-slung gun belt.

Rait took a fast step backward in response to her unexpected advance. "What are you doing?" He grabbed her shoulders and hauled her upright.

Katy was disappointed. There wasn't a single notch in the handle of his gun. Maybe he wasn't a gunfighter at all. Maybe he was a train robber. She'd never read anything about train robbers putting notches in their guns. Yes, that had to be it. She was standing right beside a train and he was surely a badman of some sort, so he must be a train robber. How exciting! She was about to see her first crime.

The only problem was that he seemed more interested in her than the train. Another possibility occurred to her. Maybe he was going to rob her!

Oh happy, happy day, she sang silently and beamed up at him again. "I'm ready whenever you are. Don't go too fast, though. I want to be able to remember everything so I can make notes later. What do I do first? Put my hands up? Or do I give you my bag first and then put my hands up?"

Katy's dime novel-inspired imagination added a new twist to the plot.

"Are you going to kidnap me, take me hostage, demand a ransom? Are you going to use me as cover against a lawman's bullets? Are you going to shoot me in the stomach and leave me to die a horrible, terrible, lingering death?" She paused for breath. When he didn't do anything, she tapped her foot impatiently. "Well? What are you just standing there for? Pull your gun and get on with it."

Rait had never heard anyone talk so much, so fast, or about so much nonsense. "If you're Richard Halliday's daughter, you can get right back up on that engine, because you're going straight back to New York, favor or no favor!"

Her smile was saucy. "I'm not Richard Halliday's daughter, so I guess that means I get to stay." She started to add that it wasn't any of his business who she was or whether she stayed or not until she realized if he knew her uncle, then she knew him. It also meant he wasn't a gunfighter or train robber or kidnapper or anything remotely similar.

He was Rait Caldwell, and Rait Caldwell was a lawman.

For Katy, the word "lawman" evoked bigger than life images from a page in Western history written by Bat Masterson and Wyatt Earp. It was five years ago that those two legendary lawmen shot their way into national headlines by taming what the newspapers had called "the wickedest city in the West," Dodge City.

And now here Katy was . . . talking to one of their kind.

Though she'd known that she was headed for an encounter with the marshal of Durango, the town's recent reputation for tameness had caused her to think he would be a stodgy old coot with a big paunch and no guts.

This unexpected turn of physical events made the missing notches an important issue again. Surely he'd killed at least one man. Western lawmen killed lots of men and for every badman they blasted to boot hill, they put a notch in their gun handle. Katy knew this for a fact, not only because she'd read every dime novel ever published about the lives and habits of lawmen, but because she'd also read every newspaper article written about them. Nearly all those stories had made reference to notches, and everyone knew newspapers *never* lie.

There was something else missing, too. "Where's your badge? I thought marshals were always supposed to wear their badges. Otherwise, how will criminals know it's the long arm of the law reaching out to stop their dastardly deeds and not just some gunslinging social climber trying to shoot them down like a dog in the dirt in order to assume their rotten reputation?"

"Who *are* you?" Rait asked again, this time in the intimidating tone of voice that had once been

17

so effective in cowering even the rowdiest trouble-makers. It didn't make much of an impression on this yellow-clad girl, though, except to cause her to quirk a delicate eyebrow at him as though questioning his sanity.

"Katy Halliday, of course," she said and laughed, which caused the rainbows in her eyes to shimmer again. "And you're Rait Caldwell, the man who's supposed to meet me, and this is Durango, Colorado, where I'm supposed to be met. Uncle Richard said he would wire all this to you and obviously he must have, because otherwise you wouldn't be here meeting this train and you wouldn't have thought I was Uncle Richard's daughter, which I didn't lie to you about before when I said I'm not his daughter . . . though I'm sort of like one since he raised me, but legally, I'm just his niece. Now that's all straightened out, we can move onto more important issues, like what happened to your badge. Did you lose it, or was it the job you lost?"

Rait's usual reaction to that question was to smash his fist into the questioner's face. He was so relieved Katy had stopped talking, though, it never occurred to him to get angry. "No, I wasn't fired, and the only thing 'Uncle Richard' wired me was to take delivery on a piece of yellow baggage."

Katy laughed. "That's what he calls me, a piece of baggage. He does it to make me mad, only it doesn't. And this isn't yellow, it's primrose, and

18

I'm wearing it because it's the brightest color in fashion this season, and I didn't want you to have trouble recognizing me. Uncle Richard told me a bow would do, but I didn't want to be overlooked so I had this outfit made special. Now that we really do have everything straightened out, here are my baggage checks. I only have a few pieces, so it shouldn't take long for you to find them. Goodness, I almost forgot, I have a letter for you." She handed him an envelope.

Rait ignored the brass baggage checks. "I'm not a porter," he said, but did take the envelope, which he ripped open.

Inside were two sheets of paper, the first a document naming him guardian of Katy Alice Halliday, ward of Richard Tarrance Halliday, while the latter was out of the country on business. The second paper was a letter from Halliday. It revealed little more than his telegram: "Caldwell, this temporary guardianship transfer is required by Katy's court-controlled trust. I'll wire you before I leave for Europe and when I get back. I know I can trust you to take good care of my girl. My gratitude for your hospitality, R. T. Halliday."

Rait folded the two papers and shoved them back in the envelope. Two thoughts instantly struck him. First, Katy's comment about having her dress specially made; now a legal document transferring her guardianship. Both proved Halliday had known for weeks, maybe months, that he was sending his niece to Rait, but hadn't bothered to inform his victim until yesterday.

So I wouldn't have time to get out of it. I've got news for you, Halliday. I'm getting out of it anyway.

"Let's go," Rait said. He grabbed Katy's right hand and pulled her through the thinning crowd and into the station house. "Give me your return ticket," he said. She looked confused, but handed over a ticket with a long attachment of transfer coupons. He gave it to Jimmy Baskins, who was wearing a green visor and working behind the ticket counter. "I want to exchange this for an immediate return ticket to New York City, Jimmy."

"You can't do that," Katy said.

"I just did."

"Sorry, Mr. Caldwell, the lady is right. This ticket is nonexchangeable and nonrefundable. It's stamped under the printed contract."

He handed it to Rait, who scanned the back of the ticket.

"If Halliday thinks this is going to stop me, he's wrong." He yanked out his wallet. "Give me one ticket, one way to New York on the next train out of Durango."

"Emigrant class?"

Rait glared at the man so intently that Katy thought he was going to shoot him. Her excitement at the prospect of gunplay was dashed when all Rait did was growl, "First class, with a sleeper berth."

"That leaves at 9:30 A.M. tomorrow morning,"

the clerk said.

Everything was happening so fast, Katy was stunned. Before she knew what was happening, Rait was throwing fifty-dollar bills on the counter and the clerk was handing her the new ticket. The initials D&RG, for the Denver and Rio Grande Railroad, were at the top. Then, instead of showing transfers to the Denver Pacific and the Union Pacific, like her original ticket, this one transferred her to the Atchinson, Topeka and Santa Fe Railroad. She stared at the AT&SF initials, unable to believe her eyes.

Rait noticed how she was looking at the ticket and surprised himself by feeling sorry for her. She'd just arrived, and now was being sent back without so much as a chance to catch her breath. But hell, what was he supposed to do? Halliday was the one to blame.

"Listen," he said, "I know this is a shock to you. Tonight I'll take you to Elitch's Oyster House for dinner. It's the best restaurant in Durango. That should make you feel better, and tomorrow I'll show you around town before your train leaves. Would you like that?"

Katy's shock had already worn off, though. "Excuse me a minute," she said to Rait and placed the ticket back on the counter. She caught the clerk's eye and pointed at the AT&SF transfer coupon. "Does this mean I'll be going east across southern Kansas?"

"Yes, ma'am. I could route you through Denver

like your other ticket, but it would mean a delay in Pueblo to make the connection north."

"No," she said and pulled the ticket out of his reach. "This is fine. I was just trying to remember where the Express stops for lunch. Dodge City, isn't it?"

"That's right. It gets into Dodge at 11:40 A.M. There's a Fred Harvey's lunch counter in a railroad car beside the station. You'll have twenty minutes before the train starts rolling again."

Twenty minutes. I'll have plenty of time to get my bags off the train.

She turned her attention back to Rait. "There's no need for you to apologize, Mr. Caldwell. I understand your decision to send me back. As for dinner tonight, oysters sound wonderful. Since I left New York, almost every meal I've eaten has consisted primarily of a lump of unidentifiable food floating in a sea of grease. I would also love a tour of Durango tomorrow morning. I will need to visit a bank before I leave so we can cash the drafts Uncle Richard gave me."

She paused, waiting for a reaction. Nothing. Apparently the drafts were another subject her uncle had neglected to include in his correspondence to Rait Caldwell. She smiled.

"I believe they've finished unloading the luggage. Shall we go see how much damage they've done to my hatboxes?"

She swept out of the station house with a lot

22

more style and elegance than Rait had given her credit for possessing. Of course, it was easy to misjudge a woman who had several hundred dead bugs splattered on the front of her jacket.

It was those bugs that aroused his suspicions. It didn't fit that a woman spunky enough to tolerate getting plastered with insects just so she could be thrilled by a ride on the cattleguard would so readily accept an abrupt termination of her holiday plans. Then there was that business about stopping at Dodge City for lunch. Why would she know where an eastbound AT&SF train stopped when she'd been ticketed to return to New York on the Union Pacific?

He pushed her original ticket across the counter at Jimmy Baskins. "Is this nonexchangeable, nonrefundable clause standard?"

"It would be on an emigrant or special tour package ticket, but that's first class, Mr. Caldwell. Whoever purchased it had to request that be added to the contract."

Rait went to the station house window and looked out at Katy. She was seated on a bench under the eaves of the station house while she wrote in a pocket notebook with a stubby little pencil. She looked quite pleased with herself and the world in general. He rubbed his thumb across the back of the ticket before folding it into his pocket.

"I want to send a telegram," he said to Jimmy, who handed him a blank telegraph form and a

23

pen.

Rait wrote several lines in a quick, sure hand. "I'll be at the Grand Central Hotel. When my reply comes in, see that I receive it immediately."

Katy was still writing when Rait came out of the station. "Where are those baggage checks?" he asked.

"I gave them to a porter." She closed her notebook and slipped it, along with her pencil, into her bag. "He's finding everything for me now. He's over there," she said, and they went to where the uniformed porter was adding a trunk to a mountain of luggage already so large that it deserved a name and a snowpack.

Rait walked around it, surveying the heap with a skeptical eye. There were three traveling trunks, half a dozen gripsacks, as many hatboxes, and one carpetbag tagged as carry-on baggage.

"A few pieces," he said and looked at her.

She had the good manners to look guilty. "I exaggerated a little."

"You exaggerated a lot."

Her blush deepened. "It wouldn't seem like so much if I were staying a month instead of one night. All I need tonight is this," she tapped the lid of the trunk closest to her, "the carpetbag, those two cases, and the blue hatbox under the small trunk beside you." Small, Rait realized, was apparently a relative term. His father used to work in mines that weren't as big as her small trunk.

24

"You need all this for just one night?"

"I want . . ." she hesitated, uncertain how to tell him she needed fresh undergarments. She'd exhausted the supply in the carpetbag that morning. "Clean linen," she finally said. "I don't remember precisely where it's packed, just that it's in one of those pieces."

Rait mentally weighed the selected baggage. Only a madman would attempt to lift it, much less try to carry it anywhere. "I'll need a wagon," he said. "I'll walk you to the hotel first."

"Hotel? I thought, I mean, I assumed I'd be spending the night with you and your wife."

Never in her life had Katy seen anyone turn so violently pale. It was frightening and revealing.

"So," she said softly, and again took the measure of this man she scarcely knew. "You lost her, too."

There was pity in her eyes. It saved Rait, pulling him back from the sharp edges of his guilt and his inadequacy.

He picked up the two grips, the carpetbag, and the battered hatbox with one hand, hoisted the trunk onto his back with the other and began walking, not looking left or right or at Katy or anywhere except straight ahead.

Chapter Two

In *Pete Pander's Big Bonanza; or, The Bungled Robbery of the Wobbly Frame Mine by the Black Hills Gang*, the hotel in the mining town of Deadwood, South Dakota had been built from old packing crates and canvas held together with wolf dung.

The Grand Central Hotel in Durango, Colorado had gold leaf French mirrors, crystal chandeliers, and was managed by Thomas Rockwood, who was the son of British nobility in the person of Sir Richard Rockwood, currently of Boston.

Thomas Rockwood stood very erect, which kept him from looking as short as he actually was. He was a little overweight and seemed to enjoy everything and everyone. He laughed at Rait's portage of Katy's luggage, complimented his strength and endurance, and suggested that a career as a jackass might better suit Rait's personality than his current occupation.

The joke wasn't well received, and roused Katy's curiosity as to what that occupation might be. Before she could ask, Thomas Rockwood was filling the lobby with laughter again and offering her sympathy for having such a bad-tempered beast of burden. Then, pretending to be cowered by Rait's glowering visage, Rockwood started issuing orders to every employee in sight, and a few who weren't.

"Ferny, take Miss Halliday's trunk to room 315. Francisco, you take the grips and the carpetbag. Polly, you have charge of the hatbox and Miss Halliday. Pearly Baker, I want you to tell Mrs. Houlihan to start heating bath water, then you go get the bathing tub in the storeroom and take it to Miss Halliday's room. Go, go, go!" He clapped his hands and people scurried to carry out his commands. "Now, Miss Halliday, if there's anything you want, short of having Caldwell put out of your misery, just ask Polly."

"Damn it, Rockwood," Rait grumbled. "Keep this up and I'm taking my business to the Inter-Ocean Hotel."

"Good, then I won't have to listen to your braying. Braying, get it? Jackass, beast of burden, braying? Ha, ha, ha!"

Katy realized that Rait's bad humor had somehow been tempered by Rockwood's teasing. She was grateful to the Grand Central's proprietor, and though it was hard to resist laughing along with him, she decided not to tempt fate.

* * *

Room 315 was big and airy, a welcome change from the confinement of the train. Because the room was on the top floor of the hotel, its north-facing window provided a spectacular view. It was from that window that Katy got her first real look at Durango. It was as surprising as the Grand Central.

The houses perched on the slopes of the mesa east of town were built in classic Victorian styles and grand enough to grace the most discriminating of New York's residential streets. Durango's business district was a well-designed area with many of its larger buildings constructed of brick. The streets were crowded with people, wagons, horses, and buggies. They gave the town a busy, excited appearance as they bustled back and forth on the long, straight avenues.

From her window, Katy could see not only the train depot, but also its roundhouse, service yard, and a set of silvery tracks slicing north through the city. The train tracks served as a dividing line between the attractive business district and a shantytown section. Katy guessed the shantytown served as Durango's red light district and the last stronghold of the town's old fire and brimstone spirit.

The red light district's narrow streets and ramshackle buildings covered every inch of space between the railroad tracks and the Animas River, which looked capable of breaking over its banks at any moment and sweeping the whole untidy mess away. On the other side of the river was the town's ore smelter. It poured ugly smoke into the air and across the barren slopes of the hill behind its fuming stacks.

Though intrigued by the town, Katy's attention kept straying to the view beyond Durango. In the distance, looming great and beautiful against the sky, were the majestic peaks of the San Juan Mountains. These weren't hills shaped like mountains, but true mountains whose lofty heights gleamed white with lingering winter snows.

Some of that snow, Katy knew, was eternal, never melting, always shining bright and bold against the porcelain skies. How strange it must be in the summer to see snow.

"Your bath is ready, Miss Halliday," Polly said.

Bath. The word was like music. Katy had never felt so dirty in her life, not even the time she spilled printer's ink all over her. It had taken weeks for the permanent stain to wear off. She hoped the week's worth of transcontinental dirt which stained her now would be easier to wash away. Without even a moment's regret at abandoning the lovely vista outside her window, she began undressing.

* * *

She washed and soaped and scrubbed and shampooed and washed again. Polly slathered strange smelling concoctions on Katy's face, hair, and hands. The concoctions were allowed to dry, then scraped off, along with several layers of skin. Only after both Katy and Polly were satisfied that not a single gram of grime could possibly have escaped their labors did they begin the tedious task of getting Katy ready for dinner.

First came her hair, which had to be untangled, dried, brushed and arranged into a delicate arrangement of dark curls and tortoiseshell combs. A creamy softening lotion was rubbed on selected parts of her body, powder was dusted on others, perfume sprayed on the rest. Then they began sorting through the contents of the trunk, grips, and hatbox in a quest to decide what she should wear.

The decision kept getting delayed by yawns. The effects of the long train ride and the exhausting bath had made Katy so sleepy, she could hardly see straight. She longed for a nap, but Rait had sent word that if she wasn't in the lobby at 6:30 P.M. sharp, "I won't wait and you won't eat."

Because her hunger was just as great as her need for a nap, Katy refused to even look at the big iron bed with its soft feather mattress and big fluffy pillows and clean crisp sheets and snugly down comforter in fear that she would nod off just at the thought of how wonderful it would be to lie down on a real bed again.

Polly suggested Katy select something warm to wear because the high altitude often made spring nights in Durango quite cold. Katy appreciated the advice and chose a peacock-blue dress made of Zephyr wool. It was very stylish with its tight sleeves, layered draperies that fell to the floor in a train, and delicate edging of black lace on the collar and cuffs, bodice and draperies. With that decision made, the dress was sent to the hotel laundry room for pressing while the layering of undergarments began.

First came a lacy pair of drawers, which Katy called pantalettes, even though that fashion item had gone out of style twenty years ago. "Drawers sounds like I'm putting on a piece of furniture," she explained, causing Polly to break into a fit of giggles.

The chemise, which was just as lacy as the pantalettes, came next, then a corset. Shaped by gussets and stiffened with whalebone, it hooked in the front, a design intended to make dressing easier. However, by the time an increasingly sleepy Katy had hooked it up crooked twice, both she and Polly were laughing so hard that they thought they were going to have to send for reinforcements to get the thing on right.

31

Finally, breathless and a little punchy with laughter, Katy let Polly handle the chore and soon her natural shapeliness was transformed into a French corset maker's idea of proper fashion form.

Her stockings were black with tiny flowers embroidered over each ankle with sparkling jet beads. The stockings were normally held up by suspenders fastened at the waist, but she'd forgotten to put them on under the pantalettes and wasn't about to undo everything and start again. Instead she unearthed a pair of garters from the bottom of the trunk and bound the tops of her stockings with elastic. Then she pulled the elastic cuffs on her pantalettes legs down over them. Between the two layers of elastic and the corset, Katy felt like a dumpling that was about to implode.

"How many petticoats?" Polly asked.

"Just three tonight," Katy decided. She sorted through her extensive collection of petticoats until she found the three that would best enhance the lines of the blue dress.

Polly fastened the petticoats around Katy's waist with their wraparound tapes and Katy fluffed the stiff organdy ruffles on the back of the top petticoat to give just the right amount of lift to the draperies on the back of the dress.

"I'll see if Mrs. Houlihan's finished pressing your dress," Polly said.

Katy spent a few minutes rearranging her hair, then drifted to the window again. A gentle wind was ruffling the tops of Durango's few trees. She opened the window, pulled a chair close, and sat down to wait for Polly's return.

This was the first chance she'd had to relax since her arrival. It felt nice. The breeze coming through the open window was cool and fresh. It smelled of pine and the river, of wood smoke and the moist, rich earth.

Katy folded her arms on the windowsill and rested her chin on her arms. With a soft sigh, she watched the entire western sky turn a beautiful rose pink that reflected on the slopes of the distant mountains and flamed like firelight on their snowy crests.

New York, the train, even Dodge City seemed very far away.

And while the lamps that lined the street below her were lit, one by one, so that their hazy, yellow light could chase away the deepening twilight, Katy forgot how angry Rait would be if she was late for dinner. She forgot how pale he'd turned when she mentioned his wife. She forgot everything except how long the sunset was lasting and how blue his eyes were and what a pity it was that she couldn't spend a little more time in Durango.

She hadn't expected to feel this way. She could blame her interest on Durango being such a pretty town. Or that its history was interesting. But the truth was that it simply wasn't every day a woman came face to face with a man who looked exactly like a dream come true.

It was 6:35 P.M. Rait felt like he'd spent all day waiting for this girl.

"Five minutes?" Thomas Rockwood asked. "That's nothing, Rait. Women are always a half hour late, at the least. Sit down, have a drink, smoke a cigar, do anything, but stop pacing around my lobby. You're making my other guests nervous."

"I'm not waiting a half hour. I told her that I wouldn't wait one minute."

"Then why did you wait five?"

"Because I have a soft heart," Rait said.

Rockwood burst into laughter. "Soft heart, that's a good one! Ha, ha, ha!"

"Keep it up, little man, and I'll put another hole in that head of yours."

Thomas Rockwood laughed louder.

Rait scowled at him. "You could at least have the good manners to pretend to be frightened when you're being threatened by a man wearing a gun."

"Frightened by what? That you might shoot me? Shooting people is a crime in this city. We both know that you'd rather be eaten by cannibals than commit a crime. That little lady upstairs is something you should be afraid of, though. Those eyes and that smile of hers might just make you remember that there's more to life than earning money and threatening your friends."

"Enough," Rait said and took the steps two at a time to the third floor.

The maid that Rockwood had instructed to help Katy was in the hall outside room 315.

"Where is Miss Halliday?" Rait asked.

The girl's arms were full and she was struggling to open the door. "She's dressing, sir."

"Maybe if you were helping her, she'd be finished by now."

"I am helping her. This is her dress, only I can't get the door open without dropping and wrinkling it."

"Here." Rait threw the door open, but instead of letting the maid enter, went in himself.

The place looked like the aftermath of a ruffle factory explosion. The whole room was swathed in frothy female finery. It spilled from the trunk, was strewn across the gripsacks, covered the bed, and dripped from the washstand. And not just ruffles. There was lace, too, and ribbons and bows, buttons and embroidery, silk and satin, and cotton so fine that it was almost transparent.

The maid rushed into the room behind him. "Sir, you shouldn't be in here!"

She was right. This was the last place on earth Rait should be, but he was unable to leave. He'd never been in a room so full of soft things.

At the end of the ruffled gauntlet of under-clothes was Katy. She was curled into a chair in front of the window that framed the last breath of sunset glowing on the distant snowy peaks like a picture. She was asleep, her head propped on her arms, her face turned toward the mountains.

He'd noticed her eyes before and the masses of her dark hair. He hadn't noticed her face, though. Now it captured him with its gentle repose, its soft features, the color that warmed her skin like a shy blush.

Angie had been beautiful. She'd also been delicate, like spun sugar. Sometimes Rait had been afraid that if he touched her, the warmth of his hands would cause her to melt away. And when he did touch her, she had shivered beneath his caress.

Only it hadn't been a shiver.

Katy wasn't like Angie. She wasn't made of spun sugar and she wasn't beautiful. She was pretty, though; the kind of prettiness that made him think of laughter and teasing and having fun. When he'd first seen her, he'd thought of her as a child. Then, when she accepted his dictate that she return immediately to New York, she had displayed the maturity of a woman. Now, again, she was a child, reaching out to him with innocent appeal, reminding him how long it had been since he had wanted to do any of the things her pretty face promised. Laughing. Teasing. Having fun.

"Shall I wake her, sir?"

Rait shook his head. "Let her sleep."

"In the chair?" The maid sounded horrified.

He considered the option. He didn't want to touch her, to feel that young body in his arms, to touch the ruffles and lace that she wore. Angie had never worn lace. She had worn plain cotton and stiff wool and starched muslin. No silk. No satin. No ruffles that looked as soft as moonlight.

"Clear off the bed," he told the maid, and walked slowly across the room.

He bent to take Katy in his arms. He felt the warmth of her body and smelled the scent of her perfume, like spring wildflowers, like sunlight, like a Sunday picnic in the country. She turned and curled into his embrace, exhaling a little sigh as her head fell against his chest.

He was sweating. Cold sweat. Fear sweat.

He turned and moved to the bed. He put his burden on the snowy white sheets and stepped quickly back so the maid could pull the comforter over the still sleeping Katy.

37

"I'll check on her later, sir," the maid said.

Rait felt clumsy and stiff as he walked to the open door and the lamp-lit hallway beyond. Hanging from the footboard of the bed was a waterfall of petticoats. They brushed against his hand. His heart stopped beating. His legs would not move. His palms turned clammy and his arms went numb. Only his fingertips were still alive, and they reached out to touch the alien softness of a ruffle. Rait held it for a moment, then let it go, the way he'd never been able to let Angie go.

Chapter Three

Rait entered the Grand Central's dining room with enough force to cause people to turn and look at him. The only one he looked at, though, was Katy, who was the only person in the room not looking at him.

She was at a table near the center of the room, her dark head bent, her attention directed solely on the plate before her. Actually, it was plates, a good half dozen of them already empty and another three still containing food, from which steam rose to waft and curl around her head like wisps of smoke.

It irritated Rait that she didn't have enough sense to order food like a lady.

As he stalked into the room, the other diners pretended they hadn't been staring at him by concentrating on their own breakfasts. By the time he reached Katy's table, everyone in the room was eating so fast that the noise of their forks hitting their plates sounded like gunfire.

Katy didn't appear to notice it or him. She just kept devouring a serving of poached eggs with an intensity that implied her life depended on it. Rait yanked out the chair across the table from her, turned it backwards and straddled it, using it as a barrier between them.

She wasn't wearing yellow today. She'd chosen something more suitable for travel, a charcoal gray suit with a snug jacket trimmed with twinings of narrow black braid. The charcoal and black colors made her hair look darker and richer. Beneath her jacket, she wore a white blouse with lace cuffs that decorated her wrists and a lace collar that stood up around her throat in a pretty ruff.

It reminded Rait of the petticoat he'd touched last night, how soft and feminine it had been. He shifted uncomfortably in his chair and tried not to wonder if she was wearing that petticoat now.

His movement in the chair drew her attention. Her face brightened and she smiled.

"Good morning! Isn't it a lovely day? I haven't been out but I've looked through nearly every window in the hotel and it's a beautiful morning. Thank you for letting me sleep last night, though I do wish we'd had a chance to eat. I was so hungry when I woke this morning,

40

I was afraid I would starve to death before I could dress and come down for breakfast. I ordered for you, too, only I didn't know what you like, so I just ordered everything. Most of it, I'm embarrassed to admit, I've eaten myself, but I left the best for you. This trout, which looks divine, the biscuits, and a cup of coffee."

Rait was amazed. Didn't she ever breathe?

"I'm looking forward to seeing Durango this morning," she said, and he realized that he'd just missed the only opportunity he might have to speak all day. "I want to see where Henry Moorman was lynched for killing a man on a Sunday, where Ike Stockton's gang of rustlers shot it out with New Mexico cowboys, and where Clay Allison robbed the Durango stage. Oh, and I don't want to forget to cash those drafts before I leave. Mr. Rockwood told me both the First National Bank and the Bank of Durango are just a few blocks away, which means it won't take long to finish my business."

Katy didn't want to linger too long on the subject of the drafts, but couldn't afford to ignore it, either. A town tour was interesting, cashing those drafts was crucial.

"Were you the marshal who shot Ike Stockton to death when he tried to resist arrest?" she asked and her eyes widened suddenly. "I'm so sorry, I shouldn't have asked that. I realize

41

you're sensitive about losing your job. I hope I haven't upset you."

Rait didn't feel in the least upset. He felt murderous.

She was concentrating on her plate again. Her eyes closed and her face assumed an expression of ecstasy as she ate the last bite of bright, yellow egg yolk.

She gave a little sigh of regret that the meal was over. "Those were the most delicious eggs I've ever eaten."

"They were snake eggs," Rait said. "Rockwood keeps a shed full of snakes out back. He prefers them to chickens because they lay more than one egg at a time."

She went as pale and stiff as the starched cotton tablecloth. And her eyes, those incredible rainbow eyes, stared at him in an expression of horror. "Excuse me. I left something in my room." She ran out of the dining room like a schoolboy who had just taken his first sip of rotgut whiskey.

Rait allowed himself a silent chuckle before turning his chair around so he could eat. When Katy returned several minutes later, she looked shaken and subdued. She sat with an almost hesitant uncertainty, as though afraid that before she got all the way down, she would need to run out again.

The waitress came rushing to the table. "Are you ill, miss?"

Katy shook her head. "I'm fine. Will you take this, please?" She shoved the yellow stained plate away.

"Did you want something else, miss?"

"Yes," she said, and Rait could see the effort it was taking for her to control the tremor in her voice. "I'd like another serving of eggs, please."

He was so surprised, he spilled coffee all over the table.

Katy sat as silent and pale as a marble statue until the waitress returned with her second order of eggs. There was no doubt in Rait's mind that his young charge would rather face a hangman's noose than have to look at them. He pushed his plate back, tipped his chair onto its rear legs, crossed his arms over his chest and waited to see what happened next.

With a shaking hand, Katy dusted the eggs with salt, picked up her fork, and began to eat.

Bite after agonizing bite, she lifted the pieces of egg to her mouth, where she thoroughly chewed each one, then swallowed. It felt like hours before the last morsel of slippery white matter was forked, lifted, and swallowed. She could feel it sliding down her throat and all the way to her stomach.

The task completed, she forced herself to carefully place her fork on the side of her plate so as not to give Rait any clue to her inner turmoil.

"That was . . ." She couldn't make herself say delicious. The very thought of the word made her stomach heave. "Excu . . ." She abandoned her pretended calm, along with her chair, and bolted from the room.

The stairs to the upper floors of the Grand Central were at the far side of the lobby. She knew without a doubt that she would never make the staircase, much less her room.

"Katy?" It was Rait. He was towering over her like the mountains that towered over Durango.

She opened her mouth to speak, couldn't, and covered her mouth with the back of her right hand. She clenched her left hand into a fist and pressed it to her rebelling stomach.

Rait didn't need to know anymore. "This way," he said and put an arm around her for support.

He half-pulled, half-carried her down the hall at the back of the lobby and out a shadowed door into a bright alley. A row of slop cans lined the back wall of the hotel. He threw off the lid of the nearest one and pushed Katy against it. He kept one hand around her waist and put the other on her forehead to hold her steady while her body relieved itself of its second helping of snake eggs.

When she was left with nothing but the aftertaste of being sick, Rait propped her against the wall and handed her a clean handkerchief.

"Is this why you left the dining room the first time?" he asked.

She nodded. She'd never been so humiliated, or so sick, in her life. She'd have wished for death, but she didn't want to do anything to jeopardize getting on that train to Dodge.

"Then why did you order another serving?"

"I wanted to be able to say that not only did I eat snake eggs for breakfast, I had seconds."

Rait laughed. He couldn't help it. She might be an irritation and inconvenience, but she wasn't boring.

"I want to show you something," he said. Taking her hand, he led her down the alley to a ramshackle shed surrounded by a fenced yard. Inside the yard and the open shed were chickens, dozens of them cackling, scratching, and preening.

"You lied," Katy said. Her stomach was beginning to feel better.

"I wanted to get back at you for this." Rait took from his pocket the telegram he'd received early that morning. "It's from Basil Pellingham."

"Uncle Richard's secretary," Katy said. "Why did he send you a wire?"

"To answer the wire I sent your uncle telling him that he was a gutless son-of-a-bitch to send

45

you out here without checking with me first, and to let him know I was sending you straight back to New York."

"Uncle Richard's already sailed for England, though. He was scheduled to leave New York two days ago."

"I know that now. The letter you gave me yesterday, though, said that he would wire me before he left."

Katy smiled. "He's like that. He thinks about doing something, then later believes he's already done it. The day after he agreed to let me come out here, he looked at me like he'd seen a ghost and said, 'I thought you'd left already.' "

"When was that?"

"Last month."

"The first I heard about it was from a telegram he sent me the day before you arrived."

"Then he did wire you before he left." Her smugness irritated Rait. "Mr. Pellingham probably reminded him just as he was about to leave. I can see them now—Uncle Richard dictating your telegram as he runs up the gangplank, which is already being pulled aboard the ship, so he has to jump the last two feet. I don't know how he's going to manage in England without Mr. Pellingham there to look after him."

Two of the chickens were fighting over a tidbit that one of them had scratched out of the dirt.

Katy watched them peck at each other so she wouldn't have to look at Rait. He was leaning against the shed, arms crossed over his chest and those blue eyes fixed on her so intently, it was making her nervous.

"I guess you're wondering why I'm here instead of in England with Uncle Richard. I love Western dime novels and want to write one myself. I've actually written several already, only Uncle Richard won't publish them because he says all I've done is rewrite other people's stories."

"I thought all dime novels were the same story written different ways."

"Oh, no, they're not at all. There are Indian and cowboy stories, mountain man and lawman stories. The newest kind has a badman for a hero. Deadwood Dick is the best known in that line. He dresses like you do, all in black. That's why I thought you were going to rob me yesterday. I patterned Matt Rash, the fictional hero of my books, after my real hero, Bat Masterson. And because Matt Rash is the antithesis of Deadwood Dick, he always wears white. White hat, white horse, sterling white heart. Good idea, don't you think?"

Rait could see in her face how much her writing meant to her. He remembered when he'd felt that way about a dream. He also remembered how it had felt to turn his back on it.

"Why didn't your uncle come with you on this quest for a story?"

Katy shifted her weight from one foot to the other. Her shoes were new and a little tight. She didn't want to appear rude, but she was tired of standing beside this chicken coop, and she was worried about the drafts, and Rait was still looking at her with that intent expression that made her think he knew a lot more than she wanted him to know.

"When Uncle Richard decided to go to England to see why our books aren't selling as well as our competitors', I convinced him to let me come out here so I could find an original story to write. I promised him that if after that, he still thought I was the worst writer that God ever put on the face of the earth, I'd never write another word as long as I live."

She tried to look concerned that she might have to keep her promise, but not so worried that Rait might change his mind and not let her get on that Dodge-bound train.

"It's getting late," she said. "We should find a bank and then go straight to the station. I've already inconvenienced you enough. I don't want to miss my train."

"You won't," he said, but she didn't believe him. The sulphur smell of the smoke from the train was already heavy in the morning air. To emphasize her doubts, the whistle blasted out a bellow of sound that made her jump and set her heart hammering.

"Tell me about the drafts, Katy."

Her heart stopped its pounding pace with a jolt that almost caused her to gasp. "I need to cash them," she said cautiously.

"Why?"

"I need money for meals and incidentals."

"Incidentals?"

"Books and newspapers." She tried to think of other things sold by the trainboys. "Candy," she remembered. "I have a sweet tooth that won't be denied. Then there's my meals. It costs seventy-five cents to eat every meal. That's three meals a day times five days to New York makes a total of . . ." She couldn't think under all this pressure. ". . . a lot. To pay for all that, I need to cash Uncle Richard's drafts, only he made them payable to you instead of me, so you need to sign them before I can cash them."

She was saying too much, but she couldn't make herself stop. She was just so nervous thinking about that train that was about to leave Durango. She wanted to be on it more than anything in the world, except for getting those drafts cashed. She needed money for a hotel and for meals while she was in Dodge, not that she was ever going to get there if this overtly suspicious man didn't stop lounging around this smelly alley and get moving.

"Let's go," he said. Without warning, he grabbed her hand and began to run.

She'd done more running today than in her entire life. And considering that she'd never had a man hold her hand before yesterday, she was becoming well acquainted with what that felt like, too. It felt good, or at least she thought it did. It was hard to tell while being pulled along like a reluctant cow to a branding fire. (She'd read that description last week in *Big Jim Corbett and the Big Roundup at Big Rim Ranch*.)

"Where are we going, pard?" she shouted at Rait's back.

"The train!"

"But my drafts!"

"You don't need them!"

"Yes, I do, I really do! Please, Rait, it will take just a minute!"

"I'll buy you whatever you need!" The train blasted its whistle again. "Come on! We're going to miss it, Katy, if you don't run faster!"

"We? What we?"

"You and me!"

"You're going to New York with me?" Katy had never been so horrified in her life. What had she done to deserve this? All she wanted to do was see Dodge City. Was that so terrible a sin that she deserved this as punishment?

"You're not going to New York!"

They were finally within sight of the station. The train was already moving. Rait ran faster and Katy gasped louder.

"Where am I going?"

"Silverton!" he shouted, and made a desperate grab for the railing on the last car. He caught it and pulled himself and Katy aboard.

She didn't even know what Silverton was or where it might be. She did know that this train was going in the wrong direction for Dodge City. It was chugging north past the red light district of Durango. She saw the Clipper Theater go by, then the Big Two, whatever that was. There was a sign that just read Bessie's and another that read Jennie's. She did know what those were and craned her neck to see if either Bessie or Jennie were in sight.

"What about my luggage?" she asked after she'd given up trying to see her first whore. "It was tagged to go to New York."

Rait was adjusting his hat. "I had it changed."

"My hat! I don't have my hat, either."

"I'll buy you a new one."

There was nothing more irritating than a man who had an answer for everything.

"And my journal. I left it in my room, too,

51

and you can't just buy me another one. It has all my notes from the trip out here. I have to have it, Rait. We'll have to get off at the first stop and go back."

"When we get to Silverton, Katy, you'll probably find everything that you're missing was packed for you by the maid, along with everything else you managed to unpack last night." He looked directly at her, then away. "Let's find a seat."

"I don't want a seat." She was going to cry. Her throat ached, her eyes burned, and her empty stomach felt like it wanted to be sick again.

It was so unfair. All she'd ever wanted in her whole life, at least for the last five years of it, was to see Dodge City so she could walk the streets Bat Masterson had walked and see the graves he had filled.

No matter how hard she tried to get there, everything just kept getting turned around. First, there was Uncle Richard with his clever idea about the nonexchangeable ticket and the uncashable drafts. Now she was being dragged off to a place she'd never even heard of before by a has-been lawman.

"What's in Silverton that's so important we had to go running through town like a pair of bank robbers who forgot where they left their

52

horses?" That wasn't bad. She wished she had her journal so she could write it down before she forgot it.

"My job," Rait said in answer to her question.

She gave a scoffing laugh. "As what? An abductor of innocent, unsuspecting tourists?"

"I manage a saloon." He also owned a share of another saloon. It had taken every cent he'd earned managing other people's bars for the last year to buy into that partnership. It had been a smart investment, though. The Hub was an immensely profitable operation.

Rait Caldwell would never need anyone's help again, and he would never owe anyone anything, either. Especially favors.

Katy was astounded. It was unbelievable. Her uncle had spent an entire month plotting how to keep her out of the reach of anything that even remotely resembled sin, then sent her straight into the clutches of an unmarried man who ran a saloon and looked like Satan in black denim pants and snakeskin boots.

"Uncle Richard will have a heart seizure when he hears about this."

"As soon as your guardianship is transferred back to him, Richard Halliday can have any type of seizure he wants."

Katy stared at Rait as she realized that this excursion to Silverton wasn't just a temporary side trip before he sent her home.

"You're not sending me back, are you?"

"I owe Richard Halliday a favor and I'm going to repay it."

Katy didn't care about favors or repayments. She just wanted an answer. "You're not sending me back?"

"Basil Pellingham, along with two Durango lawyers, confirmed this morning that the guardianship transfer is legal and binding. I'm stuck with it, and with you, too."

Katy was threatened by tears again. "You're not sending me back."

"No," Rait said.

It felt as though he'd pulled the train out from under her and left her hanging in midair. This was the worst day of her life. She didn't even care that he looked as miserable as she felt.

She turned to look back at Durango, and what might be her last chance to see Dodge City, but it was already out of sight.

Chapter Four

Rait and Katy searched through two passenger cars before they found an empty seat. He let her go in first. She sat, fluffed her hair, straightened her jacket, and arranged her skirt. Once she was settled, she realized that Rait was still standing in the narrow aisle and was staring at her with an expression that bordered on fear.

"What?" She jumped up, certain some dire and dreadful creature must be sharing the seat with her. "What is it? A spider?"

"You have a bow where your bustle should be."

She glared at him. "You frightened me half to death because I broke a fashion law?" She plopped back onto the seat and let out an exasperated sigh. "It's bustles that should be outlawed, not the absence of them. You can't imagine the discomfort of having to sit on one of those things for a few minutes, much less a thousand miles. Not even a padded Pullman seat helps for long. Besides, I like bows."

Rait forced himself to ease down onto the seat beside her. He couldn't get the image of that big taffeta bow out of his mind. Before he'd adjusted to having to sit beside something that pert and pretty, he noticed her high button shoes. They were made of black kid, had little scallop cutouts accenting the buttons, and around the ankle seam, a ruffle. A flirty, frilly ruffle the same smoky-gray color as the bow on her bottom.

It had taken Rait a long time to accept the changes that losing Angie had caused in his life. He didn't want to relive those months of agony. However, all the ruffles and lace and bows he'd been exposed to in the last twenty-four hours were bringing the torturous need to life again.

"You also like ruffles," he said in a voice that sounded like he was being choked to death.

"Lace, too," Katy said. "I like wearing pretty things. They make me feel pretty. Isn't that why you wear black?"

"To feel pretty?" he asked, and she laughed.

Even she could hear the note of sadness in it. *Stop moping,* she told herself. *A month is a long time. He can't watch me every minute.*

"No," she said and smiled at him. "To make you feel moody and depressed."

"I am moody," he said.

The train was following the path of the Animas River, moving upstream against its torrential flow. The narrow embrace of the valley where Durango had been now widened into a broad, flat plain that was bordered on both sides by foothills of the San Juans. Cliffs as multicolored as the fashion promenade every afternoon along Broadway in New York jutted out of the weathered slopes between the few patches of forest that hadn't fallen victim to the growing population's need for fuel.

On the valley floor itself were farms and ranches. Cattle grazed on grass as green as thoughts of Ireland, and horses, big herds of them, ran and played among fields of wildflowers.

"Look!" Katy pointed at a cascading torrent of ice-white water leaping from the forest darkness above to dash down the face of a blood-red cliff. "A waterfall! I've never seen one before."

Rait gave her a questioning glance. "Is this the first time you've ever been outside New York City?"

She nodded while twisting around in the seat to keep the waterfall in sight as long as possible. "Uncle Richard doesn't travel much. The few times he has left New York was during school term, so he wouldn't let me go with him." She faced forward in the seat again, her eyes searching the landscape for something else new and wonderful.

After a few miles of flat farmland, she turned her gaze to Rait. It was the closest she'd been to him. It was also the closest she'd been to any man, except her uncle and Basil Pellingham. She'd never had much use for the boys who tried to court her. Her dreams of romance lived only between the pages of books. No real man could match the heroes of the printed page. And now here she was with a real hero . . . or at least he used to be one.

"Why aren't you a marshal anymore?"

"We need to have some rules in this relationship, Katy. The first one is that you don't ask me personal questions."

She liked that he was the kind of man who believed in rules and regulations. She had no intention of obeying them, of course, but it was an admirable trait that hinted there was still the heart of a lawman beneath his badman wardrobe.

"I have a right to know if my uncle's trust in you was misplaced. You could be taking me into the back country of Colorado where you'll sell me into white slavery in a mining camp bordello, or maybe you're going to kill me and trade my scalp to Indians for beaver pelts or a buffalo robe, or turn me loose to wander aimlessly through the mountains until I die a terrible and grisly death!"

Her heart thumped with excitement at the horrible fates which might await her. She wished she had her journal so she could write them down. They would make great chapters in her book.

She could see it now: Matt Rash astride his magnificent white stallion riding to the rescue of his heroine, who had been abducted by a lawman gone bad. The lawman-gone-bad would be the arch villain of the book. He'd be dressed totally in black, have unnerving blue eyes, and be constantly threatening the heroine that he's about to take her in his big, strong, masculine arms and kiss her until she faints.

Katy fanned her face with her hands and wondered why someone didn't open a window.

Rait couldn't decide whether to laugh at her or send her to the nearest lunatic asylum. Her face was flushed, her eyes bright, and the pulse in her throat, just above the ruff of white lace, was racing. She was a very strange girl.

"I quit," he said. "I turned in my badge and walked away. And I wasn't the marshal, I was a deputy. I've never sold anyone into slavery; I don't trade scalps for pelts; I'm not going to let you wander aimlessly through the mountains. There are men out there who deserve a better fate than meeting up with you on some lonely mountain pass. Satisfied, or do you have any other dime novel fantasies that need to be vanquished before we put this subject to rest?"

"Why did you quit? Did you kill someone who was innocent? Were you afraid someone would kill you?"

"I grew up," Rait said. "I decided it was time to stop tilting at windmills and start earning a living like other men."

"Why did your wife leave you?"

He didn't blink. He didn't breathe.

"I never hit her, if that's what you want to know." His voice sounded as broken as he felt. "I loved her."

Katy didn't know what to say. She'd never known anyone who loved someone. Uncle Richard fell in love on the average of three times a month, but she knew that wasn't really love.

"Why is Richard Halliday your guardian?" Rait asked. He didn't look at Katy. He couldn't. But he wanted to know what twist of fate had put him in this seat beside the one person on the face of this earth who didn't care enough about her own life to keep her mouth shut about a subject that was none of her business.

"My father was a lawyer. One day he decided that his only hope for salvation was to abandon his pursuit of wealth and become a missionary.

60

He put his holdings into a trust for my mother and left for Africa on the next boat. She went with him. When she discovered she was to have a baby, she came back to New York. Word came there had been an outbreak of cholera in the Congo where my father was. As soon as I was born, my mother told the night nurse at the hospital to contact Uncle Richard about what should be done with me, and she left for Africa. That was the last anyone's heard of her or my father."

Rait wasn't a man who shocked easily. He was shocked now, though. From the first moment Katy had stormed into his life, she'd been a volcano of emotion. But now, nothing. She sounded the way he wished he could feel about Angie. Empty. Distant.

"I inherited my father's estate," Katy continued in the same emotionless voice, "which includes an interest in Uncle Richard's publishing house. Because he's my guardian, the court took over control of my trust to insure he didn't try to take financial advantage of me. When I marry, I get control of my money. There's quite a lot of it, I understand."

Rait was again shocked. "You don't know?"

"I can't spend it, so what does it matter? And even if I could spend it, it wouldn't change the fact that my father thought saving his soul was more important than being with my mother when I was born, or that my mother thought dying with Father was more important than giving me a name."

Rait's problems stemmed from not having money. Katy had it, but hadn't been shielded from being hurt, too. Maybe that old saying was true, money was the root of all evil. Funny. He couldn't even think of a moral to the story that didn't require cold, hard cash. Maybe that was the moral, you had to have it before you could moralize about it.

No matter how tragic her beginnings had been, though, the fact remained that she had money. She would never know what it was like to not have enough money to buy a coffin for the only family she'd ever known.

The train was slowing. Katy saw a cluster of buildings ahead. She tried to lower the window. "Is this Silverton?"

"No."

"What is it?" The window was stuck.

"I'm not a tour guide," Rait snapped.

"If you don't like the questions," she snapped back at him, "send me home." She slapped the stubborn window with her fist.

Not once in the two years he was married to Angie had she ever answered him back like that. He knew he'd deserved it a few times, just like he deserved it now.

"Trimble," he said. "It's a hot springs resort."

"Thank you." Katy got up onto her knees in the seat and put her whole body into the task of getting the window open. "Are we very far from Silverton?"

"Forty-five miles." Rait pretended not to notice that her bow was almost in his face. "Give or take a few inches."

Heavens, Katy thought. *Isn't it bad enough, God, that I have to spend a whole month with him? Do I have to sit beside him for forty-five miles, too?*

"It's a five-hour ride because of the mountains," he said. Katy had to bite her tongue to keep from groaning.

"Silverton is also the end of the line for the D&RG," Rait added because he was desperate to think about something . . . anything . . . other than that bow.

"Great," Katy said, grunting the word out as she gave another straining push on the window. "I've always wanted to visit the last place on earth."

"Do you need help with that?"

"Heavens, no!" she cried in horror. "I wouldn't dream of imposing on you by asking you to perform manual labor. Please, just sit there and don't move an inch on my account." *Please,*

God, make it open so I can jump out.

The train, which had been taking its own sweet time covering the last five hundred yards to Trimble, came to a sudden stop, almost throwing her through the closed window.

Rait looked past Katy's outflung arms at the lone passenger waiting to board at the Trimble station. It had been six months since the last time he'd seen that familiar face. He refocused his attention on Katy. She'd managed to stabilize herself, but he knew that it wouldn't take much to set her off again.

"I'm going to the smoking car," he said. He handed her a ticket to Silverton. "The conductor will want to see that after we leave Trimble."

Katy hurriedly sat down before the train could make another attempt on her life. "This is my sixth straight day on a train, Rait. I may not know how to open a window, but I have managed to gain a working knowledge of tickets and conductors."

"Fine, then I don't need to tell you that the rules of the railroad are posted at the back of the car and that you should read them."

She turned around. "Don't expectorate," she read.

"The other one," Rait said. "The one that warns passengers not to stick any part of their body outside the car. Maybe that's why the window won't open. The railroad got tired of picking up the heads that were being cut off and sealed the windows shut. Don't leave this car, Katy, and don't stick anything out of it."

Rait was tempted to wait outside the car to see how long it would take before she decided to see if her head would really get cut off. He didn't want to take a chance on the owner of that too-familiar face appearing in this car, though, and set off to find his old friend and keep him out of sight.

Chapter Five

Katy wasn't afraid of heights, but she wasn't fond of them, either.

Not long after the Silverton-bound train left the broad Animas Valley floor, it had begun to scale the sides of a narrow gorge that the conductor told Katy was called the Canyon of Lost Souls. It was an interesting name, she'd thought at the time. She hadn't realized how appropriate it was until a few minutes ago when she'd concluded that, at any second, hers was going to be the next soul lost.

The problem started when Katy began wondering if the train had ever been robbed. "It's been tried," the conductor had said. "We were headed for Durango with a carload of silver smelted in Silverton. Two men blocked the tracks south of Elk Park and tried to take off with their saddlebags full of shiny new bars of silver."

"What happened?" Katy had asked in a voice breathless with anticipation.

"Rait Caldwell's what happened. He was on the train and he picked those boys off with two shots, and them riding away." The conductor shook his head and laughed. "When we got to Durango, first thing he did was make the D&RG agent pay him for the two bullets he used. Funniest thing I ever saw."

That had started Katy thinking that if she were a train robber, instead of stopping the train and alerting any train-riding heroes that something was afoot, she would do her robbing while the train was moving.

The only way she could figure to do that was crawl on top of the express car, which was where trains always carried their loot, drop through the vent on the top of the car, force open the locked door, throw the loot off the train at a predetermined spot, then jump off and head for the hills.

It would make an interesting chapter in her book, she decided, to have her arch villain attempt such a crime. But only if it were a feasible plan. She wanted her book to be not only original, but realistic. To make certain her plan would work, Katy had decided to try it herself.

She'd encountered her first problem when trying to reach the express car. Between it and the passenger cars was a combination car, which was part baggage car, part smoking car. Standing in the doorway to the smoking car was Rait. He had his back to her and was talking to an over-dressed dandy with a bowler hat and a gold-handled cane.

Katy had realized immediately that it would be impossible to get on top of the combination car without being seen. The solution had been simple, though. She went to the rear of the car she was in, climbed onto the railing around the outside platform, and dragged herself up onto the roof. It had been a struggle, but when she'd finally hoisted herself over the edge of the roof and onto the top of the train, she'd felt a great rush of satisfaction.

The train at that point was moving along the face of a solid granite wall on a narrow ledge seven hundred feet above the rushing, roaring rapids of the Animas River. From her perch on top of the train, it hadn't taken Katy long to figure out how the canyon got its name.

If she'd been wearing anything other than two-inch heels and a leg-strangling skirt, it might have been easy to run along the top of the moving train and jump from the roof of the passenger car to the roof of the combination car. Though it wasn't easy, it was fun. What wasn't fun was trying to hang onto the top of the combination car while the train threw itself around a sharp curve. That was when Katy went sliding over the side of the car, the train, and almost the canyon.

Now she was hanging by her fingertips from a slender gutter above the smoking car window. Each time the train took another turn along the inwardly curving wall of the canyon, Katy smacked up against the car like a moth against a lantern. Occasionally, just to keep things interesting, the meandering path of the silver tracks caused the train to swoop around an outwardly facing curve. Then Katy went swinging out over the seven hundred foot drop with nothing between her and death except the tips of her fingers.

Between the breathtaking and the life-threatening curves, she just hung there and looked into the smoking car. There were eleven men in the car, including Rait and his dapper friend. Not one of those eleven men seemed to have even the slightest interest in the spectacular scenery of the Canyon of Lost Souls, because not once did any of them even glance at the window where Katy was hanging like a curtain.

Things could have been worse, she reasoned. She could have fallen off the left side of the train, which was so close against the side of the cliff that she could occasionally hear paint being scraped off. Instead, she'd had the luck to fall off the side of the train where she didn't have to worry about being crushed to death. Instead she had to worry that her hands were starting to go numb and her arms were being pulled out of her shoulders.

She needed to do something. The choices were to admit she needed help or drop to her death on the rocks below.

"HELP!"

Eleven faces turned to look. Ten of them assumed an immediate expression of surprise.

Rait stepped out of the smoking car, leaned over the platform railing, and made a desperate lunge for Katy. He caught her on the first try, dragged her to him, lifted her over the railing, and lowered her to the floor. He didn't release her, though. He couldn't. He was too damn scared.

Katy thought about demanding that he release her. It simply wasn't proper for him to hold onto her like this with his long, lean body pressed against parts of her that were never intended to be pressed against in public. She didn't say anything though, because her legs weren't yet capable of supporting her. Besides, she wasn't certain that she could make herself release the death grip she had on him.

She decided to take advantage of the situation of not being responsible for her own weight by leaning the upper part of her body back out over the railing. She looked up, then down, up again, down again. "It's really strange how I get dizzy when I look up, but not down."

Rait was getting dizzy watching her. He pulled her away from the railing. "What were you doing out there?"

"Trying to rob the train. I thought I'd figured out a way to do it while it was moving, only I didn't figure on all these curves. Beautiful view out there, though. I could look straight down between my feet at the river. I bet I'm the only person in the world who's ever seen it that way."

Her legs were still unsupportive, but Rait didn't seem inclined to release her, so she busied herself with straightening her hair. "I must look a mess," she said as she smiled at Rait's companion.

He was the only person in the smoking car who wasn't gaping at her. He was laughing at her. Actually, guffaw was a better term for the noise he was making.

How rude, Katy thought, and decided to put him in his place with a display of impeccable manners.

"We haven't met," she said and extended her hand while taking in the details of his appearance, listing them like a description in a newspaper article: gold-handled cane, elegantly cut suit, diamond stickpin, perfectly coiffured

71

moustache, pearl-gray bowler.

"I'm Katy . . ." she said, then let her voice fade into a chasm of silence.

That description. She *had* read it in a newspaper . . . and more than once. She'd not only read it, she'd created Matt Rash in its image!

Her legs collapsed and she sagged against Rait like a limp printer's rag.

Rait had been holding onto Katy because not only had she almost frightened the life out of him, but he wasn't certain she wouldn't try to do it again if he let her go. When she suddenly melted against him, he held onto her for another reason as her softness began to breathe life into embers that had laid too long cold within him.

He pulled her closer, wanting to breath in the wind-fresh scent of her and feel the touch of her hair on his face. He wanted to see her delicate lashes casting shadows across her eyes, which surely must be dark with the same passion he felt. Otherwise, why would she be as breathless and flushed as a schoolgirl before her first kiss?

Only she wasn't looking at him. She was looking at the man Rait had tried to prevent her from meeting.

His quickly kindled desire sizzled out like a fire doused with water. He released Katy just as quickly.

She didn't even notice.

"Bat Masterson," she said, whispering the sacred words as though in church. "You're Bat Masterson. *The* Bat Masterson. The one, the only, the legendary Bat Masterson. You're him. You're really him."

"Yes, I am," he said and reached to take her still-extended hand. "I should hire you to make all my introductions. You make me sound so impressive, people might pay money just to meet me."

She transferred her stare from his face to his hand as it closed about hers. This was *the* most exciting moment of her life. So exciting, in fact, that she didn't know if she would live through it.

"Oh, my." She sagged back against Rait. "I never, I really never ever." She lifted her gaze back to her hero's face. "I wanted to, but I didn't. I was afraid to even dare. That's why I wanted to go but Uncle Richard bought my ticket so I couldn't, but then Rait was angry and I thought finally, but he changed his mind and I thought I'd missed my only chance, and then I did that and got pulled in here, and there you are, and I can't believe this."

"Neither can I," Bat said. He was smiling at her.

Bat Masterson is smiling at me. And touching me. He's holding my hand and smiling at me and speaking to me. Katy wondered if maybe

73

she had fallen off the train and was now in heaven.

"Are you going to Silverton?" she asked.

"Yes, I am. It's a good town for itinerant gamblers like me to make a few dollars on a turn of the cards."

Katy was overwhelmed with amazement. Bat Masterson was going to the same place as she was. The same town. On the same train.

"We're going there, too," she said, unable to believe it until she heard it said aloud.

"Then I guess I'm on the right train," Bat said. He transferred his amused gaze to Rait. "She's a delight, Caldwell. When did you get married again?"

"Good God, Bat, I'm not married to this half-wit."

"He owes my uncle a favor," Katy said. "I'm it."

"You're in good hands," Bat said, then laughed as Rait shoved Katy away from him again. "Unfortunately, he has no sense of humor."

"I've noticed," Katy confided. "Incidentally, I never finished introducing myself. I'm Katy Halliday from New York."

"You're the first female train robber I've ever met, Miss Halliday."

Katy laughed self-consciously. "I'm not really.

I'm a writer and I had an idea for a story and wanted to see if it would work."

"At the risk of your life?"

"I always think about things like that after I get into trouble, not before. Uncle Richard says it's a serious character flaw."

Rait was irritated by their little tête-à-tête. "Katy's uncle is out of the country and he stuck me with temporary custody of her." It irritated him that he felt the need to explain their relationship. He glowered at Katy as though it were her fault. She smiled at him and then at Bat.

"I'm his ward," she said. "Which means he's my warden."

Bat thought that was almost as funny as Rait's obvious attack of lust when he'd been holding Katy earlier.

"If he tries to lock you in a jail cell or anything," Bat said, "just let me know. I've never tried to break anyone out of prison before, but I think I could manage it."

"May I ask you a question?" Katy said. "It's personal."

"Certainly. If it's all right with your warden, that is."

Rait glowered at both of them. "You got yourself into this, Bat. You can get yourself out of it."

"Ask away," Bat said to Katy.

"Were you really shot in the leg during an argument over a whore, and is that why you carry a cane? Did you really lead your first posse as sheriff of Ford County, Kansas, the same day you were sworn into office? Were you really almost killed while playing cards with Doc Holliday the night Eddie Foy performed at the Comique Theater in Dodge City and Wyatt Earp had to shoot a man to save you? Did you really go all the way from Tombstone, Arizona to Dodge City and fight the Battle of the Plaza to save your brother's life, and is that really why you missed the gunfight between Wyatt Earp and the Clantons?"

Bat laughed again with that big guffawing sound. He didn't seem much like a gunfighter. Yet, the way the other men in the smoking car watched him with cautious, awestruck expressions, Katy knew that his current happy-go-lucky demeanor wasn't his only persona. Lurking beneath the surface was a gunfighter ready to kill at the drop of a hat.

"You know more about my life than my mother, Katy," Bat said. "Let's see. First the leg. You're right. I was shot in the leg, but not over a whore. It was a dance hall girl named Mollie Brennan. I carry a cane more out of habit now than need. My first posse wasn't until I'd been in office a few days. As for that boy Wyatt

76

killed when Eddie Foy was in Dodge, Doc and I had moved our card game to the floor when the shooting started, so I wasn't paying much attention to anything but making certain that damn dentist didn't try to cheat. What else? Oh, yes. The Battle of the Plaza. It wasn't much of a battle, just a few men shooting at me and me shooting back at them, but it was to save Jim's life. He was all right, though, and I was arrested as soon as the shooting was over, which is why I couldn't help Wyatt with his trouble in Tombstone." Bat considered for a moment. "Did I miss anything?"

"No," Katy said. She had another question, but knew asking it would be considered rude. She didn't want Bat Masterson mad at her. She also didn't want Rait to strangle her. If she could get a look under Bat's jacket, she wouldn't need to ask it at all. She twisted her head this way and that, turned it sideways and almost upside down trying to see past the fashionable cut of his coat.

Bat was looking at her like she had a contagious disease. "What are you doing?"

Katy gave an exasperated sigh of defeat. "I was trying to see your gun, Mr. Masterson. I wanted to know if you'd really killed twenty-six men but thought it might be rude to ask, so I figured if I could see your gun, I would just count the notches. Only I can't see anything because of your suit jacket being so long."

"Notches," he said with a shake of his head. "I'd like to know who thought up that bunk. Notches unbalance a gun, Katy, and a man can't shoot straight with an unbalanced gun. Only green kids who want a reputation as a killer carve notches in their gun. They don't live long enough to carve too many of them, though. As for killing men, I've performed that regrettable task only four times, all for good reason."

She was bitterly disappointed. Gunfighter notches was one of the great legends of the West, as was the number of men Bat had killed. Was everything a lie?

"You really don't have notches?" she asked in the hope that he was just being modest.

Bat pulled his gun to show her. "See?" He rubbed his thumb over the hard, black, rubber handle. "No notches, not even any fancy engraving. Though a few years ago I did have a pearl-handled Colt carved with Mexican eagles. That's another reason most men don't notch their guns. They pay too much for fancy handles, like the one you're carrying, Rait. That silver mirror strapped to your leg must have set you back a few dollars."

Rait didn't confirm or deny it. His silver-handled gun had been costly, but its flashiness invoked a lot of respect from his rowdier customers. To date, not a single one had tested his talent with the big Colt.

"You can hold it, if you want," Bat said. He handed his gun to Katy.

"Keep your fingers off the trigger," Rait said. "Don't point it at anyone and don't drool on it."

"Very funny," Katy said. A heartbeat later, she was holding Bat Masterson's gun.

This was the most exciting moment of her life.

It felt warm and deadly and the threat of it weighed heavy in her hand. She'd never held a gun before, had never even seen one until she reached the Mississippi River. From there to Durango, though, there had been one strapped to almost every male leg she'd seen.

"Why did you get rid of the gun with the Mexican eagles, Mr. Masterson?" she asked. That Colt was as famous as his twenty-six notches.

Rait caught Bat's eye and nodded toward the interior of the smoking car. Several men were showing too much interest in the gun display. Rait stepped between Katy and the interested observers in the car, then turned to face the men, revealing his own gun and his willingness to defend his famous friend.

"It drew too much attention," Bat said. He

took his Colt back from Katy and secured it in his holster, then dropped his jacket over its threatening presence.

"Why don't we find a seat in one of the passenger cars?" Rait said. "We'll be stopping at Needleton soon to take on water. We'll be in the way of the people trying to board if we're standing here."

Katy led the way into the nearest passenger car, where there were plenty of empty seats. Rait insisted they keep going until they were in the last car. They sat in the last two seats, which faced each other. It seemed to Katy that both Rait and Bat were trying to act invisible. She felt quite the opposite. She wanted everyone on the train to know she was with Bat Masterson.

Bat took the aisle seat beside Katy. Their backs were to the wall and they faced the interior of the car and the rest of the train. Rait sat across from them and kept his eye on the observation platform. Both men positioned their hands close to their guns. They also kept a discreet watch to see that Katy didn't notice anything unusual in their actions.

Now that the river had risen to the same height in the canyon as the train, there was a lot of lush, beautiful scenery to distract her from getting curious about their caution. Rait pointed out two more waterfalls and listed the names of the Needle Mountains as the train passed beneath their lofty slopes. Bat identified trees and flowers.

"The trees with white trunks are aspens. You should see them in the fall. Spectacular. That's a Blue Spruce over there and those are pines, I think. Columbines are the blue flowers. Beautiful, aren't they? The yellow ones? Those are dandelions, Katy. I've never met anyone who didn't know what a dandelion was."

After the Needleton stop came and went without incident, both men relaxed a little. Apparently the smoking car contingent hadn't proven dangerous.

"I must admit," Rait said as he settled more comfortably in his seat, "I'm a bit surprised that you aren't still carrying that pearl-handled Colt, Bat. Are you finally getting tired of being famous?"

"Famous, no," Bat answered. "Infamous, yes."

"Oohh," Katy said. "That's good. I wish I had my journal so I could write that down. It would make a great scene in my book. Let's see, I could have you, Mr. Masterson, and my hero, Matt Rash, riding together on a train. Suddenly, a green kid, who wants to put a notch in his handle with your name on it, jumps into the car with his gun drawn. Matt says, 'Don't you ever get tired of being famous, Bat?' just before the bullets start to fly and blood begins to pour."

She acted out the action as she described it, almost decapitating Rait in the process of drawing her imaginary gun. When she finished, she sat down again and gave both men a questioning look. "Did that sound original?"

"Halliday," Bat said slowly. He lifted an inquisitive eyebrow in Katy's direction. "You're not related to the R. T. Halliday who publishes that Double-Nickle and Half-Dime Library trash, are you?"

Katy stiffened in anger. "Buffalo Bill Cody has a Wild West show, but that isn't considered trash. Newspapers write stories about the West, but they aren't considered trash. So why is it when someone prints a Western story in a paperback book, it suddenly turns into trash? Last year Uncle Richard published *Jack Graham, Rebel of the California Gold Fields; or, The Treasure that Walked Away.* We sold 400,000 copies of that book, Mr. Masterson. That's not trash, that's good business. And the people who read it weren't stupid or dumb. They just wanted to be entertained, and they were. That's something wonderful, not something to be laughed at or looked down on. It would be the proudest day of my life if my uncle were to publish one of my manuscripts as a dime novel."

Bat looked humbled. "You're right. Please forgive my churlish attitude. It's difficult, though, to think of those books as anything other than trash when they're responsible for people believing that I've killed twenty-six men."

"I read that in the *New York Times*."

It was Rait's turn to laugh. "You might as well give up, Bat. She's not going to let you win. I've known her less than twenty-four hours and I've already admitted defeat."

"Speaking of defeat," Katy said, "if you had told me that Bat Masterson was on this train, you wouldn't have had to drag me aboard. I'd have been dragging you."

"I didn't even know he was in Colorado until I saw him waiting at the Trimble station."

Katy couldn't believe it. "So you just naturally decided to keep him as far away from me as possible? That's mean. Who else do you know that you don't want me to meet? Wyatt Earp? Doc Holliday? Buffalo Bill Cody? How about Sitting Bull and Calamity Jane? Do you know them? What about Deadwood Dick? I know he's a fictional character, but there are people who think Bat Masterson is a fictional character, too. Come on, speak up, Rait. I want a full confession."

"She talks faster than Wyatt can shoot," Bat said, and Katy felt a shiver of delight race through her.

It was the best compliment she'd ever received. She couldn't wait until they got to Silverton and she could unpack her journal and write it down, along with everything else that had happened to her today. Her uncle was never going to believe that all his careful plans to keep her away from ex-lawmen turned gamblers had delivered her directly into their midst.

Uncle Richard probably wouldn't let her out of his sight again as long as he lived.

Chapter Six

Silverton. The name brought visions of glitter and a tingle of excitement to every prospector in America, for the mountains encircling the town were rich with not only the town's namesake, silver, but also gold.

The mountains were as awesome as their treasure. Magnificent in size and beautiful in grandeur, their slopes were steep and rocky and stained with mine tailings stretching out like comets from a hundred mines. The immensity of the mountains was intimidating to even the people accustomed to living beside them. To a newcomer, they were overwhelming.

Silverton was located in the center of a mountain park, one of the largest in the San Juans. Parks are flat, open areas set high among the mountain peaks. Silverton was in Baker's Park, which was ten miles long and two miles across at its widest point. It was startling to see so much openness in the middle of such a vast range of immense mountains.

The Animas River was the principal watercourse in Baker's Park, but two smaller courses spilled out of the mountains to the level valley floor, too—Cement Creek and Mineral Creek. Both of the creeks joined the roaring waters of *Rio de las Animas Perdida,* the River of Lost Souls, before it began its run through the canyon. Silverton had been built on the triangle of land surrounded by those three waterways. It was an excellent location, high and dry, wide and flat.

Until the Denver & Rio Grande Railroad cut its perilous route through Animas Canyon last year, the town had been a small, isolated mining community of several hundred residents. The number changed drastically with the seasons. In winter barely a handful of people could be found in the town. Most of those came and went from their houses via trapdoors in their roofs because of the deep snows. There were over a thousand permanent residents now and more coming everyday. Silverton was rich; it was wild; it was growing.

The train depot was far enough away from Silverton's business district to warrant a need for wagons and carriages to transport businessmen, salesmen, miners, and tourists from the depot to the hotel of their choice. Rait commandeered the biggest wagon for Katy's luggage, which drew its own crowd of sightseers.

Her awestruck attention was elsewhere, for covering every uninhabited inch of Baker's Park were dandelions. Hundreds of them. Thousands. Millions. Each as bright and beautiful as a droplet of yellow sunshine. It was the most unbelievable sight she'd ever seen or ever dreamed of seeing.

"Dandelions," Rait said as he came to stand beside her at the edge of the depot platform. "They do this every spring."

"It's beautiful," she whispered, unable to believe the sight of the lake of dandelions, the incredible mountains, and the breathtaking sky. It was the prettiest shade of robin's egg blue she'd ever seen and stretched from mountaintop to mountaintop like a silk scarf trimmed with white fringes of cloud. "Now I know where God was standing when He thought up the name for heaven."

"It doesn't last," Rait said. "In a few weeks, they'll turn to seed and blow away."

She looked up at him. "They don't really do that, do they? How could anything so beautiful just go away?"

He turned away from her. "It happens. Petey's waiting for us."

They rode with Bat in the wagon with her mountain of luggage, his one gripsack, and a driver who smelled worse than his mules. When they passed a street of houses sheltered by shade trees and surrounded by dandelion-decorated yards, Katy turned to Rait and asked, "Where do you live?"

"A hotel."

She was disappointed. She and Uncle Richard lived in a hotel. She'd been looking forward to spending the first night of her life in a real house.

"Where's your saloon?"

"In the hotel," Rait said.

"How convenient," she said, but was thinking, *how inconvenient*. It would be a lot harder to escape his overseeing eye than she'd hoped.

"Way over yonder beside Cement Creek, that's the smelter," the driver said to Katy. He pointed at the far end of the park where a large building belched smoke. "Over here beside Mineral Creek is the brewery. It's got a tap on it so even a man that don't got a cent to his name can still take a nip now and again."

"We don't need a tour, Petey," Rait said.

"I do," Katy replied. "Do the mountains surrounding the town have names?"

"Sure do. Back where you came out of the canyon, that's Sultan. Behind it's Black Ball.

88

Across the river Kendall and Hazelton and back there, that's King Solomon. Directly behind the town is Anvil. They all got mines on 'em, too. We got more mines around here than we got men to mine 'em."

Silverton was a rougher looking town than Durango, principally because most of its buildings were made of slab-sided wood. There was a lot of new construction going on, too. The sounds of hammering, sawing, shouting, cussing and more hammering filled the air, making it seem like a big, loud song of building noise coming at them from all sides.

"This here's Blair Street," Petey said. "Forty saloons per square inch and more gettin' built everyday. We got dance halls and gamblin' parlors and pleasure palaces, too. Last count, there was 117 prostitutes in town. Most of 'em live right here in this two block stretch. It's a hot place, all right."

"That's enough!" Rait ordered. "Miss Halliday isn't interested in Blair Street."

He was wrong. Katy was very interested.

Petey looked abashed. "Sorry, Rait. I didn't realize she weren't a line girl. With so many of 'em comin' in every day, I just natural get to thinkin' anythin' in a skirt is lookin' for business. Hotel's just ahead."

"Are you staying in the same hotel as we are,

Mr. Masterson?" Katy asked, drawing his attention from the multitude of gambling opportunities surrounding him.

"I wouldn't miss the opportunity to be close to you for the world, Katy."

"You can put a rein on that thought right now," Rait said in a tight, low voice. "As far as you're concerned, Katy is your little sister."

"Understood, friend. She's all yours."

"That's not what I meant."

"This is me you're talking to, Rait, not the inside of a whiskey glass. Instead of trying to drown your demons, why not let Katy help you get rid of them? I saw the way you reacted to her on the train."

Katy turned around and looked at them. "What are you two talking about? I can't hear a single word."

"I'm telling your warden that he's a fool if he doesn't fall in love with you."

"Isn't being stuck with him as my guardian bad enough?" she said and joined Bat in his hoot of laughter. Even Petey thought it was funny. Rait just sat there and practiced his scowl.

A block west of Blair Street was Greene Street. On the corner of Greene and Twelfth, which also bisected Blair's two busiest blocks, was the Grand Hotel. It was a three-story structure built of local stone and brick intended by its builders, the Thomson brothers, for retail stores, offices and apartments.

The ground floor supported two men's clothing stores and a large hardware store. Most of the offices on the second floor were being used by the government of Silverton while the new city hall was being built. When the railroad reached town last year, bringing with it a flood of tourists, the plan to install apartments on the third floor was changed to hotel rooms.

A sign emblazoned with the name of the hotel spanned the front of the building and a flag forty feet high flew from the roof. The corner retail space had been converted to a hotel lobby, and in the substreet level was the Grand Hotel Bar. It supplied a convenience for the guests, but drew little business from the rest of the town.

The saloon Rait had bought into last month was the Hub, which was located in an unattractive frame building a block from the Grand Hotel. The Hub was popular with not only Silverton's sporting crowd, but drew gamblers from all around Colorado and the west.

Rait believed the Hub would be even more popular and profitable if it was located in the Thomson Block, which with the opening of the hotel had become the social and business center of Silverton. No deals had been signed yet, but Rait knew it was only a matter of time before the Thomson brothers saw things his way and replaced the Grand Hotel Bar with the Hub.

The street outside the hotel was so busy, it took several minutes for Petey to maneuver the big wagon through the pack trains, carriages, and pedestrians to pull close to the boardwalk. While Rait supervised the unloading of Katy and Bat's luggage, she leaned close to Petey and whispered, "Are there really 117 prostitutes in Silverton?"

"That many's paid the monthly fine for May, so I reckon so," he wheezed back in a hoarse imitation of her whisper.

It was staggering. It was also exciting. With so many "fair but frail" packed into such a small space on Blair Street, it shouldn't be hard for Katy to meet one of them.

"Inside," Rait told her.

The entrance door to the lobby of the Grand Hotel had the state seal of Colorado engraved on the door handle. Once the seal was turned and the door opened, Katy stepped from the rough world of a boomtown into the lush world of the Grand.

The lobby was beautiful. All the woodwork was painted in shades of chocolate and cream. There were chandeliers, oil paintings on all the walls, and beveled mirrors reflecting the lacy fronds of potted palm plants. Two uniformed porters waited to take guests to their rooms, a dignified-looking room clerk was handling the duties of the registry desk, and the manager of the Grand, Mr. M. T. Mizony, who was taller than Thomas Rockwood in Durango but every bit as efficient and kind, greeted every new guest.

A group of people from the train were already registering at the hotel's front desk. Bat Masterson's entrance caused a stir. He was hurried to the front of the line, given a brass room key, and cheered as he signed the register with a flourish. While Rait checked Katy in, Bat came to talk to her beside the biggest palm in the room.

"I'm off to find the best game in town, Katy. It's been a pleasure meeting you. We'll see each other again before I move on."

The thought that he might leave Silverton hadn't occurred to her. "Move on? Where are you going?"

"The trains run everywhere now and I like to go with them. I promise not to leave without saying goodbye." His easygoing smile took on a firm seriousness. "I want to caution you not to take Rait's rumblings too seriously, Katy. He suffers from a determination to pursue the wrong

93

occupation, and it makes him a bit harsh some-times." He touched the brim of his hat to her and went out into the crowded street.

Rait brought Katy a key. "Room 303," he said. "Sam will take you upstairs. I'll meet you in front of the dining room at six. I have a few matters to take care of in my office until then."

Because saloon managers were never mentioned in dime novels, Katy had no idea what Rait's job entailed. She had a vague notion of him dragging noisy drunks out into the street and shooting gamblers caught with cards up their sleeves. She didn't get a chance to ask what he really did before Sam, the black porter, was ushering her upstairs.

"These are temporary stairs, Miss Halliday, so be careful when you use them. This hotel is a fine place, but they're not finished building her yet, so things change nearly every day. Last week, the dining room was in the basement. This week it's on the second floor beside the mayor's office. Next month, it'll be beside the lobby. The cook is having a fit over all this moving, says his food is suffering from being carried all over the place by waiters that can't remember where they're supposed to serve it."

They reached the third floor and Sam led her to the end of the hall. "You'll have a fine time here, Miss Halliday. Silverton's a good town. She has a few wild parts, but she'll settle down really fine someday." He opened the door to room 303 and stood aside for Katy to enter.

The room was lovely. It had a big four-poster bed smothered in a red velvet spread. Overhead was a red and gold brocade canopy. A frothy pile of lace pillows were banked against the headboard on the bed. In front of them was an assortment of red cushions decorated with gold braid and tassels. A cherrywood commode was on the other side of the bed and a writing desk that cried out to be tested was in the far corner. There was an armoire big enough to hold all her dresses, a chest of drawers, a red-patterned carpet so thick, Katy's feet sank into it with each step she took, and red flocked wallpaper that begged to be touched. There was also an over-stuffed chair and ottoman beside a tea table, a rocking chair draped with a bed scarf, and a highbacked wooden chair positioned close beside the writing desk.

An iron stove to warm cold evenings and a bucket of coal set against the wall beside the door. Sconces fitted for gaslight adorned the walls, the nightstand held an oil lantern with a red shade and beaded fringe, and a candlestick with a new beeswax candle was poised on the writing desk.

Best of all, on the wall opposite the door,

were two curtain-draped windows that gave a sweeping view of east Silverton, the Animas River, and Kendall Mountain.

"What a beautiful room," Katy said.

Sam nodded. "This is the prettiest we got, except for the honeymoon suite. Mr. Caldwell tried to rent that for you but a couple checked in there yesterday. If there's anything you want while you're here, Miss Halliday, you send for Sam and I'll take care of it."

"I already have a list of things I need, Sam. Hot water to wash, a maid to help me unpack, and I'll need to have a dress pressed for dinner tonight."

Sam grinned. "I already sent for Bessel to tend you. She's my wife and the best lady's maid in Silverton. There's a bathroom right here on this floor that's got hot and cold running water, but if you want water brought to your room, Bessel will fix you right up. I'll go get your luggage now."

Katy went to the window closest to the writing desk and looked out across Silverton. One avenue away was Blair Street. She could see a big false fronted building with a sign that read "The Diamond Belle Dance Hall." To the left of the Diamond Belle and a few buildings down were two other false fronted structures: Riley Lambert's Dance Hall and Tom Cain's Dance Hall.

Between were smaller buildings without signs, or with signs too small to read at this distance.

The block south of the Diamond Belle was dominated by F. O. Sherwood's Bordello, which appeared to be even larger than the Grand Hotel. On the corner facing Sherwood's was the Alhambra Theatre, which was still being built. Men carrying lumber were walking across the unshingled roof.

There were other buildings, too; both under construction and already open for business. Some of the latter had unreadable signs; some didn't need signs. The scantily dressed women hanging out of the upstairs windows were all the advertising necessary.

Katy's run of bad luck had finally ended. First, she hadn't fallen off the train. Second, she'd meet her favorite hero in the whole world. Third, she could observe a goodly portion of Silverton's nightlife without even leaving her hotel room.

Sam was right. She was going to like it here.

Chapter Seven

For dinner that night, Katy wore the peacock blue dress she'd planned to wear the previous night. It was one of her favorites, plus it was the only thing she owned that didn't need pressing. She'd used every packing tip she'd ever read in *Godey's Lady's Book,* but to no avail. Everything she owned looked as though it had been dragged behind the train all the way from New York to Silverton.

Bessel sent the whole mess to the hotel laundry. "Tomorrow mornin', all your pretty things will be back lookin' good as new. Now, let's see to that hair. Land's sake, child, you got a lot of it, and curly, too. I've never seen the like on a white person before. But soft, like it's been washed in rainwater."

She skillfully manipulated the dark tresses into a tumbling waterfall of curls held in place by black silk ribbons that matched the lace trim on the Zephyr wool dress. The dangling tips of the ribbons tickled the back of Katy's neck and made her feel flirtatious. After receiving Bessel's approval on everything from petticoats to the lace handkerchief tucked into the hidden pocket beneath the layered draperies, Katy was ready for dinner.

As she came down the stairs to the second floor, she received more than one lingering glance of interest.

Rait noticed every one of them. He'd spent most of the afternoon processing the paperwork that had been threatening to crush his desk. He'd barely had time to dress for dinner before he was scheduled to meet Katy. Then he had to wait fifteen minutes for her to make her appearance.

Even he had to admit it was worth the wait.

She looked lovely. The blue dress restored the aura of elegance and maturity that had been missing from her behavior all day. It was hard to believe this was the same wildcat who had been hanging by her fingernails from the side of the D&RG smoking car.

Though Rait answered the glances of her other admirers with a scowl, he greeted her with a smile.

"You look nice," he said.

She laughed. "So do you."

No longer was he dressed as a dime novel bad-man. He was now a nickel library gambler. He had on a black suit and white silk shirt, black string tie, and a silver vest with fancy black stitching. He looked as though he might whip out a pack of cards and start dealing at any moment.

This was the first time she'd seen him without a hat. His hair was as dark as her own, a little shorter than she'd expected without the weight of his hat to press it flat, and looked as though it was trying to escape its hair tonic imprisonment.

It was strange, but without his hat, he looked taller. Maybe it was the lighting. The hallway was lit only with the sparkling magic of candle-light to disguise the businesslike atmosphere of the city offices. Anything was possible in this lighting. Katy once again felt secretly attracted to Rait. He was tall and arrogant, she felt beguiling and bewitching. If this were a novel, he would sweep her into his arms. Then they would waltz until they were breathless and in love.

"Are you hungry?" Rait asked and broke the magic spell by reminding Katy of the indelicate noises her stomach had been making while she dressed.

"Famished. I could eat snake eggs."

He laughed, which was what she'd intended. The only way to survive a month with him was to keep him laughing. That way he wouldn't have time to be angry or suspicious of her. And she wouldn't have time for silly thoughts about falling in love.

He took her hand, tucked it under his arm, and led her into the dining room. Though this location was only temporary, no detail had been overlooked in making it as beautiful as the finest restaurants in New York. Marble sideboards lined the walls; carpets covered the floors. The tables were spread with linen tablecloths and set with china that looked too delicate to withstand a single washing, much less a trip into the high country of Colorado. There were candles on the tables, too, weaving their special magic and romance in the room.

The room was filled with diners. Katy was pleased to note that Rait was easily the most handsome man in the room. She enjoyed the looks she received from the fashionably dressed women with their glittering diamonds and jealous expressions. None of them need know that Rait wasn't with her by choice. All they needed to know was that they weren't with him at all.

The menu offerings were as elegant as the decor. Blue Point oysters, California salmon with butter sauce, pork tenderloin, boiled ham with champagne sauce, and fresh lobster were the entrees. Soup of the day was vichyssoise. Side dishes were sweet corn, mashed potatoes, French peas and Hubbard squash. There was also steamed plum pudding with brandy sauce and lemon meringue pie, Malaga grapes and Edam cheese, Roman punch, St. Julian claret, and a selection of French and Rhenish wines.

Katy hadn't exactly expected ragout of prairie dog, grizzly bear steaks, or fricassee of horned toads, but she was surprised by the offerings. There wasn't one Western-sounding meal on the menu. No deer. No steak. No fowl.

"Impressive, isn't it?" Rait said.

Not really, Katy thought. "Wonderful," she said. "I'll have the oysters," she told the waiter, who had appeared at her side wearing white gloves, a condescending smile, and a pair of pants that were the strangest shade of green she'd ever seen.

"What else?" he asked after giving a nod of approval at her choice.

"Lemon meringue pie, two pieces. I love lemon meringue pie."

"I meant, what vegetable?"

"Anything that isn't green." His pants were making her nauseous.

"Do you want the soup?"

"No, but I will have a glass of wine."

"Good try," Rait said to her, then to the waiter, "No to the wine, yes to the soup, give her

102

the squash, hold the second piece of pie until she finishes the first. I'll have the salmon with French peas, Malaga grapes, a wedge of the Edam cheese, and a bottle of Meursault."

"No soup," Katy said. "I don't like eating anything that requires learning a foreign language before I can order it."

"No soup," Rait said and sent the waiter away.

"There wasn't any need for you to get upset about the wine," she said. "I drink it occasionally."

"Not this month."

"Does that mean I can't drink at all this month or I can drink frequently this month?"

"Don't get smart."

"You'd make a wonderful father," she said. "You already know all the retorts."

"That reminds me," Rait said. "I have a list of rules which you're to follow during your stay. The first . . ."

"We discussed that one on the train. No personal questions."

"The second rule is don't interrupt."

Katy began to laugh. "Are you really serious about this?"

"Yes," he said, but it was hard to be serious about anything while she was looking at him like that. Her eyes were so bright, so full of fun. He remembered how it felt to hold her against him today, and suddenly had the urge to kiss her right here in the middle of the dining room.

This has got to stop, he told himself and frowned at her.

"You already know that I don't want you here, Katy, and I know that you don't want to be here, either. Basil Pellingham's telegram confirmed my suspicions that your restricted ticket and the drafts made out to me, instead of you, were intended to keep you away from Dodge City. Your uncle wanted you under my care, and that's where you're going to stay. The only way this will work is if we both know what to expect from each other. Rules will help us do that."

Katy's run of luck was over. Any hope of following Bat if he decided to leave Silverton had been shot down by Basil Pellingham's obsessive need to answer every question with excruciating detail and accuracy. As far as Katy was concerned, those jealous women could have Rait . . . and Basil, too.

"Forgive me if I hold my applause for that little welcoming speech until after I hear the rest of the rules," she said.

"You're making this very difficult, Katy."

"I'll try harder," she said and answered his deepening frown with a calculating laugh. "I meant that I'll try to make this less difficult, not more. Go on, list your rules. I promise not to say another word until you finish."

"Rule number three, the bar downstairs is off-limits," Rait said, "along with every other saloon in town, all the dance halls, and, well, everything on Blair Street. I don't want you any closer to that street than this dining room. About my work, I manage the bar downstairs and I own a piece of another one in town called the Hub. I spend the evenings after dinner downstairs, the rest of the night in the Hub, and I sleep mornings.

"Rule number four is you're not allowed out of the hotel during those hours since I won't be available to supervise your behavior. Sundays are the only exception. I will accompany you to morning services then.

"Rule five, we'll meet here in the dining room every day for lunch. Most afternoons I'm in my office doing the books for the hotel bar. When I can get away, we may go for walks if you like or shopping if you need anything. The afternoons that I do work, you may still go out, but not without an escort . . ."

"Which you must approve, of course."

Rait sighed. "You promised not to interrupt again, Katy."

"No, I promised not to say another word until you finished, but I was lying when I said it."

It was difficult to be strict with someone who

refused to be intimidated. It would be a struggle to keep Katy under control for an entire month. To add to his growing list of complaints about her, he'd also discovered that she had an embarrassing lack of respect for social amenities.

The waiter had served their entrees during Rait's attempt to put an end to the chaos of their relationship. Katy had eaten her first two oysters with a deft handling of the special fork provided with the shellfish. When her laughter had drawn a frown of disapproval from a woman wearing several pounds of carats around her neck and on her earlobes, Katy had responded to the silent reproach by discarding the oyster fork and slurping the oysters down like a starving cowhand.

Rait had been determined to ignore her little display of childishness. She was enjoying herself so much, though, that she looked not only ridiculous, but also adorable. His desire to kiss her was getting out of control.

"Stop that," he said, but she'd finished her last oyster seconds ago, so the order was really directed at himself. "Eat your squash."

"I can't eat anything that sounds like something you do to a fly." She grimaced at the squash on her plate. "It looks like a squashed fly, too, those big juicy ones that invaded the train after we crossed the Mississippi. I think the army should stop worrying about Indians and start shooting at flies."

Rait didn't know if he'd ever be able to eat squash again. "Rule number . . ." Damn. He'd forgotten what number was next.

He hadn't had this much trouble trying to reason with someone since the time he'd ordered Billy the Kid to leave Durango. The Kid could have talked his way out of hell, but he was an amateur compared to Katy's diversionary tactics. Rait decided to forget about the numbers and just concentrate on getting his point across.

"You may associate with any of the respectable women in town, go to their homes for tea, or whatever it is respectable women do in the afternoon."

Katy had popped the fruit garnish on the side of her plate into her mouth, only to discover it was a peeled slice of lemon. She tried to look normal while her mouth turned inside out and her tongue braided itself around her teeth. "I'm respectable," she said with a shudder, "and spend my afternoons with printers, writers, and accountants."

"I don't think that can be considered normal."

She tried to drown the effects of the lemon by drinking a whole glass of water in one big swallow. It helped a little. "Good," she said and sighed with relief. "I'd hate to think that all the women in Silverton were running secret printing operations out of their parlors."

Her relief dissolved into a strange quietness. She looked almost wistful as she toyed with her empty oyster shells.

"I've never been inside a real house," she said. "For all I know, maybe they all do have printing presses in their parlors."

The waiter brought their dessert. Katy's pie was beautiful. The filling quivered with style and grace, and there was enough creamy meringue to fill the Canyon of Lost Souls.

"Impossible," Rait said while she began devouring the pie. "You must have been in a house at one time or the other."

She shook her head. "We live in a hotel. We eat in restaurants. Until this trip, I'd never tasted food that wasn't prepared by someone with a French accent. It's a very isolating way of life. I even eat alone most of the time. Uncle Richard is out with a different woman almost every night. When we do eat together, all we do is talk about the books we just printed or will print or should have printed. I'm surprised I'm not stunted socially."

It was a pitiful story. Rait would have been more deeply moved if she hadn't managed to get a dollop of meringue on her upper lip part of the way through the recital. He wiped the meringue away with his napkin. She regarded him solemnly with those beautiful eyes while being dabbed clean.

"We'll have dinner together every night," he said because it was on his list.

"May I have my second piece of pie now?"

"No, you've made quite enough of a spectacle of yourself for one evening." He pulled out her chair and escorted her out of the dining room and into the hallway. At the foot of the stairs to the third floor, he said, "Good night, Katy," and waited for her to ascend.

"What? No kiss? No bedtime story?"

"Those are for good girls, not hellions who disrupt the dining room with silly pranks."

"Tomorrow night I shall be a perfect angel," she said with a teasing smile before climbing the stairs.

Rait was tempted to let himself get swept up in the flirtatious game she was playing. But what if the longing he'd felt for her today, and was feeling now, wasn't enough to overcome the guilt?

That was a risk he didn't want to take.

Katy bundled into her blue chenille robe and wrapped the bed scarf around her shoulders so she could sit in the rocking chair beside the open windows. A wind as chilling as Rait's dislike for her breezed through the open casements, along with the sights and sounds and smells of Silverton at night.

By day, the town had busied itself with work and duty. At night, it turned all its energy to having fun. Music from a dozen different songs sparkled in the air like the stars that filled the midnight black of the sky. Those stars, like the music, were as bright as crystal. They seemed to be dancing to the pulse of the town, glowing and changing color with every blink of Katy's sleepy eyes.

No matter which direction she looked, but especially on Blair Street, was light. Every window flamed with brightness; every doorway spilled a welcoming warmth into the dark streets. The streets and the boardwalks that lined them were crowded with people. Miners with the bottoms of their pants rolled up over the tops of their boots, workmen in bib overalls with knotted bandanas around their necks, gentlemen in tailored suits and bowler hats. And there were women. Not the women of the Blair Street bordellos, but women as respectable as that frowning female in the dining room were on the street below Katy's window, hurrying from one exciting entertainment to another.

Everyone was out tonight and everyone was having a good time. Katy wanted to be down on

110

the streets with them, going to and coming from the brightly lit establishments. She wanted to be part of the city, not an onlooker from a third-story window in a dim and shadowed hotel.

But not all the Grand was dim and shadowed. From the sub-street level trickled a sparkling of light, a piano trilling a tune, and the tempting sound of laughter being shared by friends and strangers. Katy could imagine the scene with roulette wheels spinning, poker chips clicking, glasses of liquor being poured and being emptied.

There must be women who worked there. Maybe they had feathers in their hair and rouge on their faces. Maybe their lips were painted and their skirts hiked high to show their pretty legs. They would be wearing red satin dresses and black stockings, three-inch heels on their shoes, and perfume in places that Katy had never dared put hers.

Did Rait like that kind of woman? Was one sitting on his lap right now? Was he smoking and laughing and drinking and losing all his money to Bat in a poker game? Was he playing faro or roulette? Was he pitching balls in a Bee-hive game or kissing a painted pair of lips in the shadows behind the coat rack?

Last night Katy had wished for a little more time with a man who looked like a fictional hero come to life. Since then she'd met a real hero, but her thoughts didn't insist on lingering with Bat. They settled defiantly on Rait. It was his blue eyes and cold smiles and grim expressions of distaste that kept her sitting beside this window even though she was freezing to death. And no matter how often she told herself that she was sitting here to see the nightlife on Blair Street, the real reason was the sounds drifting up from the bar below, because maybe, just maybe, one of those voices she heard laughing might be his.

Chapter Eight

Katy breakfasted in her room on biscuits, country cream gravy, crisp slices of bacon, and eggs, which she tried to eat, but couldn't. Immediately after she finished her last sip of English breakfast tea, she seated herself at the writing table and began to fill page after page of hotel stationery with notes on yesterday's adventures.

Her journal, which hadn't been packed in her trunk as Rait promised, was being sent by train later that day from Durango. A telegram from Thomas Rockwood had been delivered with her breakfast informing her of the special shipment, which would also include her hat. Meanwhile, Katy took advantage of the stationery.

After writing her pen dry several times, she paused to read over her notes. What she discovered didn't please her. Her prose contained more observations about how it felt to be held by Rait than how it felt to be inches from

113

death. There was only a brief mention of the terror she'd experienced when jumping from one moving railcar to another, and yet she'd wasted a whole page describing how Rait had looked standing in the doorway to the smoking car.

The man was determined to not only dominate every movement she made in Silverton, he was also taking over her subconscious. Last night she'd spent more time thinking about what he might be doing at that very moment downstairs in the Grand Hotel Bar than she'd spent watching the parade of Silverton's nightlife past her window.

And right this very minute, she realized with a guilty start, she was sitting here in her room like the good little girl he wanted her to be instead of taking advantage of his sleeping habits to see what a saloon looked like.

"Enough of this," she announced.

She left her notes on the desk, shed the wrapper she wore, and took out her seal-brown skirt. She chose a cream-colored shirtwaist with lace insets on the bodice and down the outside of both sleeves to wear with it. She pinned a corsage of pinks to her belt. A delicate broach with a blood red garnet was pinned to the center of the blouse's high collar. Brown shoes with a low heel finished the outfit.

It was getting close to noon when she hooked

the last button on her shoes. She didn't want to waste anymore time, so instead of styling her hair, she just pulled it back with a brown ribbon and let it fall free down her back. A quick glance up and down the hall showed no sign of Rait.

The lobby was empty. Not even the room clerk was there. And right behind the temporary stairs to the upstairs' floors was the temporary entrance to the downstairs' bar. The only thing between Katy and that door were three potted palms.

This looks too easy, she thought, and slipped from plant to plant in a stealthy approach of her target.

The entrance to the Grand Hotel Bar was only inches away now. The air was so thick with sin and vice, Katy could almost taste it. Her heart was racing like a mustang with a burr under its saddle. She reached out to touch the big, brass door handle.

It was warm and slippery. She turned it. Pulled. Just a little, just enough so she could put her head inside.

It was dark and smelled of cigars . . . and felt exciting! She pulled the door open a little farther. Her eyes were adjusting to the darkness. There were steps leading down to the saloon. She crept in a little farther, frightened that at

115

any moment she would come face to face with Rait.

Down in the pit of the bar, she saw glass-globed chandeliers whose light was reflected in arched mirrors mounted behind an ornately carved bar. It was breathtaking. Bottles and glasses lined the counter against the mirrors, and there were men standing against the front of the superstructure.

She heard a sound like cards being shuffled. It came from deep within the pit of sin, beyond her field of vision. She wanted to know who it was shuffling those cards, what game they were playing, and if gambling tables were really covered with green felt.

Emboldened by her success so far, she took another step forward.

A hand gripped her shoulder like a bear trap. Of course, she'd never actually felt a bear trap, nor had she ever seen one, but she'd read about them in *Seth Parker, Big Game Hunter of the West; or, The Grizzly That Wouldn't Die.* There was no doubt in Katy's mind that the hand clamped on her shoulder right now would have killed that grizzly in the first chapter.

She turned around, or rather, the hand turned her around. Even in the dim light, she recognized the cold stare bearing down on her.

"Don't you get tired of always looking dis-

116

agreeable?" she asked. "It must be exhausting to keep your face squinted up like that all the time."

"Rule number three," Rait said. "The Grand Hotel Bar is off-limits."

"Along with all other saloons, dance halls, and Blair Street." She smiled. "See? I was paying attention."

"Then what are you doing in here?"

"Looking for you," she said, and it wasn't even a lie. "It's close to noon and I didn't know where to find you. Will you have to work this afternoon? I was hoping you could take me out to see the town, plus I need to make a few purchases."

"I'm working."

"Oh." Now what? She didn't exactly have a long list of acquaintances to call upon for an escort. "I spent an entire week locked up inside a train and now I'm stuck inside this hotel. I was really looking forward to going out today." She lowered a soft fringe of dark lashes over the blue and gray of her eyes.

There wasn't a doubt in Rait's mind that she was going to cry. She looked very young standing there with that little bunch of flowers pinned to her waist and her hair tied back off her face like a schoolgirl. He almost relented.

"What's this?" The voice boomed out from

the bottom of the steps leading down into the bar.

Katy's head popped up so fast, it looked as though it were mounted on a spring.

"Mr. Masterson!" she cried, and Rait resented her eagerness.

"In the flesh," Bat said as he came up the stairs to them. "Is Rait trying to force you into servitude in this fancy saloon of his, Katy? That might not be such a bad idea. You'd look fetching in one of those red costumes he has the girls wearing."

Katy could see herself serving drinks to famous gamblers and dangerous gunfighters. "Maybe I should apply for a job," she said.

"Absolutely not," Rait said.

"You could keep an eye on me all the time," she said, and Rait felt his chest tighten. Watching her parade around in a saloon girl's dress would be the last straw. It was hard to believe he'd only known her for three days. It felt like he'd been besieged by her bows and ruffles for months. This morning it was lace and silk flowers. He wasn't going to last much longer if he didn't do something soon.

"I wanted to go out," Katy said to Bat, "but Rait is resisting my efforts to persuade him to be my escort."

"Then I volunteer."

Her mouth fell open. "Really?"

"Certainly. I've just finished emptying the pockets of all the players in the Grand and need a little fresh air. Where do you want to go?"

"Everywhere," she said, "including lunch. Let me get a hat and I'll meet you in the lobby."

"Come to my office, Katy. Bat and I need to talk before you leave," Rait said. This whole affair had gotten out of hand so quickly, he needed to exercise some control. Besides, he didn't like the way the two of them were looking at each other.

"I won't be a minute," she said and ran out the door and into the lobby.

"I'm not going to stand here and listen to you give me a lecture," Bat said.

He was in Rait's office. A large wood desk took up most of the room. The cubbyholes in the desk were neatly filled with envelopes, stationery, and other paraphernalia associated with office work. A leather sofa big enough to sleep a moose reclined against a wall beneath the moose's mounted antlers. Bat thought the room reflected Rait's personality well, masculine and obsessively neat. He'd been an excellent lawman, but would make a good housekeeper, too.

"I'm not giving you a lecture," Rait said. "I'm

119

reminding you of our discussion yesterday."

"I'm not the one who spent the night drinking up the profits of two bars. I remember yesterday very clearly, though I'm surprised you recall it." Bat sighed. "I'm not going to seduce the girl, Rait. All I want to do is show her a little of Silverton, give her some attention, let her have a bit of fun. That's more than you'll do for her if she stays here a year instead of just a month."

"I have work to do," Rait said. "I can't tell the world to stop revolving just so I can spend time with Katy."

"Why not? The world doesn't need to keep spinning all the time."

Rait paced across the room and back. "You've spent too many years traveling around from card game to card game to remember what it's like to have a steady job."

"What do you think I've been doing for the last six months? I've been wearing a badge, old friend. Marshal of Trinidad, Colorado. Dirty piece of business, Trinidad. They have the type of crime there that gives lawmen nightmares. I put a stop to the worst of it, but it was hard work, so don't give me that holier than thou speech about steady employment. I had it and I didn't lose myself in it. I still had time to treat a lady to a pleasant afternoon."

"I'm here!" Katy announced as she rushed into the room. She was flushed and breathless and wearing a polonaise that matched her skirt, gloves that matched her polonaise, and a hat that matched everything.

She paused in the doorway to adjust its tilt, which hadn't fared well during her rush down the stairs. She hadn't had time to do anything fancy to her hair, so had just pinned it up in a knot and balanced her hat on top of it. Now everything was slouching sideways. She pushed it back into place and adjusted the pearl hatpin in the back until it felt more secure.

Her hat was the very latest in head adornments. It was made of straw and the high crown was decorated with a broad band of cream, pink, and brown velvet. Katy had pinned a filmy piece of cream netting over the brim and secured it with seashell-decorated pins. She'd moved her corsage of flowers to the brim, and at the last minute added a shopping bag to her toilet. It dangled from her right hand, had fringe decorating the bottom and a bow on the handle.

It brought a glare from Rait that almost wilted her silk flowers. He pulled his disapproving gaze away from her long enough to open his wallet and take out a dollar, which he handed to her. She regarded it solemnly.

"You said you needed to buy something," he said.

"Yes. A sticky bun and some chocolate and maybe ice cream if I can find any and a journal to use if mine doesn't make it here from Durango today and a new pencil, only now that I'm not on a train anymore, a pen and ink would be better. A dollar won't do it."

"I'll buy you whatever you need," Bat said.

Rait stiffened. "I bring in a thousand dollars a week between my job in the hotel bar and my interest in the Hub, Bat. I can afford to buy Katy a bottle of ink."

"I should think so, raking in money like that. Maybe I should have given up my silver star a little sooner and looked for work in a saloon."

"You've given up a lot of silver stars," Rait said. He looked saddened by the idea. "How much do you need, Katy?" He had no idea of the cost of anything on Katy's shopping list and didn't even know what a sticky bun was.

She needed $2.33 if everything cost the same in Silverton as it did in New York, but recognized an opportunity when she saw it glaring at her. "Five dollars," she said. The whole thing was silly considering she had five hundred dollars in drafts in her room.

Rait gave her ten dollars, but only because Bat was watching and even if she were plotting to leave Silverton, ten dollars would only get her as far as Durango. Besides, while Bat was in town, Rait would bet his share of the Hub that Katy wasn't going anywhere.

"Shall we go?" Bat asked.

She linked her arm with his, waved goodbye to Rait with her other hand, and was out the door before he could think of anything more to say.

"Don't go near Blair Street," he remembered to call after them.

"We won't," Katy called back.

"Where would you like to go?" Bat asked when they were on the street outside the Grand Hotel.

"Blair Street."

"Sorry, honey. If Rait doesn't want you on Blair Street, we're not going. Besides, not all the entertainment in Silverton is on Blair. Right here on Greene there are a number of interesting establishments. What if we stroll along Greene and explore what it has to offer, then stop at every corner to see how much of Blair we can view from a block away?"

"You're a genius," she said. "And thank you for volunteering to pay for my purchases."

"It was the chivalrous thing to do. Besides, it's embarrassing for a man to stand by while a woman pays for her own ice cream."

123

"That's as silly as Rait giving me ten dollars to buy that ice cream with," Katy said. "But I'd be honored to have you treat me to this afternoon's entertainments."

The tour began right in front of the Grand Hotel. Directly across the street was Westminster Hall, known locally as the Sage Hen's Dance Hall. The Sage Hen, whose real name was Jane Bowen, also owned another dance hall. It was behind the Westminster on Blair Street. It contained not only a dance floor, but rented out rooms upstairs that were furnished with a bed and a prostitute.

Bat wasn't shy about pointing out the shadier parts of Silverton life. Soon Katy had seen everything from cribs, which were tiny houses with a front room where line girls entertained customers, to bordellos and brothels, which were smaller and, according to Bat, raunchier than bordellos.

They saw the Hub Saloon, which was a small building with a false front and a fancy sign hanging over the door. "Popular place," Bat said. "Rait keeps the games clean, the liquor flowing, and the women friendly."

Bat showed Katy dance halls, gambling parlors, and more saloons. He also told her stories about some of his adventures in the gambling parlors during his last visit to Silverton six months ago, and a few of the girls he'd met then in the dance halls. All the stories were funny and a few were ridiculous. Katy laughed, Bat acted gallantly, and they had a wonderful time.

She didn't meet any of the "brides of the multitude," but he pointed out one of them coming out of a hat shop. She was blonde and only a few years older than Katy and very pretty. She wore regular everyday clothes, but they looked flashier on her. She smiled at Bat when he tipped his hat to her.

"That was Lilly Gold," Bat told Katy. "She runs her own brothel over on Fourteenth Street. She's a well educated woman. I believe she went to college back East somewhere."

Katy was so shocked, she barely tasted the sticky bun Bat bought for her at the Silverton Bakery a few doors down the street from the Arlington Saloon.

"Wyatt Earp deals faro here when he's in Silverton. He also spends time at the Great Northern Saloon."

Unbelievable. She was eating a sticky bun paid for by Bat Masterson and discussing Wyatt Earp's gambling habits.

Ice cream came from a confectionery across

the street from Goode's Saloon and was eaten while they read a flyer distributed by a boy in a baseball cap. He'd appeared out of the storefront office of the *La Plata Miner,* one of the town's newspapers, carrying a stack of the flyers and handing them out to everyone who passed.

"My dad plays for the local nine," he told Bat when asked about the origins of his hat. "They practice across from the school."

"Shouldn't you be in school now?" Katy asked.

"I'm gettin' twenty-five cents to pass these out. What do I need school for? Here, take another one."

The flyer was advertising Silverton's big Fourth of July fling. The premier event of the week-long celebration was to be horse racing at the new racetrack being built by the members of the Jockey Club on the outskirts of town.

"That should be exciting," Bat said. "The betting will be good, too. I'll have to visit the livery stables to get a fix on the favorites."

The Silverton Fireman's Association was promising to take back the championship belt and Silver Trumpet Trophy from last year's winner, the Durango Hook and Ladder Association. That explained the team of men Bat and Katy had seen carrying a ladder while they

126

dashed up and down Thirteenth Street. They were all dressed in white shirts and crimson knee britches and had expressions of intense determination on their sweating faces as they charged around pack teams and women in flouncing hats.

The entertainment for the Fourth included a baseball game with the Silverton team taking on all comers. Rifle and shotgun matches were scheduled. Miners' events were also promised. Double-jack drilling led the list for prize money being offered for the mining contests.

Boxing and wrestling matches were also listed on the flyer, along with John Robinson's Combined Circus and Menagerie, which was heralded as "The first circus to appear in the San Juans!"

"I wish I could be here for this," Katy said. "I've never seen a circus."

Bat laughed at the thought of her coming all the way to Colorado to see her first circus when there was one appearing in New York almost every week.

Between the sticky buns and ice cream, they had ruined their appetites for lunch. They abandoned their search for a restaurant and just strolled along. The Silverton Cornet Band was playing in front of the Odeon Dance Hall south of Twelfth Street. Katy and Bat stopped to listen, then wandered on down Greene in the direction of Mineral Creek and the brewery.

It was a beautiful day for walking, cool but not cold. The sky was clear, the mountains stunning. Bat pointed out some of the mines on the nearby slopes of Anvil Mountain and explained that the pack trains of mules and burros they'd seen stringing along the center of the wide city streets were hauling ore to the smelter and supplies to the outlying mines.

South of Eleventh Street, they came across a Chinese store with a sign that read "Silks, Slippers, Candy, Beads, Porcelain, Nuts, and Ladies' Underwear."

"Surely there's something in here we can buy," Bat said.

They ended up with paper firecrackers, which Bat suggested they light and toss in the potted palms at the hotel, a green silk nightshirt with a purple dragon sewn on the front for Rait, a crimson bathrobe with a huge gold dragon on the back for Bat, and a pair of slippers for Katy made of quilted white silk that was as pale and soft as moonlight. Bat also bought her a red hair ribbon, "because I like red hair ribbons," and they went out again laden with their purchases and laughing at the thought of Rait wearing his purple dragon nightshirt.

"Here's what we need," Bat said and pulled

Katy into a photography studio. "We want our picture taken," he told the man behind the counter.

"Oh, yes!" Katy cried. "What a good idea!"

They posed in front of a painted screen of a street cafe in Paris. Bat was standing and Katy was seated on his left. The photographer wanted them to look serious. Neither of them agreed with his opinion.

Katy insisted that Bat's gun be displayed, "Otherwise no one will believe it's really you." So he stood with his suit jacket pushed back with his hand on his hip and a look on his face that made it appear he was threatening the photographer.

A flash of light, and the two of them were frozen in time.

"Let's do another one," Bat said. "Pick a screen with a Western theme this time," he told the photographer. "Make it a bar if you have one."

While the screen was changed, Bat browsed through the clothes on a rack hanging on the back wall of the studio. Because not everyone in Silverton owned a fancy set of clothes and because most people wanted to look their best for the camera lens, the studio supplied suits and dresses for a fee.

The recent influx of tourists into the San

Juans had inspired the photographer to take the idea of supplying clothes one step farther. He had a wide range of attire including a buffalo hunter's hide coat, a gambler's fancy suit, a cowboy hat and chaps, a dance hall girl's dress, and a set of miner's gear complete with pick, shovel, and a lump of rock painted silver. The prize of his collection was a wedding ensemble for the happy couple that was in too much of a hurry for anything except a picture and a hotel room.

"Put this on," Bat told Katy and handed her a feathered thing that was meant to be worn on top of her head. The dance hall girl's outfit was tossed at her next. "I'll be the slick gambler," he said.

Katy was unpinning her hat. "You already look like a gambler."

"Then I'll be Deadwood Dick."

She howled with laughter. "So much for your highfalutin' speech about dime novels being trash. How do you know about Deadwood Dick?"

He winked at her. "Stop talking and get dressed."

Katy went behind the dressing screen. "Undressed, you mean," she said when she held the dance hall dress up against her. It was designed to uncover more of her than it covered.

By the time she'd taken off most of her own clothes and put on the dress and pinned the feathered thing on her head at a jaunty angle, Bat had transformed from his everyday gambler persona into the toughest looking desperado in dime novel history.

All day, men had been covertly watching Bat from under the shadow of their hat brims. There had also been those men in the smoking car on the train yesterday who had looked at him with fear and respect. But until now Katy had seen only the happy-go-lucky Bat who teased and laughed at everything.

The Bat she saw now was the one all those men had seen: a dangerous, steely-eyed man who was fast with a gun and not afraid to kill. There wasn't a man on earth fearless enough to face down this Bat Masterson. He looked mean and tough. He also looked like Rait.

Here again was the hard-edged man she'd seen that first day beside the train in Durango. Here was the strength of will. Here was the type of man who, although he looked dangerous, also inspired immediate trust. She'd felt it that first day with Rait and now, looking at Bat, she realized it was because not only did they display confidence and strength in every move, they also displayed their hearts. They were men who

131

were willing to risk their lives to uphold the law.

Real heroes, she thought, and smiled.

"You look mean and dangerous," she said to Bat as they took their positions in front of a saloon scene complete with whiskey bottle, spittoon, and a picture of a naked lady hanging above the bar.

"And you look good enough to eat. Rait might rethink his decision to hire you once he sees this picture."

"He might kill both of us if he sees this picture," Katy said.

She followed Bat's instructions to put her arms around his neck and press close against him in a most embarrassing manner. Then he leaned her backwards like he was planning to kiss her, leered up at the camera and pointed his gun directly at the photographer. With her right leg kicked high into the air and her left leg revealed well up past the knee, Katy gave the camera what she hoped was a seductive expression and waited for the flash. Nothing happened.

Katy was uncomfortably aware of how good-looking Bat was and how close he was holding her. She was also uncomfortably aware that it was Rait she was thinking of while Bat held her in his arms.

"Hurry," Bat said to the photographer. "Otherwise I'm going to have to either drop her or marry her."

Katy giggled, Bat guffawed, the flash went off, and they had to take a third picture.

"I want two sets of all three photos, regular framing size for the lady and a smaller set for me. Something I can carry in my pocket," Bat told the photographer. "I'll pick them up in a day or so."

"They'll be ready, sir."

While they were walking back to the Grand Hotel, Bat stopped to look in the window of a millinery shop while Katy moved on down a few doors to a hardware and sporting goods store. Behind the dusty glass of the front window was a display of pistols.

When Bat joined her, she pointed at a single action Colt .45 with a hard rubber handle. "That's just like yours, Mr. Masterson."

"Enough of this Mr. Masterson nonsense, Katy. I'm twenty-sseven, not seventy-two, but that's how old you make me feel every time you pull that mister business."

Incredible. She was discussing guns on a first-name basis with Bat Masterson.

"I'll try," she said and added, "Bat." She felt silly.

"That's better, honey. Now let's look at this

133

gun." He regarded it carefully. "The barrel's the same length, four and three quarter inches. That's considered short by some men but I like it that way. It comes out of the holster clean and fast. That one's nickel-plated like mine, too. I like my front sight a little higher and thicker than standard sights, though, and I like a coy trigger, so I order my Colts custom-made from the factory."

"Coy?" Katy asked.

"Hair trigger. When I'm looking down another man's gun barrel, I want an instant understanding with my trigger. See the difference in the sight?" He pulled his gun and rubbed a finger across the enlarged sight.

Katy could barely see a difference between Bat's specially ordered sight and the standard one. She read the price on the Colt in the window. Forty dollars. It was a lot of money, but wouldn't it be something to have a gun almost exactly like Bat Masterson's?

"Let's see now," Bat said as he and Katy approached the Grand Hotel. "What do I know about Wild Bill Hickock? He was a nervous man. He used to check and double check all the doors before he went to bed at night and never slept in line with a window. Before he went to bed, he spread the floor with newspapers so if

134

someone sneaked into the room, he'd hear the papers rustling. Strange to think of him being that cautious and still getting shot in the back. We're here," he said and opened the door for Katy to enter.

The lobby was in the same type of turmoil as when Bat had checked in yesterday. Hotel staff were flitting around and a clump of guests were standing beside the potted palms, whispering among themselves and trying not to look as though they were staring at the tall man registering at the desk.

"I'll be fried in snake oil!" Bat thundered out. "Reach for the sky or grab for your gun, *compadre!*"

The tall man spun while his hand dropped to the gun on his hip. Katy froze.

"Bat, you old possum poacher!" The tall man relaxed his defensive posture and crossed the lobby with an extended hand, which Bat accepted. They shook hands vigorously, slapping each other on the shoulder and back while they grinned at each other like long lost friends. "What are you doing in Silverton?"

"Winning all the money," Bat said, "so you might as well leave. Is Josie with you?" He looked around the lobby.

"Already upstairs. We came over the pass from Ouray and she nearly froze to death.

Must've been ten feet of snow up there." He glanced at Katy, whose mouth was hanging so far open, her tongue was getting dry. "Is she yours, Bat?"

He shook his head. "Katy's here visiting Rait Caldwell. Katy? Are you all right, honey? You look a little pale."

"Wyatt Earp," Katy gasped. "He's Wyatt Earp."

"She's easily impressed," Bat said. Wyatt whacked him on the shoulder.

"I'm standing here with Bat Masterson and Wyatt Earp." Katy felt like she was going to faint. "I don't believe this. I think I'm going to be sick."

"Women usually have that reaction when they're with Bat," Wyatt said.

"Katy!" The shout caused her to blink her way back to reality. She turned and saw Rait coming toward them. She looked back at the blond Apollo standing before her.

"Wyatt Earp," she said. "I found Wyatt Earp."

"Stop gawking at him," Rait said. "Sorry, Wyatt. Katy gets a bit carried away. When did you get in town?" He shook hands with Wyatt.

"Just now. Josie and I came over the pass from Ouray." He threw back his head and laughed. "There we were, wading through snow

136

to our waists, or I was. I hired a mule for Sadie to ride. We thought we were the only people on earth, just us and the mountains and the snow, when suddenly two men appear over a ridge and start interviewing me. Reporters from some paper in Chicago. Can you believe it? Just happened to be passing by."

"Who's Sadie?" Katy asked. She was also trying to figure out who Josie was and what she rode over the pass if Sadie was on the mule.

"My wife, Josephine Earp. I call her Sadie."

Wife! Katy was surprised. That was one detail the press had missed while chronicling Wyatt's legendary life.

"Is Doc here, too?" Bat asked.

Katy knew she would faint now. There was only one Doc famous enough to be discussed by Wyatt Earp and Bat Masterson: Doc Holliday.

"He was in Leadville the last I heard," Wyatt said.

"You stay here long enough and he'll show up," Bat said.

Rait was frowning. "Marshal Ogsbury won't be happy to see him. Silverton's already keyed up waiting for the party on the Fourth to get under way. If Doc shows up here now, it would be like throwing a lit match into a keg of powder."

Wyatt looked displeased by the comment.

137

"He doesn't go around looking for trouble."

"No," Bat said. "But he finds it anyway. The man's a menace."

"It's the drink, not the man," Wyatt said.

"And it's the man who takes the drink," Rait said. "I wouldn't want him in my town if I was the law."

He didn't say it in the mocking, cynical way he'd talked about his past profession on the train. He made it sound like the noble profession Katy knew it to be.

"When are you going back to marshaling, Rait?" Wyatt asked. "I thought you'd have tired of being a saloonkeeper by now."

Rait's hands clenched into fists that he held stiffly at his side. "Never," he said. "I own part of one of the bars I'm running now and I'm happy with the work." He didn't look happy, though. He looked like a thunderstorm that couldn't quite work itself into releasing its fury.

"So," Wyatt said, "How's the gambling in town, Bat?" It was obvious he was trying to relieve the tension of the moment by changing the subject.

"I just got here yesterday. It was good last night, though. I picked up enough to cover my train fare."

"I'm headed out to do a little playing right now," Wyatt said.

"At the Arlington," Katy said.

Wyatt smiled at her. "That's right."

"Faro," Katy added.

"Right again."

"How does she know about the Arlington?" Rait asked Bat. "What have you two been doing?"

"Shopping." He gave Rait the package with the nightshirt. "We bought you a present."

Rait took the bundle with all the enthusiasm of a man being handed a stick of lit dynamite.

"Did you throw away your manners with your badge?" Bat asked. "Most people say thank you when handed a gift."

Rait shot him a deadly glance. Then he turned on his heel and stalked away.

"Still touchy, I see," Wyatt said.

Bat was looking after Rait with a concerned expression. "He's eating himself up with it."

"With what?" Katy asked.

"It's Rait's problem to tell, honey," Bat said, "not ours."

"Speaking of badges," Wyatt said, "I thought you were still down in Trinidad, Bat."

"Quit last month. Wasn't much fun after the crooks left town. Why don't we have dinner tonight and talk?"

"Good idea," Wyatt said. "Pleasure meeting you, Katy." He left, stepping out the front doors into the bright sunlight that glistened on his golden hair like a halo.

"I'm going to the Hub for a drink," Bat said. "Katy, I had a wonderful day today."

"So did I," she said and stretched to kiss his check. "Thank you."

"I can't wait to see Rait's reaction to our pictures."

She grimaced. "I can."

Bat laughed. "Maybe I'll have to marry you to preserve your honor and my life."

"And I'll write a book about our whirlwind romance and title it *The Shotgun Wedding of the West's Greatest Lawman; or, how Bat Masterson Met his Doom in Front of a Camera in Silverton instead of in a Shoot-out in Dodge City.*"

"Think it'll sell 400,000 copies?"

She shook her head. "Not enough blood and gore. A hundred thousand tops."

"Maybe I'll have to let Rait shoot me so we can sell another 300,000."

Katy laughed. "No way. All I've ever wanted is to write a big-selling dime novel, but I'd rather give up writing than have either of you get into a gunfight."

And it was true. Two days ago, she'd have paid money to see Bat Masterson in a gunfight. Now, she'd give her whole trust fund to keep him safe. And Rait. She shuddered to think of losing him, even though he'd probably prefer to be shot in the stomach than put up with her for one more day.

After dinner that night, Rait again walked Katy to the bottom of the stairs leading to the third floor.

"You were quiet at dinner," he said.

"I told you that I'd be an angel tonight." She hid a yawn behind her hand. "Good night, Rait."

He didn't want her to go yet. "What did you and Bat do today?" The question had been eating at him all through supper, along with the way she was always looking at Bat as though he was the greatest hero in the world. It wasn't that Rait was jealous. It was just that it was his responsibility to make certain she didn't get carried away with her fantasies and get hurt.

She gave him a sleepy smile. "Everything. It was a perfect afternoon, except you weren't there." She was standing on the bottom step, but still had to reach up to kiss his cheek. "Good night."

She stifled another yawn as she climbed the stairs, leaving Rait to wonder why Richard Halliday had to have such an artlessly charming niece. His life before her arrival hadn't been perfect, but it had been adequate.

Now it seemed as empty as a dry well.

Chapter Nine

Katy came skipping down the stairs to the second floor the next morning, hoping to eat breakfast with her heroes. Bat and Wyatt were nowhere in sight. Rait was. He was coming up the stairs from the lobby.

"I thought you slept late in the morning," Katy said. He looked as though he hadn't slept at all. His eyes were red and bloodshot. He hadn't shaved and his face looked craggy beneath a day's growth of beard.

"Today I didn't."

"Good," she said. "You can have breakfast with me."

The dining room was almost empty. Katy ordered flapjacks. Rait ordered coffee, black and strong. They didn't talk. She concentrated on eating. He watched her.

She was wearing a pretty pink dress trimmed with violet and white lace ruffles. The skirt was full and made her waist seem incredibly tiny. Her cheeks were flushed, her eyes brighter than a thousand stars. Just looking at her made Rait's headache worse. How could anyone be so full of energy and enthusiasm this early in the morning?

"Good morning!" It was Bat. He strolled into the dining room and over to their table like he owned the hotel. "What did you do last night, Rait? Try to drink up all your profits again? If you don't lay off the bottle, you're going to end up like Doc Holliday."

"Mind your own business," Rait muttered.

Bat sat in one of the empty chairs at their table and turned his smile on Katy. "How's my girl today?"

"I dreamed last night that I was eating ice cream in a gambling parlor while you were playing poker and Mr. Earp was dealing faro."

"Could happen," Bat said.

"Better not," Rait threatened.

"It's too bad you're not in a better mood, Caldwell. It would make it easier to tell you my news. Josie and Wyatt are on their way down for breakfast, and guess who's with them?"

"Doc Holliday," Katy said, and Bat nodded.

"You win the prize, honey. He surfaced last night at the Arlington. He's not staying in the Grand, though, so you can be grateful for small favors, Rait."

"Tell him to stay out of the dining room, too."

"You tell him. I'm headed for the train station."

Katy was aghast. "You're leaving?"

"Headed for Denver on the first train out of Silverton today."

It was the worst news she'd ever received. "What about our pictures?"

"What pictures?" Rait asked.

"Wedding pictures," Bat said. "I'll be back in a few days, Katy. We can pick them up then. Take my advice, Rait, stop tipping the bottle in your own direction."

Bat kissed Katy on the forehead, which almost caused her to fall out of her chair with delight. He strolled out of the dining room just before Wyatt Earp entered with the most exotically beautiful woman Katy had ever seen.

Behind them was a man who lacked any of the hero qualities of Bat, Wyatt, or Rait. He was thin and his skin was sallow. He gave her a creepy sensation that reminded her of the rats that scurried through the alleys in New York.

"Rait," Wyatt said. "Good morning, Katy. I'd like you to meet my wife, Josie. This is the girl I told you about who's visiting Rait for a few weeks."

"It's nice to meet you, Katy," Josie said. She had lustrous black hair and brown almond shaped eyes. Her dress was dark and flowing, giving her a mysterious, almost mystical quality.

Katy was immediately intimidated by her and jealous of her for the way Wyatt treated her. It was as though she was a precious crystal that relied totally on him for protection. He held out her chair and, when she was seated, gently slid her close to the table. He rested his hand on her shoulder until he was certain she was comfortable, then pulled a chair from a neighboring table to sit beside her, leaving the other empty chair at the table for the man with them.

"Dr. John Holliday," Wyatt said, introducing him to Katy. "The best dentist west of the Mississippi and a good friend. John arrived in Silverton late last night."

"We heard," Rait said. His tone and his manner were hostile.

"I just came by to see Wyatt," Doc said. "It is indeed a pleasure, Miss Halliday. Our names are remarkably similar."

"Yes, aren't they?" She was too overwhelmed by his negative personality to be impressed by meeting him.

"When are you leaving?" Rait asked him.

The way Doc fingered the front of his suit coat made Katy think he was planning to throw it open and go for his gun. "I guess now is as good a time as any." He slid his hand away from his lapel. "Wyatt, Josie, I'll see you tonight. Miss Halliday." He touched the brim of his hat and left.

"I know you don't like John," Wyatt said to Rait, "but that's no reason to be rude to him. Yesterday you were talking about the way he drinks, but it looks like you hit the bottle harder last night than John has in the last month."

"I need to get some sleep," Rait said. "Are you finished yet, Katy?"

She was but didn't want to leave. She also didn't want to argue with Rait. After they'd climbed the stairs to the third floor, he stopped her.

"Katy, John Holliday is a dangerous man. He kills more easily than any man I've ever known. I want you to stay away from him. Do you understand me?"

"Is he really that dangerous?"

"He's deadly. If his whore is in town with him, she's just as bad. Big-Nose Kate Elder is her name and she'll gut you with a dull knife if she thinks you've had anything to do with him."

Katy shuddered. Most of Rait's warnings and rules she had taken lightly. This one she didn't. Not just because Doc Holliday frightened her, but because he frightened Rait.

"I promise to stay away from him." She regarded Rait solemnly. "Did you really have a lot to drink last night?"

"I drink every night. Last night I had a few more whiskeys than usual."

Heroes never had flaws in dime novels. She hadn't expected real ones to have them, either.

"I have to get some sleep," he said. "I'll come by your room to take you down to lunch."

Once she was in her room, Katy opened her new journal, dipped her new pen in ink, and began chapter one of a brand-new story. At the top of the first page she wrote:

Matt Rash, U.S. Marshal, Meets the Deadliest Man in the West; or, Face to Face With the Devil in Denver

Chapter One: Matt Rash Meets the Devil

It was spring in Colorado. The mountains were shiny with snow and dripping with silver. Legendary lawman Matt Rash came to the Rockies to find a few days of peace. What he found was danger. . . .

Chapter Ten

It was Katy's thirteenth day in Silverton. She and Josie had become friends, which gave them both something to do besides sit in their hotel rooms while Wyatt gambled, Rait worked, and Katy waited for Bat to return.

Together, the two women explored Silverton. They went to the meetings of the Silverton Literary Society in the home of Emma Happs Tinker and listened to a reading from a book being compiled about the pioneers of the San Juans. They had tea in Amanda Cotton's home and saw the first piano brought to Silverton on the backs of pack mules.

They watched the baseball team practice in the field across from the schoolhouse and cheered the hook and ladder boys as they dashed around town. They listened to the Negro orchestra practicing for the Fourth of July celebration. They even toured the smelter, which smelled awful but dazzled them with stacks of silver and gold bars awaiting shipment to Durango and Denver.

Katy told Josie about her attempted robbery of the D&RG train, and Josie told Katy about how she'd married Wyatt on a boat in the Pacific Ocean beyond the three-mile limit.

"No preacher? No license?"

Josie shook her lovely head. "Just us and the captain. My parents aren't very happy, but I am." Josie Earp was a woman very obviously in love. She glowed with it. Every thought, every word, every movement she made was centered around Wyatt.

It was on this unlucky thirteenth day that Josie decided to go to the Arlington to watch Wyatt deal faro. Katy was devastated by the thought of being trapped indoors all day when Rait did something heroic. He volunteered to accompany her on her afternoon walk.

Katy was giddy with relief. "You can't imagine how happy I am not to have to listen all day to how wonderful Wyatt Earp is." She was also excited about going out with Rait. Except for Sunday services at the First Congregational Church, this was the first time they'd been out of the hotel together.

"Does that mean Wyatt isn't your hero anymore?" he asked.

"He's still that. I'd just rather read about his exploits with a gun than listen to Josie moon over how much she likes to make lo . . ." Katy stopped suddenly and changed the end of the sentence. "Loves him."

She hooked her hand through Rait's arm without waiting for him to offer it. He looked down at her from beneath the brim of his hat, his eyes shadowed but his expression clearly one of surprise.

"Do you mind?" she asked.

"I don't mind," he said and meant it.

He'd been studiously keeping his distance from her. Lunch and dinner were the only times they met, and then it was across a table and in a dining room filled with people. The only time they were alone was at the bottom of the stairs every night as he bid her good night before going to the bar. She hadn't kissed him again—to his relief and disappointment.

He'd also stopped drinking. Not since the day Doc Holliday appeared in Silverton had Rait touched a drop of liquor. He didn't know how much of his willpower came from wanting to be ready if Doc started trouble, or whether it was the disappointment that had dimmed Katy's eyes when she'd learned Rait drank. Either way, he was completely sober for the first time in a long time. It felt good.

"I need a new bottle of ink," Katy told him when they came to a stationery store.

"You bought a bottle two weeks ago."

"I've done a lot of writing since then," she told him proudly. "Close to a hundred pages, almost a whole book."

He went in the shop with her. She spent ten minutes deciding whether to get blue or black ink, then another five deciding what brand she preferred. By the time they left the store, Rait was openly fidgeting and Katy was secretly smiling.

She maneuvered him in the direction of the millinery shop near the photography studio. "Oh, I almost forgot," she said when they reached the shop. "I need a new pair of white gloves. I stained mine by picking dandelions on the way to church Sunday."

"I told you to leave those weeds alone."

"They're too pretty to be weeds. The preacher liked them, too. He said they looked cheerful setting on the pulpit beside his Bible."

Rait glanced into the millinery shop. There were half a dozen ladies inside. It had taken all his patience to wait in the stationery store while Katy made her choice. He wouldn't last a minute in there with all those women.

"I'll stay outside." He took out his wallet. "How much do you need?"

"Twenty dollars," she said.

He almost dropped the five-dollar bill he'd taken out. "For *gloves?*" he asked so loudly, people passing by stopped to stare.

"I need a few other things, too."

"I can't think of anything that could possibly cost twenty dollars, Katy. Exactly what is it you need?"

She lowered her gaze. "Female things," she said, speaking so softly he had to lean down to hear her.

Rait flushed. "Here," he said and shoved the money at her. "I'll be down the street in the cigar store."

Katy went into the shop and watched him leave through the window. This was going to be easier than she'd thought.

"May I help you, miss?" asked a saleslady with silver-blue hair.

"Yes," Katy said. "I need a pair of white gloves. Could you wrap them for me, please? I'll be right back to pay for them."

"What size?"

She paused in the open doorway. "This size." She held up her hand, palm outward, and then slipped out of the shop and ran down the street in the opposite direction as Rait.

She entered the hardware store breathless from her run. "I want to buy a gun," she told the man behind the counter.

He lifted one eyebrow and regarded her with a distasteful eye. "Ah, yes. The latest fashion accessory for a young lady's wardrobe. We've a nice .22 calibre pocket pistol, just the right size for an evening bag. It has a lovely pearl handle which should go perfectly with all your gowns."

Katy lifted one eyebrow and regarded him with a disdainful eye. "I want a Colt .45 calibre New Model Army Metallic Cartridge Revolving Pistol with six chambers in the cylinder, four and three-quarter inch barrel, nickel plated with a rubber stock. The one displayed in your window will be perfect. I'll need a box of .45 calibre metallic, self-exploding center-fire cartridges, too. And hurry, please."

The man's mouth was hanging open. "I guess you know a little about guns."

"Bat Masterson taught me," she said because it sounded more impressive than, "I read about them in a gun catalog I found on the train in Omaha."

"That will be forty dollars for the gun and one dollar for the cartridges. Do you need a holster or cartridge case?"

"No, I'll just carry everything in my shopping bag." She counted out the ten dollars Rait had given her the day she went out with Bat, the fifteen she'd managed to save since then by not spending a single penny on anything, not even ice cream, and sixteen of the twenty dollars Rait gave her today.

The salesman handed over the gun and box of cartridges. Katy dropped them in her bag. They barely fit and weighed a ton. She shoved the sales slip in with them and dashed back to the millinery shop. It felt like she was dragging an elephant with her. She ran inside, snatched up the package with the gloves, paid out two more dollars, and made it back outside just as Rait came out of the cigar store.

"Ready to go back to the hotel?" he asked.

"How about some ice cream first?" She brandished her remaining two dollars. "I'll buy."

She ate vanilla and he had strawberry. She finished hers first and he let her have the last bite of his.

"I like this better than my vanilla."

"I'll buy you strawberry tomorrow."

She was so surprised, she stopped licking ice cream drips off her fingers. "Really?"

"Unless you want chocolate," he said and tried to ignore that the way she was looking at him made him feel ten feet tall.

Katy smiled. "I'll have both."

When they reached the hotel, he went to the bar to check on business and Katy went to her room. She dumped the contents of her shopping bag on the bed and took a step back while she stared at the gun and the spilled box of cartridges.

She didn't have the slightest idea what to do with them. She didn't even know how to load a gun, much less fire it.

She bundled them in a Gypsy print scarf and hid it in the deepest corner of her bottom bureau drawer. Then she stood in the middle of the room and stared at the closed drawer. Knowing she had a gun in there was thrilling.

Even more thrilling, though, was the thought that maybe Rait was beginning to like her.

Chapter Eleven

Katy was up to her neck in threats and gun-fire. Bullets were flying around the room, the arch villain of her book was cowering behind the rocking chair, and Matt Rash was stretched out on top of the brocade bed canopy with his silver-handled Colt .45 Peacemaker, blasting away at the villain like the guardian angel of good that he was.

The shoot-out was the climax of her book. She'd intended for it to be instigated by an attempt to rob the grande dame of the dining room of her weighty jewels. After Katy's afternoon with Rait, though, the purpose and location of the fight had changed into an ice cream shop skirmish involving a difference of opinion over which was best, vanilla or strawberry. The subject had very little to do with the plot, but Katy didn't think that would matter much if the scene was interesting, so she killed off a few spectators including a woman who looked like Josie and a schoolboy in a striped baseball hat.

Creating a lot of animosity toward the arch villain, who looked a lot like Doc Holliday and was named Ratsy McPherson, would make the ending more dramatic. Ratsy was going to be shot in the gut in a few minutes. He would run out of the ice cream shop and down the street to the smelter where he would fall into a big bubbling vat and get melted into a bar of silver that would forever after be tarnished.

The knock on Katy's door made her jump. She usually didn't write at night, but the music coming up from the Grand Hotel Bar had been so inspiring, she hadn't been able to keep her pen off the paper. The real, live Western music made the story seem so much more dramatic and real.

She ran to the door and opened it. "Bat!"

"In the flesh. I just got back in town and came straight to see you." He frowned at her chenille robe. "Why aren't you dressed? Josie's already down in the lobby waiting to go."

"Go where?"

"To the dance, honey. Surely you've heard about it. The townsfolk have rented the Sage Hen's new hall on Blair Street for the evening. It's promising to be a real foot stomping good time."

Katy had heard about the big dance from Bessel while dressing for dinner tonight. It was to celebrate the roof going up on the new city hall.

"I never go anywhere at night, Bat. Rait doesn't want me out while he's working." After their pleasant afternoon, she had expected him to ask her if she wanted to go. It had been a terrible disappointment when he'd gone to work as usual.

Bat was scowling. "A pretty girl belongs at a dance," he said, and suddenly he looked as deadly as his reputation. "You start getting dressed. I'll be back for you as soon as I talk to Rait."

"Really? You'll ask him if I can go?"

"I'm going to *tell* him that you're going. Now get dressed, honey, and don't overdo it." He pointed at the open armoire, from which spilled the skirts of a dozen fancy dresses. "This is a country dance, not a ball. Wear something simple."

He left and Katy went spinning around the room in excitement. Bat was back in Silverton, he'd come straight to see her, and she was going to a dance! She stopped spinning. What if Rait said no?

"I won't think that way. I want to go, and I'm going. Bat said so. I'll see the inside of a

160

real dance hall on Blair Street and I'll have a wonderful time!"

It had been a long time since anyone talked to Rait like Bat had tonight. First, he'd lectured him, then he'd called him a few names that would have made a prison guard blush, then he'd come close to punching Rait out for not taking Katy to the dance.

The truth was, he'd thought about taking her. Business had to come first, though. That had been a hard decision to make after their pleasant afternoon, but he'd made it. He would have stuck by it, too, if Bat hadn't threatened to hang him from one of the Grand's chandeliers and shoot his legs off.

Katy threw open the door in response to Rait's knock and greeted him with flushed cheeks and sparkling eyes.

"Oh," she said and her face fell. "I thought you were Bat. Does your being here mean I can't go to the dance?"

"You want to go to this thing?"

Her chin lifted in defiance. "Yes, I do."

"With Bat?"

"With you," she said, looking him straight in the eye. "But you didn't ask me. He did."

"Do you have something to wear?"

161

"I think so. Bat said to wear something simple."

"All right. We'll go."

Her face brightened instantly. "You, too?"

He nodded. "Be downstairs in the lobby in five minutes."

It was ten minutes before she came down. Josie and Wyatt, Bat and Rait were all waiting for her.

Katy was wearing a white cotton dress with a ruffled collar and cuffs. Over it, she wore a yellow calico pinafore which made her look about twelve years old. She'd left her hair down and tied it back with yellow and white ribbons. Her shoes had little straps around the ankles and a bow on the toes.

At the last second before she left her room, she'd unwrapped her gun and retrieved the Gypsy shawl from her drawer to wear around her shoulders. She loved its bright colors and the fringe around its edges.

She skipped down the steps, pausing when she was almost at the bottom, and held out the skirt of her dress through the open sides of the pinafore. "Will this do?"

"Perfect," Bat said, "and pretty, too."

Rait agreed. She looked country-girl fresh

162

and her eyes were filled with rainbows.

"Shall we go?" Bat asked and offered Katy his arm.

But Rait reached for her hand, capturing it in his, and pulled her out of the lobby and into the night while the sound of Bat's laughter rang out behind them.

It was the first time she'd been out at night. It was every bit as exciting as she'd expected it would be when looking down on it from her third-floor window. People thronged everywhere, most of them heading for the same place as Katy's little group.

"The Bowens have rented their Blair Street dance hall out to the town for tonight," Rait told Katy. "There's more in that building than the dance floor, though. I don't want you upstairs at all or outside without me. Understood?"

She was too busy looking at everything to speak, so she nodded her head.

"You'll have to dance with a lot of strangers, Katy. If any of them try anything, just walk away from them right on the dance floor and I'll handle the situation."

She nodded again.

"Don't drink anything that doesn't smell like punch and don't go around flirting with everything in pants."

She nodded again.

"Are you listening to me?"

"Yes, Rait." She pointed at a shady-looking building huddled in the alley between Greene and Blair. "Is that an opium den?"

"Inside," he ordered and pushed her through the open door of the Bowen hall into a different world.

It was exactly like Katy had imagined it would be. There were mirrors everywhere, dozens of them covering every wall. They caught and reflected the light from crystal chandeliers suspended from the high ceiling, bathing the hall in sparkling brightness. Chairs lined the walls beneath the mirrors except for one wall. It held a bar stretching from one end of the room all the way to the other.

On the bar were barrels of beer, cider, and blackberry wine. Kegs of wine and a huge glass bowl filled with what Josie called "schoolmarm punch" were also in prominence. More drinking glasses than Katy had ever seen in her life lined a shelf behind the bar, and a man wearing a green velvet vest and a toothy smile was filling them all to the brim with ordered drinks.

"No whiskey," Bat said to Rait.

"I wasn't looking for any."

164

A group of musicians was gathering on the stage beside the stairs to the second floor. Katy kept sneaking glances up there, but all she saw were closed doors and shadows.

The hall downstairs was overflowing with people. Every decent citizen in town was there, and they were ready to dance. The fiddle player sliced a note out of his strings, the caller came to the front of the stage and cried out, "The Paw Paw Patch!" and would-be dancers rushed onto the floor.

Josie and Wyatt were the first ones out. They stood a foot or so apart and behind them the other couples formed into lines, men in one column, women in the other.

"Let's go," Bat said to Katy.

"I don't know how, Bat. All I know is the waltz and I've only done it in dance class."

"This one's easy, honey. Just watch what everyone else does and when your turn comes, do the same. Come on."

Before Katy could think of another reason not to go out, she was being pushed into the last position in the women's column. Bat took his place across from her just as the musicians started playing a rollicking tune.

Katy had time to glance at Rait, who was standing on the sidelines with his arms crossed. She thought he was looking right at her, but couldn't be certain before the dancing began and she had to turn her attention to what she was supposed to do.

"Where, oh where, is dear Little Nelly?
Where, oh where, is dear little Nelly?
Where, oh where, is dear little Nelly?
Way down yonder in the Paw Paw Patch!"

On the first "Where, oh where," Josie turned to her right and skipped down the outside of the women's column, came up outside the men's column and back to her place. She was wearing her hair loose, too, and an emerald green dress and earrings that dangled when she skipped. Wyatt's gaze never left her.

"Come on, boys, let's go find her,
Come on, boys, let's go find her,
Come on, boys, let's go find her,
Way down yonder in the Paw Paw Patch!"

Josie again skipped around the set. This time, Wyatt led the men's column after her while all the rest of the women stayed stationary, clapping their hands and laughing at the ridiculous sight of the men skipping. Bat looked the silliest, dressed to the nines in his gambler's suit and diamond stickpin and skipping about the hall like a schoolboy until everyone was back in their original places.

"Picking up Paw Paws, put 'em in your pocket."

The partners joined hands. Josie and Wyatt turned right and skipped to the bottom of the column to stand behind Katy and Bat.

"Picking up Paw Paws, put 'em in your pocket."

Josie and Wyatt made an arch with their joined hands. Starting with the second couple, everyone skipped around and under the arch.

"Picking up Paw Paws, put 'em in your pocket."

All the couples returned to their places in the column, except for Josie and Wyatt, who were now the last couple.

"Way down yonder in the Paw Paw Patch!"

Everyone sang the last line and then the whole thing began again, with the second couple in the first round now acting as the lead couple. As the dance went on, the caller sometimes changed "dear little Nelly" to "poor little Willy." Then the lead man would skip by himself and the column of women would chase Willy around the paw paw patch.

When it was Katy's turn, she was Nelly and she skipped, embarrassed and blushing, all the way around. When she and Bat were building their arch, her side was so short that Wyatt knocked his head against her arms and they fell over in a tangle of arms, legs, and pinafore strings. The whole crowd loved it. Everyone laughed and suddenly, instead of feeling like a visitor to Silverton, Katy felt like she belonged.

Wyatt picked her up, Bat dusted her off, and Rait watched from the sidelines.

"Shoo Fly" was next. The catchy tune made Katy's toes tap. The dance was more complicated than the "Paw Paw Patch." Her partner was Wyatt this time while Bat squired Josie. The basic step was a simple walking step, which Katy handled well. It was when the caller started crying out terms like promenade, swing your partner, swing your corner, allemande left, grand right and left, and do-si-do that she became so confused, she began to not only trip over her own feet, but everyone else's, too.

The dancers took her problem in stride. Whoever was closest to her pointed her in the right direction, Wyatt shouted instructions that made almost as little sense as the caller's, and Bat laughed so loudly, no one could hear the fiddler.

"No, this way," Wyatt said and took Katy's hands. "We have to turn the corner with the left hand once and then half around in eight steps, end at the corner and switch partners. You go with the man on your left."

Her new bearded partner introduced himself as "Dr. Lawrence," and they joined hands and formed into a circle.

Harry LeRoy was her next "Shoo Fly" partner, then came "Tom Cain, happy to know you," "Pat Cain, Tom's brother," Mike Larnagan, "Butch Waggoner, ma'am," and finally "I'm Riley Lambert and don't you be embarrassed, sweetie. Everyone has trouble the first time."

Her next partner was Doc Holliday. She hadn't seen him since his first day in Silverton. He looked as mean and greasy as before and Katy shuddered when he touched her. She wondered if Rait knew he was here. She also wondered what he thought about Doc dancing with her.

Bat claimed her again as partner for "Skip to My Lou." The lineup this time was a single circle of couples, women to the right of the men and everyone facing the center of the circle. Men moved to the center in four steps, clapped their hands and moved back again. Then it was the women's turn. Up, clap, and back.

"Swing your partner with a two-hand turn

and promenade! Swing her again with a two-hand turn, promenade with your corner and keep her for another round!"

Katy was breathless and laughing after the second two-hand turn with Bat. When she turned to her corner to promenade with her new partner, there was Rait waiting for her. She was so surprised, she missed a step. He helped her recover and they went around the circle, holding hands with arms crossed over and eyes too shy to look at anything except the backs of the couple in front of them.

"I didn't know you were going to dance," Katy said halfway around the promenade.

"I didn't know you were so clumsy," he said.

She looked up at him; he winked at her; she blushed bright red. Before she could recover, the promenade was over and he was moving into the center of the circle to clap his hands. On the next promenade around, she didn't miss a step. He winked at her again before the switch of partners. For the rest of "Skip to My Lou," Katy was aware of nothing except the sight of Rait smiling down at her, his hair tumbled from dancing and his eyes bright with fun.

He danced every dance after that. Every time she looked up, there he was, either as her partner or watching her while he partnered someone else.

Katy did the wagon wheel and boxed the gnat and do-si-doed. She sashayed and half-sashayed and re-sashayed. She made chains and stars and did grand squares and danced to "Honest John" and "Dive For the Oyster."

By then it was well after midnight and everyone in the hall was hot and tired and too winded to promenade even one more step. So they drank the last of the schoolmarm punch and the blackberry wine and called the evening a success.

Rait wrapped Katy in her shawl, took her hand in his, and led her out into the night. It was cool and the stars were bright and the moon was almost full. She didn't even glance across the street to see if anyone was coming or going from Teddy Dick's crib on the corner or the suspected opium den in the alley. She just looked at the stars and caught glimpses of Rait out of the corner of her eye.

When they reached the third floor of the Grand and were outside Katy's door, she finally looked straight up at him.

"Thank you for taking me to the dance tonight."

His eyes were dark and she could feel his gaze reaching down to touch her.

"I had a good time," she said.

171

Rait almost kissed her then. She looked young and happy and prettier than anything he'd ever seen in his life.

"So did I. Good night, Katy."

He was gone before she could say anything at all.

Chapter Twelve

The midday sun bakes the earth. The street is deserted. Even the flies have left town. The silence is menacing, there is a sense of suppressed violence about to explode.

Suddenly, the gunfighter appears. His skin is the color of old saddle leather, his eyes cold and steady beneath the brim of his dusty sombrero. His holster is tied to his thigh with buckskin thongs.

One slow step at a time he moves down the street. His hands hang casually at his sides. His eyes see everything.

A face appears at a window. A dog barks, and is silenced. A hot wind slices at the gunfighter's face. He keeps walking.

At the end of the street, a man is waiting for the gunfighter. He is tall and his gun is strapped tight to his right thigh. He is ready.

For a long moment, the two men take each other's measure. Their hands jerk to the butts of their guns and the stillness of the day is shattered by the spurting flame and jarring crash of two Colt .45s being fired at pointblank range.

When the smoke clears, only one man is standing. The man with the star.

"You must be the worst shot in the whole West, honey," Bat said. "Don't whip the gun out, pull it out. And don't start firing immediately. You have to aim. Otherwise, you'll be as dead as the man beneath that tombstone you just drilled."

It was the day after the dance. Katy and Josie had been planning to have a picnic beside Cement Creek at the foot of Cemetery Hill. Before they left the hotel, Katy saw Bat, Wyatt, and Doc Holliday engaged in an intense discussion on the boardwalk in front of the hotel. Because Bat felt the same about Doc as Rait, she was surprised to see him include the dentist in whatever he and Wyatt were talking about.

"What's going on?" she asked Josie.

"All I know is Bat came back to Silverton for a reason other than to gamble. He and Wyatt have had their heads together all morning, and Bat's received half a dozen telegrams since he arrived last night."

Now the famous threesome were loading a sack into the back of the light delivery wagon Wyatt used to get around town.

"Those are the empty bottles Wyatt collected from the bar downstairs," Josie said. "They must be going out to shoot. Let's go with them."

Katy's eyes widened. "Let me get something in my room first." She left the picnic basket with Josie and ran all the way to the third floor. She was back before the men left. "I'm ready," she said and lugged her shopping bag out to the wagon.

The women hadn't exactly been welcomed with open arms, but because Wyatt suffered from the inability to tell Josie no, they were assisted into the wagon. Bat loaded their picnic basket and a few minutes later, they were on the outskirts of town and Doc Holliday was setting up bottles beside Cement Creek.

When Katy produced her gun and asked Bat to teach her to shoot, she'd expected him to laugh himself sick. He hadn't even cracked a smile.

"Does Rait know you have this?" he asked.

"Of course, he doesn't. I bought it because writers need to know what they're writing about. All I want to do is learn how to shoot,

Bat. Then I'll either sell it or give it to my uncle. I promise."

"You might as well teach her," Wyatt said. "Otherwise she'll try to learn on her own and kill herself, or someone else."

"I'll show you," Doc said to Katy. "I teach boys to shoot all the time. A girl isn't any different."

"No," Bat said, "I'll teach her, and girls are different, aren't they, Josie? Remember when Wyatt tried to teach you to shoot?"

Josie blushed deep red. "How can I forget? You remind me every time you see me."

Bat laughed. "We were on a fishing trip, Katy, and Wyatt decided Josie needed to learn to shoot. He set up a target and handed her his rifle. She lifted it to her shoulder, sighted, then dropped it and ran for the tent. We didn't see her the rest of the day. Pitiful display of female courage. You're going to do a lot better, though, honey. Any woman brave enough to crawl on top of a moving train isn't going to be afraid to fire a gun." He took her Colt and the box of cartridges. "At least you bought the best. Now, honey, if you don't do everything exactly the way I tell you, we stop immediately and I tell Rait what you're carrying around in that fancy bag."

He went into a long explanation that started

176

with listing the parts of her gun, covered every safety rule known to mankind since the beginning of the world, included a lecture about the hazards of guns in the hands of amateurs, and ended with showing her how to load her Colt.

"The main rule to remember is never fire in haste. A quick draw isn't of any use if you can't hit the side of a barn while you're inside it with the door closed. I've known men who could pull a pistol faster than I can blink, but they couldn't hit their foot if they stuck their gun barrel inside their boot before they pulled the trigger. You have to aim, then fire."

Doc and Wyatt were blasting away at bottles while he talked. Josie was watching Wyatt with love in her eyes and a fried chicken breast in her hands. Nearby, the men of the Silverton Jockey Club were working at a feverish pace to get their racetrack finished before the Fourth. And Katy was learning everything she'd ever wanted to know about how to shoot a Colt .45 Peacemaker.

Bat showed her the proper form and made her watch him blast a dozen empty whiskey bottles into shards of glass that sparkled like starlight among the dandelions beside the creek.

Wyatt Earp was good. He had style and flair and it was a pleasure to watch him shoot. Doc Holliday kept a sneer on his face all the time he was shooting, and he hit everything he aimed at no matter the distance or difficulty. But, Bat was the best. Watching Bat Masterson shoot was like listening to beautiful poetry.

Katy had read that when he killed a man, he enjoyed it. She knew he didn't enjoy the killing, though. It was the shooting he loved.

"All right, honey. I think it's time you felt how this thing kicked." He loaded one cartridge into the cylinder, closed it, and cocked the gun. "Aim it at the side of the hill behind us, Katy. That way you can't hit anything vital, like me."

She pointed the gun at the bottom of the cemetery hill. She took a bead on a scrubby growth of silvery sagebrush, and, like Bat had told her, squeezed the trigger.

The bush shuddered.

"I hit it! Bat, I hit it!" She threw her arms around his neck and hugged him as hard as she could.

"Now you know why I only put one bullet in the gun," Bat said to Wyatt, who was laughing. "Otherwise I'd be missing an ear right now."

"What I want to know is how you got that bush to move so she'd think she hit it?"

Katy pulled back and stared at Bat. "You didn't, did you?"

"No, honey. You hit it. Wyatt's just jealous

178

that he isn't teaching you to shoot. He'll do anything to get a woman to hug him."

She blushed. "I guess I got carried away."

"I enjoyed your getting carried away, but the next time it happens, put the gun down first because I'm going to put a full load in it."

Six shots later, all of which put the fear of God into the sagebrush, she strapped on Bat's holster, which wasn't easy while wearing a dress. Josie cut a little hole in the front and back of Katy's skirt, helped her thread the holster thong through, and tied it in the back.

That's when the badman in the sombrero appeared. He'd walked out of the dusty alleys of her imagination and taken up a position right in front of the sagebrush. In her haste to gun the deadly deed doer down, she'd shot a hole in some poor citizen's tombstone.

"All right, honey, try it again. Don't put your finger on the trigger until you have the gun aimed. Otherwise, you might blow your leg off. That's it. Do it slow until you get your aim perfect every time, then you can start working on speed. Aim is the only thing that matters. If you don't hit your target, you'll be too dead to tell anyone you drew first."

"What's going on here?" The voice was as sharp as the Bowie knife Doc had used to carve his name in the side of Wyatt's wagon.

179

Katy spun around and stared with wide eyes at Rait. He looked like a hurricane that was about to hit land. And he was staring at her gun.

"It's his," she said and tossed her Colt to Bat.

Rait lowered his gaze to the holster strapped to her leg.

"That's his, too." She almost tore her skirt off trying to get the holster untied. "I just wanted to see what it felt like to wear one. And the gun wasn't loaded."

Her claim might have been more believable if Bat hadn't been emptying the unused cartridges from her Colt's cylinder into his hand. She noticed Wyatt, Josie, and Doc watching her little drama unfold like it was a play being staged for their enjoyment.

"So I taught the girl to shoot," Bat said. "It's nothing to get riled up about, Rait. She did a good job. A little more practice and she'll be entering shooting matches with Annie Oakley."

Rait was glaring at Katy. "Why didn't you ask me to teach you?"

She returned his searing gaze with one just as fiery. "Because I didn't want you to look at me like you're doing right now. It was just research for my book. It's not like I went out and bought a gun."

Bat almost choked.

She ignored him and kept her angry gaze fixed on Rait. "I thought you were going to take inventory this afternoon to see how many bottles of whiskey your bartenders stole last night while you were wasting time dancing with me."

He'd caught her with a gun, but he was the one defending himself. "I came out here to deliver these." He shoved a package and telegram at Bat.

Rait had actually come looking for Katy after the room clerk at the Grand reported seeing Bat help her into Wyatt's wagon. The delivery was just an excuse to follow them.

Bat opened the package. "These are our photographs, Katy."

"Let me see!" She leaned against his arm and began to laugh. "We look wonderful!"

The rest of the group crowded around, too. When Rait saw what was causing so much laughter, his chest felt like someone had pumped a dozen bullets into it. "What do you mean posing like this with Bat's arms around you?" he thundered at Katy, but couldn't stop staring at her overexposed legs.

"We'll have to do this, too," Wyatt said to Josie. "I like this one where they're laughing the best. What were you doing to her, Bat?"

He wasn't listening. He'd moved a distance from the group and was reading the telegram. Rait forgot his anger as he watched Bat's expression turn grim. Wyatt noticed, too. Doc was watching Bat and fingering the handle of his gun. There was blood lust in his eyes.

Bat looked up and met Wyatt's gaze. Then he looked at Rait. The three men moved away from the women while Doc stood alone and waited.

"What is it?" Rait asked.

Bat folded the telegram and slipped it in his pocket. "There's been a little trouble in Dodge. You know Luke Short, don't you, Rait?"

Luke Short was one of the better known gunfighters in the west. He'd been in Dodge during its peak and in Tombstone when the Clantons were stirring up cemetery dust. Since then, he'd gone back to Dodge and bought into the Long Branch Saloon as a partner. Rait knew Luke as a straight shooter who didn't look for trouble . . . or run from it.

"I know him."

"He and the mayor of Dodge had a difference of opinion over the way Luke was running his saloon recently. Two weeks ago, Luke was arrested on a trumped-up charge and run out of town. They didn't even give him a trial, just put a gun in his back, and marched him to the depot. He wired me about it when I was in Denver. Things have gone from bad to worse since then. This wire is from the governor of Kansas. He's authorizing Wyatt and me to put a stop to the trouble before someone gets killed. It'll take more than just the two of us, though, to settle this affair without bloodshed."

Rait didn't like the direction this conversation was going. He crossed his arms over his chest. "I'm not throwing in with you."

"Doc's not going, if that's what's bothering you. I don't want him, and Luke hates him more than you and I do."

"I was glad John was in Tombstone to back me up two years ago while Bat went to Dodge to help Jim," Wyatt said, "but the truth is, John's the reason those men died in that affair. I could have talked Billy Clanton out of a fight, but John was too quick on the trigger. I don't want a repeat of that tragedy in Dodge, so I've asked him to stay out of this unless I send for him. We could use your help, though, Rait. You have a cool head and a steady hand, if it comes to that."

"You're asking the wrong man. I didn't just give up my badge last year, I gave up wanting to right the world's wrongs."

"I don't believe that," Bat said. "What's more, I don't think you do, either. All right,

Angie left you. Get over it. Stop finding ways to make yourself miserable so you can't forget how much she hurt you. It's not going to bring her back."

Rait balled his hands into fists. "I'm not getting involved, Bat."

Bat sighed. "If that's the way you want it, fine. I won't mention it again. There is one thing you should know before you turn your back on this, though. I've sent word to a few friends that Wyatt and I need their help. They're on their way to Silverton right now. I don't think you want Katy around when they get here."

"What do you suggest I do with her?"

"Take her out of town for a few days," Wyatt said.

"While Bat's here?" Rait gave a scathing laugh.

Bat locked gazes with Rait. The two men said a lot in the next few seconds, all of it in silence.

"That's something else you're wrong about," Bat said. "Only this time instead of just hurting yourself, Katy's a victim, too. You used to be a good lawman, Caldwell. Now you're nothing but a damn fool."

Rait would have had it out with Bat right then, but Wyatt stepped between them.

184

"That's enough," he said. "I want this stopped right here. Rait, back off. Bat, keep your opinions to yourself."

There were only two men Rait respected enough to take orders from, one was Wyatt. The other used to be Bat.

"I'm leaving Silverton tonight to meet Luke," Bat said. "Wyatt will be leaving tomorrow or the next day, depending on when the boys get here. If you keep Katy distracted for the next two days, Rait, maybe she won't even notice there's a convention of gunslingers in town."

It was too late to distract Katy, though.

Because Josie was telling her the tale of how she'd fallen in love with Wyatt while he was shooting at targets in Tombstone, Katy couldn't hear everything the men were talking about. She did hear, more than once, her name. When Josie finished the last chapter of her falling-in-love saga, Katy heard a lot more than just her name.

"I'm leaving Silverton tonight to meet Luke," Bat said. "Wyatt will be leaving tomorrow or the next day, depending on when the boys get here. If you keep Katy distracted for the next two days, Rait, maybe she won't even notice there's a convention of gunslingers in town."

The only other thing Katy needed to know, she learned from looking at Doc Holliday. He wasn't part of the discussion between Rait, Bat, and Wyatt, but he knew what it was about. His deadly gaze never left Wyatt's face and his hand never left the handle of the gun strapped to his leg.

Chapter Thirteen

The night was dark and cold and the streets were crowded. Katy had spent every night watching the flow of Silverton nightlife from her hotel window. Last night, she'd been a part of it herself. Now she was part of it again. Only this time, she was alone. She walked north on Green Street to Thirteenth, turned east and headed for Blair Street.

She knew exactly where she was going, thanks to Josie Earp.

After dinner while Rait was in the Grand Hotel Bar, Katy had gone to Josie's room. Wyatt was at the Arlington, and Josie had just curled up in bed with a novel.

"Do you know Big-Nose Kate Elder?" Katy asked.

"I've met her. I don't like her. How do you know about her?"

Katy shrugged. "I've read about her." She wandered around Josie's and Wyatt's room, touching bottles of perfume on the dressing table and the tie Wyatt had been wearing that day. "I was just wondering what she's like. You know, for my book. I've never met a prostitute. Is it unusual for them to follow a man around the way she does Doc Holliday?"

"Kate and John have been together for years. They took up together when Wyatt was a deputy in Dodge City. John earns enough to support her with his gambling. I don't know why she still works, but she always rents a crib in the red light district of whatever town they're in."

"So she's down on Blair Street right now?"

"Near Thirteenth Street, I think." Josie glanced at the novel lying open on her lap. "I really don't know much else about her, Katy. Wyatt makes John keep her away from me. He's so protective of me."

"I was just curious," Katy said. "Thanks, Josie. Good night."

She'd gone back to her room to wait for Rait to leave the Grand. It was almost exactly midnight when, by leaning out the window of room 303, she saw him appear on the corner of Green and Twelfth. He looked tall and handsome. Seeing him caused her breath to catch in her throat.

Before crossing the street to make his nightly walk to the Hub Saloon, he glanced up at her window. Katy threw herself back inside the room so fast, she fell over the writing desk. By the time she'd regained her balance and looked out again, this time from a more discreet position behind the curtain, Rait was walking away.

The glance up at her window was the first variation in his routine since her arrival in Silverton. It had made her so nervous, she'd almost canceled her plans. Finding out why Bat and Wyatt needed a convention of gunfighters was more important than getting in trouble with Rait, though, and so she left her room before he was even out of sight.

Now, as she reached Blair Street, she wondered what to do next. Did she knock on the door of every crib in town asking for Big-Nose Kate Elder?

Some of the little rooms bathed in the evil glow of their red lights had their doors and front windows thrown wide open. Inside were women displaying themselves in provocative clothing to the men passing by. Katy saw a man approach one of the barely dressed women. A few words were exchanged, then the man went inside. The door closed, the shade was pulled, and Katy looked hastily away. Except she couldn't make herself stop thinking about what was happening behind that closed door.

Did Rait come down here? Were the women of Blair Street the reason why, no matter how desperately she prayed, he continued to treat her like an inconvenience?

"You lookin' for company, little girl?"

Katy had been so involved in watching the women in the cribs, she hadn't realized there were men watching her. Her suitor was as big as an ox and so pale from spending the daylight hours of his life underground, the red lights from the cribs gave him a garish, unearthly pallor. "I'm looking for Kate Elder. Do you know which place is hers?"

The man pointed out the second crib from the end of the row. "Tell her if she hires you on, Black Jack Christy wants the first go. I might not turn loose of a little thing like you 'til next week. She'd make a bundle off you, that's for sure. Lordy, girl, you got the prettiest eyes I ever did see."

Katy laughed. "I'll tell her, Mr. Christy, and thank you." She walked with a saucy step to Kate Elder's door. It was closed, the shade drawn.

Now what? She didn't know how long it took for business to be conducted.

"You looking for Kate?" asked a woman standing in the open door of the last crib on the line.

"I wanted to ask her something," Katy said. She couldn't believe she was talking to a real

190

prostitute. It made her feel tongue-tied and very young.

"Ask me, doll baby. My name's Lilly Gold. Maybe I can help you out."

Katy was stunned. This was the woman Bat had said went to college in the East. She tried not to stare, but Lilly looked so different. Her pretty face and pale blond hair looked flat and ugly under the harsh red light over her door. She was wearing a dress so thin, Katy could see right through it. Under it, there wasn't anything but skin.

"I thought you ran your own bordello," Katy said.

"Things were a little tough this winter and I had to sell out. I own this row of cribs, though, and I take a cut of the girls' earnings who rent from me. I do all right." She looked at Katy a little closer. "Didn't I see you on Greene Street a few weeks ago with Bat Masterson?"

"You were coming out of a hat shop."

"That's right."

"Bat told me you went to college."

Lilly smiled fondly. "He has a good memory. I told him that last year when he was in Silverton." Her smile faded as she saw Black Jack Christy bearing down on them like a bull in heat. "What's your name, doll baby?"

"Katy Halliday."

"Well, Katy, I think you'd better come in here off the street. The lions are starting to circle because they think I'm hiring fresh meat."

Katy couldn't believe she was really inside a crib. The front room where Lilly did her street business contained an iron bed, a ladder-backed chair, and a washstand with a bowl and pitcher. A towel hung from the side of the washstand. There was an oil lantern hanging on the wall that gave off a hazy, soft glow of light.

"No, she's not," Lilly was saying to Black Jack. "The doll baby is just paying me a social call. Go find someone else to play with tonight."

After he left, she closed the door and pulled the shade. She sat on the bed and waved Katy into the chair. Beside it was a lace curtain covering what looked like a dressing room.

"Tell me what you want with Kate, Katy," Lilly said.

Both of them started laughing at the same time like schoolgirls at a silly joke. Katy relaxed as she realized talking to Lilly was like talking to any woman, except Lilly had on a lot less clothes.

"I heard Bat say there was a group of gunmen coming to Silverton. I want to know why, but he and my guardian, Rait Caldwell, won't tell me. I thought maybe Doc would, only I don't know where to find him. I was hoping Kate Elder would tell me."

"Kate would tell you where to go all right," Lilly said with a laugh. "She doesn't like women chasing after her man, especially young ones like you."

"Is she really as mean as Rait says?"

"She's as mean as they come. Two nights ago, she pulled a knife on a man who tried to get more than he paid for." Lilly pushed her hair back off her face. "Rait Caldwell's your guardian?" she asked, drawing Katy's attention away from the contents of the crib's back room.

"Just until my uncle comes back from England. Rait is a friend of Uncle Richard's. Do you know Rait?" She didn't really want to know, but couldn't stop the question from just blurting itself out.

"He's not a customer, if that's what you're asking." Lilly's face softened. "I wouldn't throw him out if he knocked on my door, though."

"Does he knock on any of the doors down here?"

Lilly was looking at Katy with an almost hostile expression. "Is there something between you and Rait?"

Katy sighed. "The only reason he knows I'm alive is because a lawyer told him he was stuck with me until Uncle Richard returns." She gave the dressing room another quick glance. "How come you're in this line of business, Miss Gold? I mean, you went to college. What happened?"

"Some women end up on the line because they lose their husbands and can't earn a living any other way. Some girls trust a man they shouldn't and get turned out by their family. And some of us do it because we like it. That's my story. I also like the money, which is good if you're running a house and not bad if you own a row of cribs."

Katy gave the dressing room another glance.

Lilly smiled. "You're so curious about what's in there, you're about ready to pop a seam, doll baby. Go on in if you want to see the tools of my trade."

Katy didn't need a second invitation.

On the other side of the curtain was a beautiful wardrobe mirror and a steamer trunk overflowing with stockings and feathers and filmy chemises and the fanciest corsets Katy had ever seen.

"Try some of it on if you want," Lilly said. "See what it feels like to dress like a line girl."

"Well," Katy said as she picked up a black lace corset. It had no lining, which made it almost totally see-through. "Maybe just for research."

Rait was so mad, he could have bitten a bullet

in half. The flash of movement he'd seen in Katy's window had bothered him all the way to the Hub. He'd paced around the gambling tables for the better part of an hour before he'd given into his suspicions and headed back to the Grand.

Sure enough, her room had been empty. When he'd gone to see if she was with Josie and heard about Katy's sudden interest in Doc's paramour, Rait had immediately stormed out of the hotel and headed for Blair Street.

Kate Elder had almost knifed him when he accused her of lying about having seen Katy. "I know she came down here to find you," Rait had argued.

"She didn't do a very good job of it, then, because I ain't seen her. Now get the hell out of my crib, boy. I got a man waiting to be serviced."

After Kate Elder slammed the door in Rait's face, he started walking the streets. He knew Katy was down here somewhere. She was so young, so innocent. If she knew the thoughts he had about her, she'd probably have Bat shoot him. There was no telling what would happen if one of these rough-minded miners tried anything with her.

When there wasn't any sign of her in the crowds milling around on Blair and he didn't find her crumpled and lifeless body in any of the alleys, Rait's concern turned to anger. Where the hell was she?

He started at the corner on Thirteenth and began asking the girls who weren't busy if they'd seen Katy. If a crib door was closed, he banged on it with his fist until the inhabitants roused themselves from their labors to see what he wanted. No one had seen her.

When he came to Big-Nose Kate's crib, he passed it and went onto the last one on the row. The shade was drawn, the door closed. He smacked his fist against the thin wood.

"I'm busy!" the owner shouted.

"Open up, Lilly! I want to ask you a few questions!"

Lilly stared at the front door to the crib. "It's the marshal."

"Open the door, Lilly!" the voice attached to the pounding fist bellowed.

"Listen, doll baby. Stay back here out of sight while I see what he wants."

She sounded worried, but Katy was too busy trying to figure out how to fit a little bit more of herself into the low-cut corset to pay attention to Lilly's agitation.

"Don't let him see you," she warned Katy again before dropping the lace curtain between them.

Katy viewed her image in the dimly lit mirror. She didn't look like herself at all. Her hair was down, loose and flowing across her bare shoulders and down her back almost to her waist. The black lace corset fit like a second skin, and she could see most of her first one through it.

Under it, she wore a tiny pair of black silk drawers. Her shortest pair at home ended at her knees. These barely covered her bottom. Between their flared hems and the top of the black stockings that she wore was bare skin.

She stepped into a pair of shoes with three-inch heels Lilly had pulled from under a chair. They were a little small, but Katy managed to squeeze her feet into them. Her stockings were held up by red garters, which matched the red ribbon she'd tied around her throat. She chose a black shawl patterned with red roses and trimmed with the longest fringe she'd ever seen in her life to drape around her shoulders.

One of the garters was slipping and letting her stocking sag. Katy put her left foot on the chair, leaned over and began straightening the stocking.

Rait was suspicious of the way Lilly Gold refused to answer his questions. "Have you seen the girl or not?"

"You're not the law anymore," Lilly said. "You can't come around here knocking my door down and demanding I answer your questions."

Rait stopped listening after her comment about his not being the law. There was someone moving around in the back room. Through the lace curtain covering the doorway, he saw a mirror. Reflected in the glass was a woman's leg. She stood with her foot on a chair, and as Rait watched, she leaned over to run her fingers up the sheer black stocking embracing her slender leg.

Her hair, black as sin and soft as an angel's whisper, fell across her face as she bent over. The shawl she wore slipped off her shoulder and revealed a softly rounded shoulder and a lace-molded breast. His chest contracted and it felt like someone had slammed a fist into his stomach.

"I thought you weren't interested in that sort of thing anymore," Lilly said.

Rait tore his gaze from the mirror. "I'm not."

"Are you telling me, Rait, or yourself? You might have convinced yourself the reason you stopped coming here was because you didn't want to associate with my kind, but we both know the real reason. But that look on your face makes me think you're ready to give the girls on Blair Street another chance."

Rait's gaze moved back to the mirror. The leg was still there. The hands were playing with a red garter positioned high on the loveliest thigh he'd ever seen.

"Who is she, Lilly?" His voice sounded pained.

"Are you interested? I want to hear you say it, Rait. You hurt me when you blamed your problem on me for not being woman enough to interest you. I want to hear you ask for my little friend in the back room."

Rait could feel the shuddering of his breath in his burning lungs. He didn't want to do this again. But, he couldn't look away, either. The girl had put her leg down, but the mirror still held her image as she turned her back to her reflection. She placed her other foot on the chair and began straightening that stocking. As she bent over, her brief drawers revealed a pale crescent of her bare bottom.

"I want her," Rait said, the confession tearing out of him. The image of Katy burned in his mind. She was out there somewhere and she needed him, but he needed this. He'd needed it for so long.

"Then by all means, let me introduce you," Lilly said. She reached for the white lace curtain and pulled it aside.

The girl turned, gasped, and it wasn't until Rait heard her surprised intake of breath that he recognized her.

"Ex-Deputy Marshal Caldwell," Lilly said in a mocking voice, "meet your little ward."

"Katy," he said, unable to even shout at her.

She was beautiful and he wanted her even more than before. He wanted her the way he'd wanted her from the first moment she'd stepped off the train in Durango and looked up at him with her rainbow eyes and sparkling laughter.

"What are you doing here?" he asked, and now the anger was back. What did she think she was doing parading around Blair Street almost naked? And she was almost naked. Every inch of her was very close to being completely naked. "You have five minutes to get dressed," he ordered. "I'll be waiting outside."

He ripped his gaze away from her and made straight for the door, but couldn't open it. He stood there for a lifetime, his eyes closed and his hand locked around the cold metal handle before he released it and turned back to face the tiny crib where the past flickered like a bonfire in Lilly's laughing eyes.

Rait looked from her to Katy. Dear God, what was wrong with him? This child was in his protection and all he wanted to do was rip that vulgar corset off and fall on her like a stallion in heat.

"I'm not waiting five minutes," he said and stripped the blanket off Lilly's business bed. He went to where Katy stood, silent and beautiful in front of the mirror.

He hesitated for a heartbeat, then wrapped the blanket around her nakedness. He picked her up and walked to the door, which he kicked open and off its hinges. He walked over it, down the street and straight for the Grand Hotel.

Chapter Fourteen

The only light in Katy's room came from the moonlight that spilled through the open windows. Rait dropped her at the foot of the bed and went to light the lantern, only he couldn't. His hands were shaking too much. His heart was beating too fast. His mind wanted it to be dark.

He'd never realized before that her room, the one he'd chosen for her, was decorated like a first-rate bordello. Maybe he had realized it. Maybe he'd wanted her here in this red room. Maybe he'd needed to put her in a place where he knew she would be safe from him. He'd proven the whores were safe, night after night, month after month until he'd finally stopped fighting the curse that was Angie's legacy to him.

He dropped the matches on the bedside table and turned to look at Katy. The blanket was still wrapped around her. Her hair, dark and beautiful and soft as the moonlight that glistened on her ebony curls, fell about her pale face and tumbled onto the blanket in disarray.

"What were you doing in Lilly's crib?" he asked.

"Does it matter?"

No, only she mattered, only Katy and her astonishing eyes that saw more than he wanted to show her.

"Things will have to change after tonight," he said. "You've broken one rule too many. The shooting today, those photographs with Bat, and now . . ."

Rait had to leave. He couldn't be in here with her another moment.

When Katy had turned from the mirror in Lilly's crib and looked into the fire of Rait's eyes, she'd wanted to be lifted into the heaven of his arms and consumed by that fire. Now he was leaving, taking with him the world she wanted, the heaven she would die for.

"Today you asked me why I let Bat hold me like that in the photography studio." Her voice stopped him before he could reach the door. "I did it because I wanted to pretend it was you."

"Katy," he said, and his voice was as broken as the pain in his heart. "You don't know what you're saying."

"I'm not a child, Rait." Slowly, like in a

dream, the blanket started to fall from her. Soon there was only the rose-patterned shawl and the moonlight on her hair. "Do you know what I wish for before I go to bed each night? I wish that just once, you would look at me the way Wyatt looks at Josie."

"Wyatt is in love with Josie."

"I know," Katy whispered. She turned her face from him, letting the moonlight touch her features. There were tears there, too. On the long walk from Blair Street to the hotel, she hadn't uttered a sound. Now he knew why.

In the last year, Rait had cursed Angie a thousand times. Now he did it again. She'd done this to him. She'd torn his soul out and turned him into the kind of man who made women cry because he couldn't let himself love them.

Only this time, he hadn't stopped his heart in time.

"I can't do this, Katy."

"Yes, you can," she said and let the rose-patterned shawl fall from her.

His desire was a living thing within him. It raged and shook at the cage he'd locked it in the last time he'd walked out Lilly's door. Now it fought to be free. It fought for Katy.

"This isn't right," he said.

"Why? Because you think I'm too young to

know what I'm doing? Or . . . or is it because you don't want me?" Her voice shook as though her heart was breaking.

"Damn you," he said, and before he could think, he was running to her, lifting her and holding her and tasting the salt of her tears as he lowered his mouth to hers.

First kiss. Dangerous kiss. Sweet, savage, wonderful kiss.

Her lips were sweet and soft and he assaulted them with an urgent, desperate desire to taste every inch of her mouth and soul and heart. He could feel her hands on his shoulders, holding him, pulling him closer, not letting him escape, not letting him run from the fury and the fear.

He was everything: the mountains, the sky, the world at their feet. She arched and ached and cried out against his lips and knew she could never get enough . . . would never want to stop.

And then he saw it. That hand. Those possessive, female fingers touching Angie's shoulder, stopping him from taking what he wanted. Stopping him from taking Angie.

"Rait?" Katy looked up into his tortured face.

"I can't do this."

He was shaking. His body shuddered like a

205

leaf in a storm beneath her hands.

"What is it? Did I do something wrong?" But that wasn't what she was thinking. *He doesn't want me. He really doesn't want me.*

Rait pushed her away. She didn't belong to him. She belonged to that creature. She had always belonged to the hands of that creature.

"Angie," he said and stumbled back from Katy. "She left me. After my father died, she left me and I went after her. She was with that woman. They were together when I met her. Friends, I thought. Just friends. I fell in love with Angie the minute I saw her. I had to have her and I wouldn't leave her alone until she said yes. I thought I would die from happiness. She was mine. Just mine. But every time I touched her, every time I looked at her, she shrank away, a little more every day until there wasn't anything left. Then one day, she was gone."

"I'm not Angie," Katy said.

"I went after her. I tried to make her come back to me. I begged her. But that woman put her hand on Angie's shoulder and said no, Angie belonged to her again. And this time, she wasn't letting her go."

"I'm not Angie, Rait."

"I tried to forget her. I tried to, but every time I looked at a woman, I saw that creature's

206

hand on Angie's shoulder and I couldn't touch them. I couldn't do anything." He drew a shattered breath and let it go. "Don't you see, Katy? I can't make love to you. I can't make love to anyone. Lilly knows. Every whore on Blair Street knows. I can't do it."

So, this was it. This was the reason for the fear Katy had seen in his eyes every time he looked at her. Until tonight.

He'd failed with the prostitutes, yet hadn't reached out for Katy until she'd dressed like them. Was the only reason he'd finally been willing to touch her tonight was because he knew he would fail?

He was at the door again, almost gone. If he left now, she would lose him forever.

"I'm not Angie," Katy said again, and he turned his pained gaze to look at her. "And I'm not a whore, Rait."

He raked his gaze down her body. "Aren't you?" he said in a cutting voice.

"Tell me," she said quietly. "Did you say that because you believe it, or because you're afraid if you can't convince yourself that it's true, you won't be able to walk away from me?"

"I didn't walk away from them, Katy. I ran. I put my tail between my legs like a whipped dog, and I ran as hard as I could."

"You're not running now, Rait."

He wanted to, only his feet wouldn't move. Or was it his heart?

"Angie made her choice and I'm making mine. I want you, Rait. And, dear heart, I know you want me, too."

He came toward her. Threw her against the wall between the windows where the moonlight shifted across his face and shadows turned his eyes black

"Is this what you want, Katy?" He put his hands around her throat, tangled his fingers in the red ribbon and tightened his grasp until he could feel her pulse against his palm. "Do you want me to treat you like the other women I couldn't make love to? Only that wasn't love, was it?" He ran his hands down her chest, onto the curve of her breasts. And still he could feel it, the steady, solid beating of her heart against his palm. "The way I do it, it isn't anything."

And he kissed her. Not a gentle kiss, not a tender kiss. A hard kiss, a ravaging kiss which shook them both and made them feel like they'd been struck by lightning. He twisted his hands in the front of the lace corset and ripped it down the front. He followed the path of the tear with his hands. Softness like he'd never felt. Heat like he'd only dreamed about. Desire so strong it was like wine in his mouth.

He drank her kiss and pressed his body hard against hers. And his hands, those searching, groping hands, no matter where he moved them, no matter what unsoiled flesh they touched, always he could feel the beating of her heart against his palm.

Katy was on fire; *his fire, her desire*. Everything she was—everything she would ever be—she offered to him with her arms, her lips, and her heart where all her hopes and dreams waited for him to love her. And not just with his body, though Katy cried out for that. She wanted more. She wanted everything. But the only chance she had of holding onto that dream was by living this one.

Rait moved his hands down her body, embracing, igniting, discovering. The silk briefs she wore were still untouched. Only when he couldn't wait another second did he push his hands down onto them, then into them. Her skin was like morning dew, wet and trembling on the tip of a spring-green leaf. Fresh, new.

The silk tore easily, then there was nothing between them but his fear. Dear God, he wanted her more than he wanted to live. He needed her more than he needed the air he breathed. If he failed now, if the guilt rose up like a snake to strike him with the poison of inadequacy this time, he would die.

Her legs parted at his touch. Her breath caught, her lips grazed his as she threw her head back against the wall and moaned a sound as raw and aching as his own need.

He pulled his hand away from the fire of her passion. "No, don't," Katy said and tried to push him back into the heat.

He brought his mouth down on hers, silencing her protests, drinking her tears in a kiss which shook her to the core of her heart. And while he kissed her, he began to undress. Shirt ripped open, thrown aside; exposing his chest and back to the bruising, searing touch of her fingers and hands.

His belt, his pants, lowering them as he lowered his mouth; taking his kiss down the front of her body, across her breasts, onto her nipples; making her cry out; causing her to arch into his sucking lips.

When he came back to her mouth, when he took her lips beneath his again, he was naked. She felt the hard, throbbing push of his manhood against her flesh, and she began to cry into his kiss because she was afraid. Katy Halliday, who had never been afraid of anything in her life, was afraid now.

He put his arms around her, pulling her away from the wall and into his embrace where he held her shivering body for a moment against him. Then he lifted her and carried her to the bed.

He laid her on the velvet spread, red as the passion in his soul, red as the ribbon at her throat and the garters on her thighs. "The shoes have to go." He slipped them from her feet, then ran his hands slowly up her legs to where the red garters looked like blood in the mist of moonlight spilling onto the bed. He put one knee on the bed beside her and lowered his lips to hers. "The stockings stay," he said, and slanted his mouth to devour hers.

Her breasts, covered by his hands, were wet with his kisses and hard with her need. Her stomach quivered beneath his touch. Her legs twisted beneath his caress.

He drank her moans, tasted her desire, caused her soul to ache with a passion that made her beg for more. And he gave it. He gave her everything.

He took her with him to the world of passion and pain, desire and fever where Angie had refused to go. But Katy—sweet, dear, beloved Katy—wanted it. She wanted him. And when he spread her legs and lifted himself above her, the inadequacy born of his guilt was gone.

He entered her fast and hard and caught the cry of her pain in his kiss. When she'd stopped shaking, he began to move inside her. Slowly, surely, he took her back up to where their fire burned the brightest. It was then, as her world shattered inside her and Rait filled her with his heart, that Katy stopped being afraid.

Chapter Fifteen

The world was so silent, Katy could hear his heart beating. She lay with her face pressed against his chest, letting the sound of it and the warmth of it seep into her. After a time, when there was nothing in the world but the rhythm of his heart, she slept.

A bold stream of sunlight stubbornly pushed past the barriers of sleep she'd erected. She tried to turn over and cover her head with a pillow, but there was someone lying in bed beside her, blocking her attempt to escape.

She sat up so suddenly, she gave herself a headache. "Ouch," she moaned and put both hands up to cradle her temples. He was still with her. Rait lay on his side, his head propped up in his hand while he watched her with those unbelievably blue eyes. "Didn't anyone ever tell you it's impolite to stare?" she asked.

"You snore," he replied. She rolled her eyes and collapsed back onto the pillow beside him.

"Just a little and it sounds very sweet, but it's still a snore."

"How romantic. I offer you my heart, soul, and body, and all you can say is I snore? This is certainly a moment I look forward to recording in my diary."

Rait played with a raven curl that tickled her shoulder. "Read something to me that you've written."

Katy was surprised by her sudden reluctance. In New York, every word she inscribed on paper was offered to every person she knew for an opinion. Basil Pellingham had recently taken to hiding under his desk when he saw her coming with a sheaf of papers in her hand.

"I can't." She buried her face against Rait's shoulder. "I'm embarrassed."

"You're lying naked in bed with a man, and you're embarrassed to show me something you're willing to let all America read?"

She nodded.

"Does that mean you think what you write isn't any good?"

She shook her head. "I just feel silly," she mumbled against his skin.

"You look pretty silly, too." He smiled as one gray-blue eye looked up at him. "And beautiful." A smile appeared. "And I would love to kiss you good morning."

"Is that why you were watching me wake up?"

"I've been waiting all morning for you to wake up."

She rolled over and offered him not just her lips but all of her.

"That's better." He gave her a kiss so soft and gentle that Katy sighed while he kissed her. He moved his lips down onto her throat and kissed the subtle pulsing of her heart while his hands slid over her breasts; warming and exciting them; then down to her waist and hips and her legs, still sheathed in the black stockings.

"Any regrets?" he asked as he nibbled her ear.

"I wish you hadn't torn that corset. I wanted to save it for my memory chest."

"You can put me in there instead and anytime you want to remember wearing that indecent scrap of lace, I'll recite the tale of the night Lee surrendered to Grant."

Katy gave an impatient sigh. "I wish men would come up with a better way to describe events other than in relation to a war. It makes life sound so violent. Why couldn't you have said 'the night I surrendered my heart to the most breathtakingly beautiful woman to ever grace my life with her smile?'"

"Women," he said in a derogatory fashion. Meanwhile he was doing something so wonderful to her ear, it gave her chills.

"We are insufferable, aren't we?" she said as he lowered his lips to her breasts and did something wonderful that gave her even colder chills.

"Barely tolerable," he said and slipped his hand between her legs to do something wonderful that turned her chills into fire.

"I'm surprised men want anything to do with us," she said and pulled him on top of her to do something wonderful that turned her fire into their inferno.

"You have your moments," he said and kept doing something wonderful until they were consumed, conquered, and contented.

"How do you know my uncle?"

"He didn't tell you?"

"If he did, I wouldn't be wasting my breath asking you. I'd be kissing you instead."

"You could do that anyway."

"Then I would never get an answer to my question. How do you know Uncle Richard?"

"He knew my mother, and through her, my father."

"And through them, you," Katy said with an impatient drumming of her fingers on Rait's chest. "Now I know all that, I still don't know anything. Why did you owe Uncle Richard a favor?"

"A year and a half ago, my father was setting charges in a mine in Rico. A stick of dynamite went off while he was rigging it with a fuse. It took Dad five months to die. By the time he did, I was so deep in debt I couldn't afford to buy him a coffin."

Rait heard again the sound of Angie's laughter. It shuddered through him like a winter wind. He tried to erase the memory of it with the warmth of Katy's body. He held her tight against him until all he could feel was the beating of her heart.

"A few days before Dad died, he asked me to send a letter he'd written to an old friend of his. It was your uncle. The day after Dad died, Richard Halliday arrived in Durango. Before I even knew what was happening, he'd paid off the nursing bills at Mercy Hospital and the doctors and everyone else in town I owed, which was just about everyone. I told him to mind his own business, I didn't need his money. Your uncle's a lot like you, Katy. He didn't listen to a thing I said. Then he bought Dad a coffin, and I stopped complaining. Before he left, he told me not to act like such a jackass the next time someone did me a favor. After I quit playing lawman . . ."

Rait balled his right hand into a fist. He clenched it so tight, all he could feel was pain.

Only then did he continue.

"After I turned in my badge, I got a job that paid real money. I repaid every cent your uncle loaned me, with interest, and told him if he ever needed a favor, there was a jackass in Colorado waiting to lend a hand."

"So he sent me to you. Only you tried to send me back."

"I thought he was presuming a lot. The truth is," Rait let his fist relax, "no matter how big the favor he asked of me, I could never repay him for how grateful I was to be able to bury my dad in a coffin."

"And then Angie left you."

The late morning sun streaming through the windows shone directly into his eyes. He closed them and stared at the blinding brightness that remained.

"Yes, then Angie left me. I was still wearing a badge, which meant I couldn't even afford to go after her until I'd sold the only thing I owned, my gun and holster. I found her in Boston."

"With that woman," Katy said and felt the skin on Rait's chest tighten.

"That's when I found out they'd been more than just friends." He looked down at Katy. "Do you know about things like that?"

"Uncle Richard told me once. I didn't believe him at first, but he told me not everyone lives the way society expects them to. He said we all have to make our own choices in life, though."

Rait stared at the red and gold canopy above the bed. *We all have to make our own choices in life.* It sounded so simple, but he knew better. It hadn't been Angie's choice to love a woman that destroyed Rait's life. It had been his love for the law that destroyed both their lives.

"What happened after you found Angie?" Katy asked. "I mean, after you tried to make her come back to you?"

"I grew up," Rait said. "I came back to Durango, turned in my badge, and started earning a living the way other men do."

"Instead of tilting at rainbows."

He smiled. "Windmills."

Katy crinkled her nose. "Same thing. I don't think you should judge whether or not to pursue a dream by how much money you can make at it. Even if I never published a word in my life, I'd still write. Yes, I want to be published, but not to make money."

"That's because you already have money."

"It couldn't get me to Dodge City, though."

Rait thought about the four men who came into Silverton on the late train from Durango last night. Jack Vermilion from Texas. Johnny Green and Johnny Milsap. Dan Tipton. After Bat and Wyatt, those were four of the most famous names to ever strap on a gun. What would Katy do if she found out where they were going when they left Silverton?

"I have to work this afternoon and it's almost noon now." He nuzzled her hair with a kiss. "I'll have a tray sent here to your room for lunch and tell the kitchen to prepare a boxed supper so we can go on a twilight picnic tonight. I should be able to get away by seven o'clock."

Katy was wondering if Wyatt had left Silverton yet. "I'd like that," she said and watched Rait leave. He carried his ripped shirt in one hand and his boots in the other.

A second after the door shut, she heard a roar of laughter, then Rait's voice saying, "Shut up, Wyatt."

Katy smiled. It was nice having her questions answered without even getting out of bed.

Chapter Sixteen

Katy was walking the rails of the D&RG extension tracks to the Silverton smelter. The extension was a mile long, but she'd only been on fifty feet or so. That fifty feet or so were as far from the depot as she dared to get. Any farther and she couldn't hear the destination of ticket buyers.

There had been a flurry of activity at the depot in the half hour since she started her stakeout. There had been a gigantic raven with a perverted interest in her hair. There had also been two tickets purchased to Denver. The first was by a schoolteacher on holiday. The second was by the minister of the First Congregational Church. "A shipment of Bibles has gone astray in Denver," he told Katy. "I'll put them back on the right path, though."

There had also been one arriving train. A flood of people had poured out of the passenger cars, searched for their baggage and then headed into town. Katy had observed them with intense interest, but hadn't been able to identify any as gunfighters. Most of them carried guns, but she'd learned since her arrival in Durango that few people fit the stereotypes made popular by the dime novels she loved.

Bat Masterson looked like himself, but was nothing like the coldhearted lawman he'd been portrayed as by every pencil-wielding writer with words to sell. Wyatt Earp was just as tall and impressive as his legend, but he spent most of his time mooning over Josie instead of habitually stalking the streets in search of order to restore.

And Rait. There was an enigma. He dressed like a blackhearted badman, ran a saloon like a slick-fingered gambler, and had the dreams of a lawman. He also had the skepticism of a broken man. And he had Katy. Heart and soul. But no matter how she felt about him, she wasn't going to let her emotions rule her ambition. There was an army of gunslingers gathering in Silverton in preparation for a heroic mission of mercy, and she wasn't going to miss one minute of the fun.

As things turned out, she missed the first three minutes. It was nature's fault. While she was in the outhouse answering its call, Wyatt Earp walked up to the depot window. Katy came out of the dim darkness of the outhouse confinement in time to hear him say, ". . . on the one o'clock train this afternoon."

The ticket agent did whatever it is ticket agents do behind their barred windows and then said, "There you are, sir, five tickets to Dodge City with an indefinite layover in Cimarron, Kansas."

Dodge City. They were going to Dodge City. Bat Masterson and someone named Luke and Wyatt Earp and four gunslingers were going to Dodge City. Or Wyatt and three gunslingers and Josie. Or Wyatt and Rait and two gunslingers and Josie.

No, Rait was going on a picnic and Josie had caught a chill by reading too late last night, so she was sick in bed with a weird-smelling towel plastered to her chest.

That meant the score was Bat Masterson and someone named Luke were being joined in Cimarron, Kansas by Wyatt Earp and four gunslingers and they were all going to Dodge City.

No, that wasn't right, either. There was another person going. Katy.

She held onto her carpetbag with both hands. It was stuffed with all her most precious treasures and a few essential things. Two changes of clothes. A new journal ready to be filled with exciting events. A pencil, a pen, and a bottle of ink to record those events with, and all the chocolate Katy had been able to buy with seventy-three cents, which was all the money she'd had.

Even if Bat didn't still have her gun and she could have sold it for the same sum she paid for it, that money added to her meager change wouldn't have bought a ticket to Dodge, which cost $48.15 with a Horton reclining chair and $47.40 without a recline. As a result, Katy had decided to invest her seventy-three cents in chocolate. No matter what happened next, at least she wouldn't be hungry.

Wyatt and four narrow-eyed men had already boarded the passenger cars at the front of the train. Katy was standing behind the depot outhouse, which was near the back of the train where three stockcars had been coupled. The last stockcar was filled with swine who were filling the air with grunts, squeals, and smell.

The locomotive gave two long blasts on its whistle to signal the brakes were being released. The conductor clicked his watch shut, called "Alll aboooard!" and climbed the steps to the first passenger car. Katy waited until all the train personnel were either out of sight or too busy to look at the outhouse, then scrambled into the first stockcar.

As the D&RG left the Silverton station on the first leg of its journey to Durango and points beyond, Katy stood at the side of the stockcar with her face pressed against the wood slats and watched Silverton roll away from her. She remembered the day she'd arrived when she and Rait had stood together looking out across the park's lake of dandelions.

"Now I know where God was standing when He thought up the name for heaven."

"It doesn't last. In a few weeks, they'll all turn to seed and blow away."

"They don't really do that, do they? How could anything so beautiful just disappear?"

"It happens."

It happened last night. While they made love, the dandelions changed into white puffs of seed and blew away.

The park was still beautiful. The sky was as soft as the inside of a sapphire jewel box, the mountains breathtaking with their slopes splashed with snow and sunlight. But the bright yellow beauty of the dandelions was gone. Just like Angie had gone.

"I'm not running away," Katy whispered as the train entered the canyon of Lost Souls. "I swear to you, Rait, I'm not running away."

Chapter Seventeen

Rait knew before he opened the door that something was wrong. It was too quiet. The air felt empty and the hall outside Katy's room had an abandoned feeling. He twisted the door handle violently and entered room 303. She wasn't there.

The logical thing to do was assume she was in another part of the hotel, but this was Katy Alice Halliday he was dealing with. There wasn't anything logical about her. The second logical thing to do was assume she was in another part of town, but six hours ago Wyatt Earp and four gunmen had left Silverton en route to Dodge City. That meant the only logical thing to do was assume Katy was gone, too.

"It was about 12:30 P.M.," the room clerk told Rait when he interrogated the staff. "She was going out to buy chocolate."

That sounded logical for Katy. She didn't have enough money for a ticket to Dodge, so she'd used what money s[...]

"She took her carp[...]
some clothes missin' a[...]
the desk."

More Katy Halliday l[...]
without ruffles and pens[...]

"I saw her lurking behi[...]
the depot just before the [...]
for Durango," Hollis Lang[...]
cleaned boots for the Gran[...] said. "I
think she jumped a cattle car [...] freeloaded her
way out of this rat-infested city of sin on her
way to bigger and better horizons on the other
side of these godforsaken mountains where a
man can lose his soul to a hole in the ground
that will never see the light of day or the glim-
mer of gold."

Obviously, Hollis Langwell had been reading
too many R. T. Halliday Half Dime and Double
Nickel Library paperback novels.

"I'm going to murder the conniving, deceitful
little she-monster with my bare hands when I
catch up with her," Rait said.

Hollis wrote the sinister threat in the little
notebook he carried in his back pocket so he
could keep track of all his ideas for writing his
own dime novel.

A six-hour lead meant Katy had reached Durango more than an hour ago. By now she was

blo. From there, she could
of several trains into Dodge.
ever be able to stop them all.
knew who could.

Katy was huddled in the corner of the stockcar behind a fort built of hay and her carpetbag.
It was dark and it had been hours since her car
stopped moving. She was desperately hungry.

Her supply of chocolate had been adequate
for her hunger needs until the D&RG pulled into
South Pueblo and she'd transferred to a stockcar
attached to an eastbound AT&SF train.

Shortly after she'd settled in, a bunch of cattle
the size of elephants and with horns like tree
trunks were loaded into the car with her. That's
when she'd built the fort from her carpetbag and
the hay scattered on the bottom of the stockcar.

One of the big cows had no respect for
boundaries, though, and had immediately invaded her territory. The brute had a sweet tooth
that was even bigger than Katy's. The creature
had snuffled and snorted and sneezed all over
her until she'd finally surrendered her stock of
imported goods. Now the beast was standing
over her and glaring menacingly at her hair ribbon.

"When God created cattle, he should have

made you smell better," she said.

The cow didn't insult easily. It just kept drooling long streamers of saliva while it stared at her ribbon.

"I'll never eat beef again," Katy promised.

Apparently the stupid cow didn't even know where this car was headed.

"Doesn't the name Chicago mean anything to you?"

It didn't.

"All right, so take my ribbon," she said and handed it over. The cow took it and bumped back into the midst of the rest of the car's doomed occupants.

"I can't wait to get off this train and eat the biggest steak I can find," Katy muttered. She wondered how long it would be before she could claim revenge.

After leaving Pueblo and entering Kansas, the train made a stop to feed and water the animals in the stockcars. The cars were unloaded, the animals cared for, then reloaded. It had been just Katy's luck to get the maniacal beast with the sweet tooth back in her car. The second time the train stopped, the stockcars were switched onto a side track while the rest of the train continued on. Since then, and as near as Katy could guess that was three hours ago, no one had been near the cars.

Now it looked like someone had at last remembered the cattle. A lantern had appeared on the other side of the rail yard and was approaching the stockcars. The light swung to and fro as if it were a basket of flowers being carried by a young girl.

As it swung close to the side of the depot, Katy saw a sign. Cimarron. She was one stop from Dodge. When the cattle were unloaded, she'd get off, too. When the next eastbound train came through, she would board one of its passenger cars. It shouldn't be too hard to avoid the conductor for the ten-mile trip to Dodge.

Of course, she would smell like a cow when she got there, but the cowboys in town probably wouldn't notice. Also, the Arkansas River ran right through the town, so she shouldn't have any trouble finding water to wash in. Finding privacy might be a problem, though.

One problem at a time, Katy cautioned herself. *If I think too far ahead, I'll frighten myself right back to Silverton.*

She didn't want to think about what might be happening in Silverton right now. Rait was probably plotting to kill her. She hoped he was, anyway. Anything to keep him off Blair Street. She wanted all his passion directed at her, even if it was of a murderous slant.

The cattle bellowed their way to freedom in a

wild stampede down the loading ramp of the stockcar. Katy took her first deep breath in hours. It wasn't much of an improvement. Bossy, Bessy, Bertha, Boris, and Butch had left behind several dozen smelly reminders of their habitation to keep her company until she could escape her bovine cage.

The sound of two-legged footsteps coming up the loading ramp caused her to sink lower behind her fort walls. Now what? Fresh hay? Why couldn't they leave smelly enough alone?

"Katy? Are you in here, honey?"

Her head popped up over the fort like a prairie dog out of its hole. "Bat?" She squinted but couldn't see anything but the light. "Is that you?"

"In the flesh."

"What are you doing here?"

He laughed and she knew it was really him. "You're squatting in a pile of manure and you want to know what I'm doing here? I'm looking for you, honey. Rait discovered your disappearance and fired off enough threatening telegrams to me in Kinsley to cost him a week's wages. I don't know why he has so much trouble keeping hold of a woman. He said you might be stowed away in one of the stockcars and told me if I didn't find you before you reached Dodge, he'd shoot me full of holes. I wired Cimarron and had them sidetrack every stockcar headed east, then came running to your rescue."

"I wouldn't have needed to stow away if Rait had signed Uncle Richard's drafts for me," Katy said as Bat helped her to her feet. "It's all those rules of his, you know. That's what makes women run in the opposite direction."

"That's the lawman in him, honey. Has to have a rule for everything." He extracted her carpetbag from the fort walls. "Come on, let's get out of here. This place smells worse than Wyatt's feet."

Katy laughed. "Now I know why Western men never take off their boots. I read that in *Rourke Ryder and the Long Walk to Boot Hill; or, A Deadshot for a Dollar*. Rourke Ryder told a 'soiled dove' south of the tracks he never took his boots off, not even for a lady, and since she wasn't a lady, she shouldn't have asked him to begin with."

"It also explains why we bury men out here with their boots on," Bat said. "Even undertakers aren't insensitive to all smells."

"Which explains why they call graveyards out here boot hill," Katy said.

"Now we have that settled," Bat said, "let's discuss how we're going to keep you alive when Rait gets here in a few hours."

Katy stopped dead halfway down the loading

ramp while Bat kept walking.

"Rait's coming here? You're not just sending me back?"

Bat looked back over his shoulder at her. "And have you jump off at the next stop and head back to Dodge?"

"It was just a thought." She ran to catch up with him. "Before we discuss Rait, tell me who Luke is and why he and you and Wyatt and four gunslingers are going to Dodge. And go slowly. I want to remember it all so I can write it down later."

It started with three "shady ladies."

There was an unwritten law in Dodge City that south of the AT&SF tracks, which not only ran right through town, but right down the middle of Front Street, anything went and usually did. North of the tracks was considered the classier section of town. A certain amount of discretion was practiced along with the vice.

As a result, while the saloons and gambling houses south of the tracks allowed women to openly conduct whatever business they wanted on the premises, the establishments receiving their mail on the north side of Front Street employed their female help under the guise of entertainers and waitresses.

233

Mostly they waited at the Dodge House and charged men $2.00 for the entertainment. To keep up appearances, though, they occasionally handed a thirsty cowboy a glass of beer or played the piano or sang a song to a weary trailhand before leading him down the street to take a room at the hotel.

One of the saloons north of the tracks was the Long Branch Saloon. Luke Short, a gunfighter whose reputation included several dead men and a friendship with Bat Masterson, owned a piece of the Long Branch. The three women working for Luke were popular with the cowboys coming up the trail from Texas, so they made Luke's place their favorite watering hole.

Next door to the Long Branch was the Alamo Saloon, which was owned by the mayor of Dodge City, Larry Deger. Deger didn't like to listen to all the hooting and hollering happening next door to his almost empty saloon. He fussed and fumed for a while, then started digging around in the city ordinances.

There, to his surprise, he found a law prohibiting vocal or instrumental music in a public place, unless intended for literary or scientific purposes. The obscure and ridiculous law had been put on the books during one of Dodge's periodic dry spells and just as quickly forgotten when the cork came off the bottle again. It was still a law, though, and Deger was determined to see it obeyed, within the boundaries of the Long Branch Saloon.

So, Luke's three ladies were arrested. He tried to bail them out but because the arrests were as shady as the ladies, his efforts were in vain.

As he was leaving the jail, Luke noticed the entertainers and waitresses in Deger's saloon were still working, as were the ones in Heinze & Kramer's and Nelson Cary's. There were so many ladies working in Brick Bond and Thomas Nixon's Dance Hall, it looked like a red satin stampede between there and the Dodge House.

Luke realized something was rotten in Dodge and figured it had to be Deger. When a few minutes later he stumbled over one of the mayor's favorite constituents in the street, bullets flew. Luke was arrested. He was denied counsel, trial, and dinner. The next day, he was given a pointed pistol salute while being marched to the depot and put aboard an eastbound train with instructions to never cast his shadow on the streets of Dodge City again.

The cowboys who had been hooting it up at the Long Branch, which was now closed, moved next door to the Alamo where music could be heard playing all night long, except when the girls were taking a little break down at the Dodge House.

235

Mayor Larry Deger thought things had worked out rather well and wondered why he hadn't thought of this a little sooner.

Meanwhile, Luke Short might have been out, but he wasn't down. He sent a wire to his old friend Bat, who complained about mayoral prejudices and the lack of due process in Dodge to the governor of Kansas. The governor agreed things were out of hand in Ford County and turned the problem over to Bat, who went to Silverton to enlist the help of Wyatt Earp and four similarly talented friends to clean up Dodge City.

That was when Katy got involved and why Rait was headed in her direction under a full head of steam and why Bat was trying to figure out a way to save her from certain doom.

"What does it feel like to be in love, Bat?" Katy was sitting on a desk in the office of the manager of the Cimarron train station. The manager was out telling all his friends that Bat Masterson was in his office. Yes, the real Bat Masterson.

"It feels like you have gas," Bat said. "Now pay attention, honey. Rait will be here any minute and we don't have our stories straight."

"It doesn't matter. He's going to kill me no matter what we say." She sighed. "I wish I could have seen Dodge first. I wanted to get the lay of the land before the bullets start to fly and the bodies start to fall and the blood starts to flow."

Bat was sitting in the station manager's chair with his feet propped up on the desk beside Katy. Now he slammed them down on the floor and jumped up, grabbed her, and gave her a kiss that smacked like a horehound drop in a street urchin's mouth.

"That's it, honey! That's our plan!"

Rait entered the Cimarron station with only one thought on his mind. Murder. He knew Katy would be expecting it and it gave him a perverted pleasure to think how frightened she must be. Every second of the long trip from Silverton to Cimarron, he'd imagined how satisfying it would be to see those blue-gray eyes go wide with terror when he put his hands around her throat and began to squeeze.

He wouldn't really kill her, of course. He just wanted her to think he might. There was something that was going to die today, though, and that was the way she'd been wrapping him around her little finger ever since they met. From now on, he was in control. The first thing he planned to control was his obsession with her. After their night together, he'd never wanted to let her out of his arms. Now he couldn't wait to put her on a train back to New York.

A single yellow-hued lantern shed a gloomy light in the empty waiting room of the Cimarron train station. Behind the station manager's office door Rait heard voices, then a sparkle of laughter. Katy.

Damn the woman. Didn't she even have enough sense to be afraid? She must have heard the train and had to know he would be on it.

Rait dropped his hand to the butt of his pistol and stalked to the door.

Bat was seated behind a desk. Katy was sitting on the desk facing him. Both of them were laughing now. Bat saw Rait first. His laughter faltered and Katy turned to see what he was looking at. Rait waited for her face to pale and eyes to widen in fear, or at least for her to stop laughing.

She didn't do any of those things. Instead, she jumped off the desk and came running to him.

"There you are!" she cried and took hold of his left hand and drew him into the room. "We have a marvelous idea! Actually, it's Bat's idea, but he said I inspired it so I'm taking partial credit."

Rait couldn't think. He took one look at that pretty face smiling up at him and forgot everything except she was all right. Bat's telegram announcing Katy had been found and was safe had reached Rait at Pueblo. He'd immediately dismissed his concern for her and begun to plot her murder. But now that he was here, all he felt was relief. Just the touch of her hands on his, proving to him that she was really safe, made him feel weak in the chest.

"What idea?" His voice sounded strangled.

The rainbows in her eyes shimmered like pots of gold. She turned to give Bat a saucy smile. "He isn't mad at me at all. We were worried for nothing."

Rait met Bat's knowing gaze and frowned. He didn't need Bat Masterson to tell him he was head over heels. He'd already figured that out for himself.

"What idea?" he asked.

Katy squeezed his hand. "We're going to Dodge to scout out the town for Wyatt before he goes in to negotiate a peace treaty with Mayor Deger. I'm going to be the telegraph contact and you'll feed me information to send Bat and Wyatt."

"No," Rait said as he looked across her head at Bat. "I won't do it."

"You have to," Bat said. "Deger wired the governor claiming to have fifty men stationed on Front Street to intercept Wyatt when he gets off the train. I can't let him go into Dodge without a scouting report first. You and Katy are the obvious choices. Deger doesn't know you and there's no one in America who looks as innocent as Katy. Deger and his supporters will never suspect a thing."

Katy was so excited, she hopped from one foot to the other. "I can see the headlines now, 'Katy Halliday, Heroine of the Dodge City War.' "

"The papers are calling it a war," Bat confirmed, "which is what it will be if they really have fifty men waiting to shoot the first familiar face that gets off the train. We need you, Rait."

"But I don't need you."

Bat laughed. The sound of it irritated Rait as much as the reason for it.

"You're not fooling anyone with that 'I don't need you' line," Bat said, and suddenly the happy-go-lucky gambler was gone. In his place was the man who tamed the wildest cowtown of them all with the strength of his reputation and the threat of his gun. He slowly rose out of the chair to face Rait. "Let's lay our cards on the table, Caldwell. We may play at being gamblers and saloonkeepers, but we both know we're really lawmen. It's what we were born to do and what we'll always be. So spare me your bullshit speech about not caring about the plight of the world and start acting like a man again."

Rait stabbed a finger at Bat. "You're out of line."

"What I am, Caldwell, is willing to risk my life to defend the law. The Rait Caldwell I used to know was willing to take that same risk."

Rait wanted to walk away. He couldn't. Just like he couldn't walk away when he was sinking into debt. Just like he couldn't walk away when he was losing Angie.

"Katy stays here," he said.

"No, she doesn't!" she cried. She'd had all she could take of watching this little passion play from the sidelines. It was time to take a stand, and she wanted to stand right in the middle of Dodge City.

Rait ignored her. "And we try to do this without guns."

"That's why Wyatt's going in first instead of me."

It was true. Men feared Bat and respected Wyatt. They would listen to what he had to say.

"And me," Katy said. "I'm going, too."

"No, you're not," Rait said without looking at her. That was the surest path to defeat. He kept his gaze on Bat. "How are you going to keep her away?"

Everyone in the room thought it was an excellent question. Especially Katy.

"I'll think of something," Bat said.

241

"Meanwhile, I'll be worried every minute that she's going to suddenly appear in my line of fire." Rait felt like a man who had just volunteered to be tortured and executed. He finally lowered his gaze to her. It wasn't fair anyone this angelic-looking could be so much trouble. "All right, you can go, but you have to promise you won't get involved, Katy."

"I promise," she said and looked up at him like he was the greatest hero in the world.

Rait knew then that no matter what happened in Dodge City, he'd already won his war.

Chapter Eighteen

Dodge City. Katy was in Dodge City. Katy Alice Halliday was really and truly in Dodge City, Kansas, the "Wickedest Little City in the West," the "Gomorrah of the Plains," the "Babylon of the Frontier."

This was the most exciting moment of her life.

She stood on the railroad embankment in the middle of Front Street and looked around awestruck at the dusty, sunbaked streets that were a landmark of history. Everything had happened here.

Right where she was standing was where Bat Masterson fought it out with rival forces in the Battle of the Plaza two years ago to save his brother Jim's life. And a few feet down the street was where his brother Ed was killed outside the Lady Gay Saloon five years ago. It was said that Bat came running with both hands filled with pistols, blasting out a hailstorm of bullets in a desperate effort to save his brother's life.

Right across the street from Katy was the Great Western Hotel. Behind it was the little house where Dora Hand, a singer known as the Queen of the Fairy Belles, was murdered by Frank Kennedy, who was in turn killed by Bat.

Down one block was Bridge Street. The toll bridge across the Arkansas River was where Wyatt Earp killed the cowboy who shot up the Comique Theatre the night Eddie Foy was performing. It was also on the corner of Front and Bridge that Wyatt faced down Clay Allison for a gunfight.

Between the depot and Bridge Street on the north side of the Front Street Plaza was the Long Branch Saloon. U. S. Deputy Marshal Harry McCarty was killed with his own gun in the Long Branch. The sporting crowd in the Long Branch had joined in the Battle of the Plaza, and it was there Frank Loving killed Levi Richardson in a shoot-out over the affections of a woman.

And now the Long Branch Saloon was in the headlines again. Coast to coast, the eyes of the nation were watching the famous saloon's swinging doors to see who came out the winner.

* * *

While Katy and Rait were waiting for the train to Dodge that morning, Bat bought a copy of the *Kansas Commonwealth* and the *Dodge City Times* so he could read the latest news about their war.

"Katy's right," he said after he opened the *Commonwealth* and began reading. "Newspapers are more unbelievable than dime novels. It says here that Wyatt and Doc Holliday are already 'secretly in Dodge.'" He roared out a laugh. "Can you imagine those two being anywhere in secret, especially Dodge City?"

The *Commonwealth* also gave the wording of the telegram Bat would send as a signal to an unnamed conspirator when Wyatt Earp was on his way into Dodge from Cimarron. "Your tools will be there at____," the blank line being where the arrival time was to be inserted. He thought that was funny, too. "'Your tools.' What a laugh! Who writes this stuff?"

The *Dodge City Times* gave a detailed report on Bat's trip west on the Cannonball two nights ago, which was one night too early but still interesting to read. It told of how the train was stopped at Dodge and searched, but the searchers "could not gain access to the sleeping car which contained the redoubtable Bat."

Bat grinned. "I like that. The Redoubtable Bat. Worthy of awe and reverence. I'd like to

245

have that on my tombstone. Here lies the Re-doubtable Bat Masterson."

"I don't think that's the way they meant it," Rait said. He was cleaning his gun. The cylinder was pushed aside, and he sighted down the inside of the barrel at Bat. "Redoubtable also means causing fear."

Bat assumed a look of astonishment. "Why would anyone be afraid of me?"

Katy laughed. He'd been cleaning his gun earlier. Now it lay across his lap like a threat few would take lightly. The image didn't match his innocent expression.

"Redoubtable also means formidable," she said. "I think that's what the *Times* meant."

"That's all right," he said and adjusted the position of his Colt so it would look a little more menacing before going back to the paper. "Listen to this, 'The country has been anticipating some fearful things judging from the promulgation of the purposed movement of a notorious gang.' "

He'd read the passage twice, then looked up at Katy and Rait, and asked, "What the hell does *that* mean?"

The only other thing of interest in the *Times* was a report that Bat had forces already in place in Dodge.

That part was now true. Katy had arrived.

* * *

"Stop gawking and get off the street before you get both of us killed," Rait hissed at her.

Oh, yeah, she remembered, he'd arrived, too.

"It's awfully quiet," she said. She'd always envisioned Dodge City as being a town of gunfights, or at least a lot of shouting and shooting and whooping, whatever that meant.

Because of Dodge's current trouble, she'd expected, if not Deger's fifty-man army, at least a few interested observers of her and Rait's arrival. There wasn't a person in sight, though, and not a sound anywhere in the whole town. Since the train left, the only noise she'd heard was the windblown dust beating against her carpetbag.

"I know," Rait said. He looked around at the empty cattle pens south of the tracks, then north to the blacksmith shop and along the street where all the stores had their windows shuttered and their doors closed. "This place feels like a powder keg that could explode at any second."

Directly north of the train depot on the corner of Front and Railroad Street was the Dodge House. It was a two-story wood frame building with an awning over the boardwalk outside. On top of the awning was a balcony that overlooked the street. To the right of the hotel was a billiard hall, which was part of the hotel. The Dodge House had thirty-eight rooms, a restaurant, a laundry, and it bought and sold horses on consignment. In short, it offered everything a visitor to Dodge could want, even a little $2.00 entertainment.

The lobby of the Dodge House smelled like cigars and cattle. There was a man cleaning out the ashcan beside the registry desk. In a chair in the corner was a man who had one leg angled over the other so his boot was resting on his knee. His hat was pulled so low over his eyes, all Katy could see of his face was his chin. While Rait registered, she stayed close beside him and watched the man's chin, which never moved once during the whole registry process.

"Upstairs," Rait said and followed her to the second floor. "We're in rooms 22 and 24."

"I thought we were supposed to be married," she said, referring to Bat's suggestion for the guise under which they were to conduct their clandestine operations.

Rait was fitting a brass key into the lock on room 22. He turned it, pushed the door open and Katy through it.

"I want my mind on business," he said, "not my hands on you."

Katy started to laugh, realized he might not

be making a joke, and fell so suddenly silent, that her chest ached.

Rait was checking the view out the window. It gave an overview of both Front Street and the alley running down the right side of the Dodge House. He let the calico curtain fall back into place and turned to see Katy's worried expression.

"Don't tell me I've finally done something to render you speechless," he said. "Tell me what it is so I can make a note about it later."

"It's the dust," she said, but couldn't stop the fear that welled in her at the thought that maybe he hadn't been joking. Maybe he really didn't want her anymore. "We should go to the Long Branch to wash the last few miles of trail out of our throats and see what's happening at the battlefront."

Rait sighed. "I wish you wouldn't talk like that."

"Wyatt talks that way."

"No, he doesn't. Besides, the Long Branch is closed, remember? And the battlefront is my territory, not yours."

"What am I supposed to do? Sit here and roll bandages?"

"I don't want you out on the streets right now. After I know how things stand in town, maybe you can go out. Until then, you're to stay in this room. I'll be gone about three hours, Katy. I'm telling you this so you won't worry and come looking for me. I can do my job better if I know you're safe."

He was leaving. Three hours was a long time and anything could happen while he was out there alone.

"I won't leave the room," she said and meant it.

Rait didn't look like he believed her, though. Katy swore a silent oath that even if the Dodge House caught fire and burned to the ground, she wouldn't leave this room.

He was back in exactly two hours and thirty-eight minutes, not that Katy was timing him. She just happened to be watching the clock and trying not to worry herself to death.

"I didn't come back early to check on you," he said as he entered her room.

"I didn't even realize you'd been gone so long," she said as she put down the clock. "Is Dodge the powder keg you thought it was?"

Rait sat on the edge of the table under the window and pushed open the curtain so he could keep an eye on Front Street. "I checked out the saloons south of the tracks, then went to the Alamo. Most of the town thinks Deger's an ass, but they're worried about what will happen when Bat and Wyatt hit town. As for Deger, he doesn't have fifty men, but he does have a half-dozen or so. They're holed up at the back table of the Alamo with enough guns and ammunition strapped to them to refight the war for Texas."

Katy was in a dilemma. This was what she'd wanted, what she'd come West for, what she'd come to Dodge for. But instead of being interested or even concerned about the events taking place around her, all she could think of was Rait's comment about not touching her.

He hadn't looked at her once since he returned. He'd entered the room, made straight for the window, and hadn't moved since. Could she really have destroyed everything between them?

"Are you ready to send your telegram?" Rait asked. She nodded, but he wasn't looking at her so he didn't see. Apparently he didn't need to, because he proceeded to tell her what to tell Bat. "Wyatt shouldn't delay any longer, otherwise the town is going to blow. Tell him there isn't an army waiting, but there are guns ready for him. Can you handle that?"

"I know what to say."

She was wearing her dark gray traveling suit with a bow where the bustle should be. She pinned on her hat, which was made of straw dyed to match the suit. It had a wide band of ribbon around the crown, a fluffy forest of brilliant blue feathers pinning up one side of the brim in a cocky cavalier fashion, and big taffeta ribbons that she tied below her right ear in a bow that matched the one on the back of her dress.

Rait had glared at the ridiculous creation all the way from Cimarron to Dodge. Now he glared at it while Katy adjusted its jaunty angle in the mirror. She picked up her purse and was about to leave, when she turned back at the door and looked him directly in the eye.

"I had to come here," she said.

She'd been holding this in ever since he reached Cimarron yesterday. She couldn't stand it another minute, though. She had to let him know why she left Silverton, even if it was too late.

"I wasn't running away from you or from what happened between us. I just had to be a part of what's happening here. Bat told me last night the West was changing and this might be the last great showdown. Imagine, Bat Masterson and Wyatt Earp, the greatest lawmen in history, in the last great showdown on the streets of the West's greatest cowtown. I couldn't stay away, Rait. If I've destroyed what we were starting to find together, I'm sorry. But if it could be destroyed that easily, it must not have been much to begin with." Before he could answer, she left to play her part in history.

Chapter Nineteen

Rait had never been so nervous in his life. He paced the narrow width of the room a dozen times, then a dozen more. Every time a board creaked anywhere in the hotel, he threw the door open to see if it was Katy coming back. When he discovered the noise wasn't her, he slammed the door shut and took up pacing again.

"I should have gone with her," he told himself a hundred times, but knew his presence at the telegraph office might alert Deger that his fifty-man bluff was being called. There was no telling what would happen then. All it would take to turn this trouble into a war was one man, one gun, and one bullet. Rait couldn't afford to let that happen, especially not with Katy involved.

Twenty long minutes after she left, he heard footsteps tripping lightly up the steps to the second floor. He flung the door open, took one look at the hat which had just appeared over the top railing of the banister, grabbed Katy and dragged her into the room. He closed the door, pushed her back against it and kissed her—taffeta bow and all.

The kiss was inspired by relief that she was safe and by her little speech before she left. He'd never doubted for a moment the reason she left Silverton. He didn't want her to think he had.

He felt her first reaction of surprise, then an immediate welcoming response. He pressed her tight against the door and did everything to her lips and mouth he'd been dreaming of doing ever since leaving her in bed two mornings ago.

When he'd fully devoured her lips, tongue, teeth, and mouth, he moved on to her ear and neck and throat. He was dismantling the fastenings on the front of her trim gray jacket before Katy regained enough breath to start laughing.

"Does this mean you're not going to keep your hands off me after all?"

"I'm wearing gloves," he said.

She laughed as she realized it was true. He was wearing black leather gloves. After he'd worked his way through her jacket, blouse, corset cover, corset, and chemise, she discovered leather felt deliciously wicked and exciting against her skin.

255

"How did the telegraphing go?" He bent his head to taste the flushed skin of her left breast.

"I was wonderful," she moaned.

"Yes, you are, but we're talking about your telegraph to Bat."

"It's hard to talk about anything when you're doing that," she gasped.

"Doing what? This?" He did it again.

She was still leaning against the door, which was the only thing keeping her from sinking to the floor. Since that was where Rait wanted her, he continued to do things to her that guaranteed she'd soon be on the floor, door or no door.

"What the hell is this?" He was trying to finish unhooking her corset, which was pink and made of satin and had a ruffle of white lace at the top. It was driving him mad. Around her waist, though, were strings of some sort that were intertwined and tied and knotted in some dangerous fashion he couldn't figure out.

"My petticoats." While she undid the tangled mess with a single finger, Rait did something with his fingers that sent her to the floor in one quick drop. He went down with her to continue teasing, tantalizing, and pleasing himself. And her, too, of course!

With the tapes undone, Katy continued to endure the tortuous pleasure being wreaked on her while she undressed Rait. It wasn't an easy task considering she had to stop every few seconds to gasp and moan.

Her corset was finally unfastened. Rait laid it carefully aside. He wanted to keep track of that thing. He also planned to buy her a dozen more just like it.

"What's this?" he almost bellowed as he came across another set of straps tied around her waist under the chemise.

"Suspenders for my stockings."

"I can't get them unfastened."

"Then cut them off." She was having too much trouble with the buttons on his pants to worry about a pair of thirty-five cent suspenders. When Rait produced from the top of his right boot a Bowie knife with a blade big enough to cut a lot more than just her suspenders with a single swipe, she wished she could snatch those casually spoken words back.

"There," he said, and before Katy could even finish getting worked up into a good panic, he'd sliced through not only her suspenders, but also her chemise and pantalettes.

"Let me borrow that," she said.

He didn't like the way she was looking at the front of his pants. He put the knife out of her reach before finishing undressing himself.

"Leave the gloves on," Katy ordered.

He answered her with a grin. "Tell me about the telegraph." Now they were both free of all unessential clothing, Rait bent his attention and body to the task laid out before him.

"I wasn't the least bit nervous," she said, "even though there was a chance every gun in Dodge was pointed at my back. *Ohhh,* do that again," she moaned, then moaned again when he did. "I gave the operator my telegraph and he asked if my uncle Mat's name might really be Bat and I said, *oh, Rait, oohh!*"

"You said that to him?"

"Be quiet and kiss me."

"You can't talk if I'm kissing you."

"I can't talk when you're doing that to me, either."

"All right. I'll do this instead," he said and did something else that would prevent her from doing much talking.

"I told him, *oohh,* that I know, *aahh,* my own uncle's name, *ooohhh,* and to just send the wire. *Rait!*"

He laughed his way back to her lips. "Did you like that?"

His devilish grin made her shiver with delight.

"Not at all," she said and kissed him on the chin. "I'll give you two seconds to start doing it again."

"I want one of these first," he said. While his dark head was bent over her breasts, she continued with her tale.

"My telegram, *oohh,* said 'Have arrived safely. Stop.' No, not you." She pushed Rait's head back down to her breast. " 'Aunt Gunny lost weight but isn't skinny. Stop. Send luggage immediately to Dodge House Room 22, *ooohhh, don't* stop. Mr. Caldwell proving to be an adequate but unimaginative guardian. Love, Katy.' "

She grinned down at Rait's piqued frown.

"I needed to let Bat know you refused to marry me so he would send the wire with Wyatt's arrival time to me with the right name," she explained with a sassy twinkle in her eyes.

"Unimaginative," Rait said with a thoughtful expression. "While we're waiting for his wire, why don't we see how imaginative I can be? How about this? Do you think that's imaginative?"

"It'll do," Katy groaned.

"How about this?"

"That's not bad, either," she moaned.

"And this? Is this imaginative?"

"It's all right," she gasped.

Rait lowered his head to a place she'd never imagined heads were supposed to go. "How about this?" he asked and began to do something that taught Katy the meaning of the word "whooping."

"That," she said when she was able to breathe again, "isn't imaginative, Rait Caldwell. It's sheer genius!"

Chapter Twenty

Uncle Mat's telegram arrived an hour later.

Both Katy and Rait were almost too exhausted to respond to the knock on the door. He finally managed to summon enough strength to get off the floor, put on his pants, and crack the door open just enough to peer through. He had his gun in his right hand, out of sight of their visitor.

"Telegram for Miss Halliday," a boy with a broken front tooth said.

Rait reached for the envelope with his gun hand. "I'm her guardian."

The boy's eyes widened as he stared at the shiny Colt being pointed at him. "You take your job seriously, don't you?"

Rait glared at him. "Damn right, son. Don't forget it."

"Yes, sir!" The boy took off down the steps at a dead run.

"Jumpy kid," Rait complained. He shut the

door, put his gun down, and opened the telegram. "The wolf howls at midnight. Stop. That's what I call creative. Stop. Maybe I should become a writer. Stop. Love, Uncle Mattie."

Katy laughed. "Bat is the funniest person I've ever met. He's also the sweetest. 'Uncle Mattie,' " she said with an affectionate smile.

Rait dropped down beside her again. "I thought I was the sweetest."

"You're the most imaginative." She kissed him on the cheek. "The next time you want to exercise your imagination, though, let's do it on the bed."

Rait was rereading the telegram. "He certainly blew your cover with this. Deger's going to know it's a code."

"I guess Bat couldn't resist making fun of that newspaper story." She began gathering the sliced remains of her underclothes.

"I wonder why Wyatt wants to come in at night? It will be a lot harder to protect him that way."

"That's not what Bat meant. 'The wolf howls at midnight' was a secret code used in *Deadwood Dick and the Danger in Dirtwater; or, Calamity Jane Rides to the Rescue*. That's my favorite dime novel and I always carry it with me. Bat started reading it last night while we waited for you. In fact, he still has it because he didn't finish it before your train came. In it, Deadwood Dick sends Calamity Jane that message, which meant he would be on the noon train tomorrow. So that's when Wyatt will be here."

Another knock on their door caused them to exchange worried glances. "Just a minute," Rait said. He shoved Katy through the connecting door into room 24 and threw her clothes in after her. When he opened the door to room 22 a minute later, his gun was the first thing the unexpected visitor saw.

"Keep your finger off that trigger, mister," the man in the hall said. "I'm not one of Deger's men."

Rait tried to see past the shadow of the man's hat.

"I saw you earlier and thought you might be Masterson's advance man," the stranger in the hall said. "The girl confused me, though."

"She's good at that," Rait said.

Katy came through the connecting door, having dressed in record time, a feat she accomplished by only putting on one layer of clothing. It felt strange. "He was sitting in the corner of the lobby when we checked in," she told Rait as she peeked around his arm at the man in the hall. She recognized his chin.

"Name's Morrow. I'm a town deputy and a

friend of Bat Masterson's. Can I come in?"

Rait let the man enter, but kept his gun ready and Katy behind him.

"The boy that delivered your telegram told me what it said. I knew it had to be from Bat," Morrow said. "He's the only man I know with enough guts to tell his enemy when he's coming after him."

"But he didn't," Katy said. She could see a little more of his face now. "You're Prairie Dog Morrow, aren't you? Bat told me that he didn't think you'd be on Deger's side." She tried to see if his ears were really pointed on top like a prairie dog's, but his hat covered them.

"No, ma'am. That's why I'm here. I thought you might like to know you had my gun on your side."

"I appreciate that," Rait said. He introduced himself and Katy. "You being a city deputy gives me an idea, Morrow, on how to give Wyatt a legal edge for his negotiations when he arrives."

2:50 A.M.: There was no midnight train to Dodge. The closest was the 2:50 A.M. run, and it was westbound, not eastbound. It wasn't perfect, but it was close enough. When it pulled into the Dodge City station, it was met by four men carrying rifles, pistols, and a warrant for

Wyatt Earp's arrest. They searched the train, argued with the engineer, manhandled the conductor, and frightened an old man with a bad heart.

When the train pulled out, the four men were left standing in the empty street with their warrant. They milled and discussed and argued for awhile, then went to the Alamo to tell Deger that the telegram from Uncle Mattie had been a hoax.

3:17 A.M.: A tall stranger in a black, low-crowned hat who had been leaning quietly against the bar in the Alamo for the last hour began to buy drinks for the house. He continued this generous practice until the four men and Deger were either under the table or asleep on top of it.

9:03 A.M.: The tall stranger in the black, low-crowned hat paid his enormous bar bill at the Alamo. He walked down Front Street to the Dodge House, where he went to room 22 and did something imaginative.

11:15 A.M.: Katy Halliday left the Dodge House with her shopping bag over her arm. She strolled down Front Street to Millicent Maury's Ladies' Wear shop and went inside. The man following her tried to look inconspicuous as he peered inside the store through the plate glass window.

Katy browsed through the ready-made dresses

on a rack near the front of the store, then moved to a display of intimate apparel on a large table.

11:23 A.M.: Fred Singer, deputy sheriff of Ford County and one of Mayor Deger's right-hand men, watched the object of his surveillance select an item and hold it up for inspection. It was a pair of lacy drawers. He jumped back from the window so quickly, he knocked up against town deputy, Dave Morrow.

"Thought I saw a spider," Fred said.

"It happens," Dave said and strolled off in the direction of the depot.

11:28 A.M.: Inside Millicent's shop, Katy finished her selection of a pair of pantalettes, a chemise, stocking suspenders, and a pair of stockings she couldn't resist. "I think I'll look at those dresses again," she told Millicent, and went back to the front rack.

11:30 A.M.: Katy looked between two dresses, out the front window of Millicent's store, and past Fred Singer, who was inspecting a knothole in the post supporting the boardwalk awning. She could see the railroad depot in the middle of Front Street where a man was sitting on a chair at the edge of the depot platform. He had one leg angled over the other so his boot was resting on his knee. His hat was pulled so low over his eyes, that all Katy could see of him was his chin.

266

Prairie Dog Morrow was in position.

11:31 A.M.: Katy asked Millicent if she could try on a hat in the display window.

"Which one?" Millicent asked.

"This one," Katy said and leaned all the way into the window. While she pointed at a robin's egg blue hat decorated with a fluttering of white feathers, she was looking at the cattle pens across the street from the depot. A man dressed in black from his low-crowned hat to his spurless boots was standing near the corral gates. He was practicing fancy quick draws with a silver-handled Colt .45 Peacemaker.

Rait was in place, too.

11:32 A.M.: Katy placed the perky blue hat on her head, tilted it this way and that. She was just taking up time, though. The moment she'd realized the entire underside of the brim was covered with ruffles, she'd known she had to have it. The ruffles were white with little blue bows scattered among their flirty depths.

11:34 A.M.: Katy handed the bonnet to Millicent. "I'll take it."

11:35 A.M.: Millicent Maury closed the lid on the cardboard hatbox containing the blue bonnet and asked, "Will there be anything else?"

Katy worried her bottom lip. It wasn't time to leave yet. "Maybe I should look at those dresses again."

11:37 A.M.: A blast from a steam whistle announced the approach of the AT&SF's eastbound train.

Katy chose a pretty blue dress with tiny white dots all over it. It would look perfect with her new hat. The back of the dress was decorated with white butterfly wing ruffles that started at the waist and fluttered all the way to the hem. She thought Rait might like them. "I'll take this, too," she said. "And I need it in a separate package, please."

11:39 A.M.: Katy paid $11.73 for her purchases just as the train chugged into view.

11:40 A.M.: Finally! The train came to a stop at the depot. Katy gathered her shopping bag, the hatbox, and the paper package with her new dress from the counter. She hurried to the front door of Millicent's shop.

Fred Singer had abandoned his assignment of following Uncle Mattie's niece. He was moving across the street to the station to see why Prairie Dog Morrow, who wasn't a Deger man, was meeting the noon train.

Katy ran out of the shop, across the boardwalk, down the three steps to the street, and right smack into Deputy Sheriff Fred Singer.

"Oh, my," she said as she lay in the dust at his feet.

268

Fred helped her up. "Golly, I'm real sorry, miss."

He gathered her scattered packages and dusted them off. Katy said she'd sprained her ankle during their collision and couldn't take a single step without his aid. He helped her down the street and into the Dodge House, where a man was climbing the stairs to the second floor just ahead of them.

Katy's ankle was suddenly much worse. She almost strangled Fred while he continued his patient efforts to drag her up the stairs. By the time they reached the top, the man was nowhere in sight. She thanked Deputy Singer and sent him on his way.

11:56 A.M.: Fred resumed his interrupted investigation of what was happening at the depot. When he stepped between two of the stationary passenger cars and onto the depot platform, he saw Prairie Dog Morrow, an officer in good standing in Dodge City, deputizing a group of men whose reputations made Fred's knees knock and his spine grow weak.

Right there in broad daylight in the middle of Front Street without a single Deger man in sight, except for Fred, were five of the greatest legends in the West: Wyatt Earp, Texas Jack Vermilion, Dan Tipton, Johnny Milsap, and Johnny Green. There was enough firepower in

269

that group to make Grant surrender to Lee.

With them was the tall man in the black hat who bought all those drinks last night in the Alamo. He was the only man who hadn't raised his hand to take the oath to become a Dodge City law officer.

"Rait Caldwell," he said as he introduced himself to Fred. "Guardian of the lady you've been spying on for the last half hour. Hope you don't make a habit of it. I'd hate to have to shoot you."

Fred felt sick. "Deger's not going to like this."

Wyatt Earp adjusted the angle of his hat. "I'll tell you what, Fred. Me and the boys are a mite thirsty. While we're washing the trail dust out of our throats, why don't you go tell the mayor that the game he's been playing with Luke Short just got serious. If he wants to talk, I'm willing to listen. And tell him we have our guns cocked and our fingers on the trigger, so talking is the only thing he'd better try to do."

Katy's sprained ankle underwent a miraculous healing. The moment Deputy Singer left her outside her hotel room, her pain disappeared. She opened the door, tossed her packages on the bed, and threw her arms around Bat Masterson's neck.

He was dressed like Deadwood Dick. She knew it was supposed to be a disguise, but because it made him look as tough, handsome and dangerous as his reputation, she was certain everyone must have recognized him immediately. Except, she realized, he looked almost exactly like Rait, which was why he'd been able to walk into the hotel and up to the second floor without being challenged by the room clerk.

"When I saw you on the stairs," she said, "I nearly choked poor Fred Singer to death trying to keep him from looking too closely at you. Now I realize he wouldn't have recognized you anyway. Why didn't you come in the back way, though, to be safe?"

"I didn't want to be too far from the station if Wyatt needed help."

"Except for Rait and Prairie Dog Morrow, there wasn't anyone on the whole street except Fred and he didn't see anything except me." Katy peeked out the window at Front Street. "There Rait and Wyatt are now. They're headed this way."

Bat looked over her shoulder. "Good. While we're waiting for them, I want to talk to you about something, Katy."

She looked at what he was holding. It was the chemise Rait had cut off her.

"Did you approve of this?" Bat looked very serious and terribly worried. She didn't have the slightest doubt he would go straight downstairs and shoot Rait right in the head if she said no, she hadn't approved having her clothing cut off with a Bowie knife.

She grinned. "I suggested it."

He looked from her to the chemise. "Maybe I should have kept you for myself instead of standing aside for Rait."

She put her arms around Bat's waist, laid her cheek against his chest, and gave him a big hug. "I'll always be a little bit yours. Don't you know that?"

"I guess that will have to do, honey." He held her gently while smiling down at the soft curls fringing her pretty face. "But if Caldwell's rules ever get to be too much for you, Katy, I'm not going to settle for just a little bit of you. I'll be coming after the whole girl."

She grinned up at him. "It's a deal."

Rait left Wyatt and the other men in the hotel bar while he went upstairs. Katy was on the bed, knees drawn up and her arms wrapped around them. As usual, she was laughing at something. Bat was sitting on the edge of the table under the window. He had his gun out and was spinning its cylinder while he watched the alley and the street.

Rait scowled at him. "When Wyatt told me you were on that train, too, I didn't believe him. What are you doing here?"

Bat clicked his cylinder closed and laid his Colt across his lap. "Did you really think I'd let Wyatt come into this town without being here to back him up if he needed help?"

"Who was going to back you up? If Deger knew you were in Dodge, it would be impossible to breathe for the bullets that would be flying through the air right now. Did you know he'd be on that train, Katy?"

"It's what Matt Rash would do, so I guessed Bat might do it, too."

"Now that you're here, what are you going to do?" Rait asked.

"Sit right here," Bat said. "Did Wyatt send word to Deger?"

Rait nodded. "Now we're going to stroll around town to let everyone see that Wyatt's here and who's with him. By sundown, Deger should be ready to talk truce."

He looked at Katy, who was smiling at him like an angel. His anger disappeared as his heart swelled within him. Maybe it wasn't such a bad idea that Bat was here. Now there was no reason to worry about her being in danger, either from herself or from any tricks Deger might try to pull.

Rait realized he'd just figured out what Bat was really doing in Dodge. Ever since the first moment Katy laid eyes on her legendary hero, Rait had viewed her worship of Bat with snide cynicism. No more, though.

He walked over and put his hand on Bat's shoulder. "Thanks, friend."

Chapter Twenty-one

"Tell me about Angie," Katy said to Bat.

They'd been talking nonstop all afternoon while he kept a watch on Front Street. The only activity in town, though, was Rait, Wyatt, Prairie Dog and the four gunfighters going from one saloon to the other. Now that she and Bat had exhausted every other subject, Katy finally turned to the one she cared about most.

"Angie was beautiful."

The way he said it sent Katy's self-esteem plummeting to the bottom of the Canyon of Lost Souls.

"The first time I saw her," he continued, "I thought, 'This is what God had in mind when He created woman.' She had hair the color of moonlight, eyes like a winter sky, and skin so pale, it was like perfect white pearls. She just glowed. She was delicate, too, almost fragile. She looked as though even the most gentle wind would bruise her. Her voice was soft and everything she said came out like a whisper so a man always had the feeling she was telling him an intimate secret. It was very seductive."

Katy felt like a stinkbug.

"Rait fell for her so hard, you could hear it a mile away. It was right here in Dodge. He was one of the town deputies, and I'd come back to help out with an election."

Surprise caused Katy to forget how sorry she was feeling for herself. "Rait was a Dodge City deputy?"

"He didn't tell you?"

She shook her head. Amazing.

"That's how I met him. He came strutting down Front Street one day and I thought, 'That's me a year ago,' only I had a better sense of humor and was too smart to let myself fall in love with a woman I was afraid of."

"Rait was afraid of Angie?"

"Not really afraid, but if she said 'Jump,' he asked 'How high?' That's why he left Dodge. She didn't like the cows and the cowboys. She came here on holiday with a woman friend, an older companion who dragged Angie around like a pet dog. Rait nearly killed himself courting her. It surprised everyone in town when she said yes barely a week after they'd met."

Katy couldn't imagine Rait courting a woman.

276

Did he bring her flowers, read her poetry, sing love songs to her from the street below her window every night? Did he buy her presents and kiss the back of her hand? What had he done for Angie that he'd never done for her?

"Did she love him?" She wanted the answer to be yes because she knew Rait had loved Angie. She also wanted the answer to be no. She felt like a hypocrite, but anything was better than a stinkbug.

Bat slid his thumb across the oversized sight on his Colt. "I remember at the ceremony right after Angie said 'I do.' She looked at Rait and there was an expression of shock on her face. It was almost as though she didn't recognize him. I've often thought she only married him to get away from her overbearing companion. And once he'd set his sights on her, I can't imagine any woman would have said no. He was bigger than life and twice as good-looking, arrogant, cocky, and every female in the county was in love with him."

Katy grinned. "That's why you thought he was just like you."

Bat winked at her. "Damn right." He looked back out at the street. "Rait took a job in Durango to get Angie away from the cattle and the cowboys and the dust and a few dozen other things she didn't like. She didn't like the smelter and the miners any better. She didn't want to just leave town this time, though. She wanted to leave the West and Rait's badge with it. She'd married the biggest piece of masculinity she'd ever seen, then realized she was terrified of it and him, too. She blamed the job. It was rough and violent and she thought if she could get him away from it, he'd be less frightening. So she turned those sad, disappointed eyes on him and asked when was he going to stop playing at being a hero and get a real job that would pay not only their bills, but his father's."

"He told me about his father getting hurt in a mine."

Bat shook his head. "That was a bad piece of business. I don't know how old man Caldwell lived long enough to get hauled out of that hole in Rico, much less last another five months. Durango was neck deep in troublemakers at the time. Rait was a powerful influence in getting the town cleaned up, and he loved his job. Quitting the law was the only thing he ever refused to do for Angie. I don't think he really believed she'd leave him."

"She threatened to?"

"Right at the end. She said if he didn't stop acting like a spoiled little boy who cared more about a little boy dream than his wife and his father, she'd leave him. Then George Caldwell died. I was working as a dealer in Wyatt's saloon in Tombstone when it happened, but I heard Rait totally broke down. He was really close to his old man. And George Caldwell was so proud of Rait, it was written all over his face. He just beamed whenever he saw his son with that shiny silver badge pinned on his chest."

"And then Angie left," Katy said. "Did you know she went back to that woman?"

Bat sighed. "I thought that might have been it. Maybe she thought marrying a real he-man would change her. She probably blamed Rait because it didn't happen."

And suddenly Katy understood. "That's why he gave up his badge, Bat! When he went after her and found her with that woman, he thought it was his fault because he didn't quit his job when Angie asked him. He thinks he's responsible for her going back to that woman."

Bat had stopped playing with his gun. He dropped it into his holster as he rose from the table. "Trouble on the street. Stay here, Katy." He was out the door the next second.

She ran to the window. There were five men crossing Front Street. They were spread out like a lawman's nightmare with their sidearms strapped to their legs and their intentions chiseled in their grim features. It was close to sundown and the setting sun cast long shadows across the wagon ruts in the dry street as they headed for the Lady Gay Saloon.

Bat's brother Ed was killed there. It was straight across the street from the Alamo Saloon. And it was the last place Bat had reported Rait and Wyatt entering on their stroll around Dodge.

Katy was out of the room before she could remember her promise that no matter what happened, she wouldn't get involved.

Chapter Twenty-two

The Lady Gay Saloon was on the southern corner of Front and Bridge Street next to the Comique Theater. History had already proven the Lady Gay an ideal location for a gunfight, which was why Wyatt and Rait chose it as the last stop on their afternoon tour of Dodge. The saloon's history would no doubt have an effect on Mayor Deger's nerves.

As Rait leaned against the bar, he could see over the saloon's batwing doors and out into the street. "Here they come, Wyatt."

"Five men," Texas Jack said. He was lounging by the front window to the left of the door. Johnny Milsap had the right window covered. Johnny Green was stationed at the back door to the saloon. Dan Tipton leaned against the wall at the foot of the stairs leading to the Lady Gay's second floor. Prairie Dog Morrow stood in the open doorway to the dance hall next door.

Wyatt Earp was standing with Rait. There was

enough distance between them for both men to clear leather without interference. They were close enough to protect each other's backs.

The rest of the Lady Gay's customers had fled when they arrived. Only the bartender, Bully Tillman, had remained. With Rait's announcement of the approach of Deger's men, Bully was gone, too.

"They all have badges," Milsap said. He cocked his Colt's hammer and settled his holster snugly against his thigh. "Fred Singer's on the left. Beside him is Bob Vanderburg, then Lou Hartman." Those were the two special officers appointed by Deger to swell the ranks of his official supporters. "Clark Chipman and Jack Bridges are on the right." Clark was a deputy marshal of Dodge. Bridges was the marshal.

Rait and Wyatt exchanged startled glances. The telegrams Deger had been firing off to the governor had implied that Bridges had refused to get involved in the current trouble. His presence with these other men, who were all known Deger supporters, meant that Rait's cover had been blown the moment he'd stepped off the train.

"Alley's clear," Johnny Green said. He closed the back door and locked it.

Tipton drew his pistol before climbing a few steps to check out the second floor. "Balcony's empty." He slid the Colt back into the worn leather, but kept it loose and high.

"Dance hall's like a tomb," Morrow said.

"Let them come in," Wyatt said. He was facing the bar. In front of him was an untouched glass of whiskey. He dropped his hand to his Colt.

Rait did the same.

The doors to the Lady Gay squealed a little as they swung open.

Deger's men stopped to look over the positions of the men in the Lady Gay. There was no way to cover them all. Vanderburg and Hartman stayed in the open doorway. Singer and Chipman angled off to keep watch on Milsap and Vermilion. Bridges fronted the group with his attention focused on Wyatt and Rait.

Wyatt turned to face the five arrivals. He put his left boot on the foot rail that fronted the bar. "Hello, boys," he said with a slow drawl.

"Wyatt," Bridges said. He was looking at Rait, though. They'd been friends once. Jack Bridges knew Rait's skill with a gun. Rait knew Bridges's flaws. "Looks like you're expecting trouble, Wyatt," Bridges said.

"That's up to you, Jack," Wyatt said. His hand was so close to his holster, daylight didn't shine through. "I'd rather talk than shoot. What's it to be?"

Bridges moved his gaze to Wyatt. "The mayor says if you want to talk, he'll listen. He's over at the Alamo right now."

"He sent all five of you to tell me that?" Wyatt laughed. "Either he doesn't trust you to get the message right, Jack," he dropped his left foot to the floor and faced Bridges straight on, "or you don't trust me."

Then Wyatt did what he was most famous for — he walked directly at his adversary without the slightest hesitation or fear.

Jack Bridges's hand twitched above his gun. Wyatt kept walking. Rait palmed the handle of his Colt. Bridges stilled his twitch.

Wyatt stopped right in front of Jack and clapped him on the shoulder like a valued friend. "Let's go see what the mayor wants to talk about." He walked through Deger's forces and out into the street.

Now the five Deger men had to decide what to do. Did they turn their backs on the men still inside the Lady Gay, or did they let Wyatt Earp walk straight across the street and into the Alamo where Deger sat unprotected?

Rait moved his hand away from his gun. "Why don't we join him, Jack?" He followed Wyatt's path across the Lady Gay. When he reached Deger's men, he accompanied them out while Wyatt's four gunmen and Deputy Morrow followed behind.

By the time Katy reached Front Street, Bat was out of sight, the five men headed for Lady Gay were already inside, and a silence had settled over the town that was so absolute that the earlier quiet seemed by comparison a riot of noise.

Katy ran down the boardwalk past Mueller's Boot Shop, Millicent Maury's store, the butcher shop, the Occident and the Old House saloons. At the intersection of Front and First, she stepped off the boardwalk and onto the dry street.

Now that she was in the open, she didn't run. She walked slowly, steadily. With every step she took, her heart leapt into her throat, trying to choke her with emotion that she couldn't afford to think about right now. History was about to happen. She wasn't going to let her common sense, which was screaming at her to run back to the Dodge House as fast as her feet could carry her, stop her from witnessing it.

She crossed the railroad tracks and passed the jail just as Wyatt Earp emerged from the Lady Gay Saloon. He was striding out into the Plaza like a man without a care in the world. Behind him were the five Deger men. With them was

Rait, surrounded by ill will and dangerous men as he backed up Wyatt's little stroll with his gun and his life.

Katy's heart plunged from her throat straight into her stomach as she was struck by a wave of fear so strong that it staggered her.

Before she had a chance to recover, Wyatt came straight at her, lassoed her with his left arm, and dragged her with him on his continuing march across the Plaza.

"Where's Bat?" he asked.

Now that Katy was part of whatever was happening, she stopped worrying about what might happen to Rait and started worrying about what would happen to her when this was over.

"He ran out of the hotel before me," she said. "I haven't seen him since."

Wyatt flicked a penetrating gaze along rooftops and into alleys. "He's here somewhere."

"Where are we going?"

"To the Alamo for a game of poker. You're going to be the wild card that helps me win, Katy."

"The ace up your sleeve?" she asked, and Wyatt laughed.

"Exactly."

Together, they climbed the steps to the boardwalk, walked across it and into the Alamo Saloon.

It was a narrow building filled with chairs and tables, a piano and bar, bottles of liquor, a painting of a naked lady, and a satin-clad saloon girl with hair as red as Sunday sin.

There was also a bartender with a handlebar moustache that swept all the way down to his tightly buttoned shirt collar. He was wearing a black vest and a red garter around his right sleeve and a nervous expression underneath his moustache. Standing in front of the bar were a couple of men wearing guns who looked sweaty and not too friendly.

At the very back of the Alamo Saloon, sitting a few feet to the left of the door to the alley, was a big, fat man. When Katy and Wyatt first entered the saloon, he had appeared confident and secure. As Wyatt strolled across the saloon toward him, his expression turned into pale fear.

"Mayor Deger," Wyatt said when he was so close he could have kicked the table over on top of the fat man. "I want you to meet Katy Halliday. She's here to remind your boys that I want this little setdown to stay peaceable."

Deger's head bobbed up and down. "That's fine, Wyatt. Miss Halliday." Deger bobbed his head in her direction. "It's a pleasure to make your acquaintance."

Wyatt pulled out a chair on Deger's right and held it for Katy to sit. He stayed standing, but took another chair and pushed it up between her and the mayor while Rait and Deger's five lawmen filed into the room, along with Morrow and Wyatt's gunmen.

He casually put his right foot up on the extra chair, leaned over to strike a match against his cowhide boot, and touched the flame to a cigarette dangling from his lips. While he inhaled the acrid smoke, he kept his foot squarely on the chair, his body angled to protect Katy's left side, and his gaze on Mayor Larry Deger.

Dave Morrow covered the cowhands at the bar. Texas Jack, the two Johnnys, and Dan Tipton took up defensive positions around the perimeter of the Alamo. Each had a Deger man move into position to keep an eye on them while they kept an eye on Wyatt. Rait moved to protect Katy's right side.

This was the most exciting moment of her life.

She glanced up at him. He was too busy watching the room to look at her, but he stood so close that he was almost touching her. He looked tall and fiercely protective and she adored him completely.

"So, Mayor," Wyatt said in a lazy drawl. "What's going on here in Dodge that's got Luke Short so riled up?"

"It was Luke's own doing, Wyatt. There's a

law prohibiting playing music in a public place. Luke broke that law in the Long Branch, so I asked Special Officer Hartman to escort him to the depot and send him on his way."

Wyatt took another drag on his cigarette and let a shower of ashes fall to the floor. "That's exactly the same story Luke told Governor Glick in Topeka a few days ago, after which the governor pointed out that a few things were missing from Luke's story. A warrant, a lawyer and a trial. What happened to those, Mayor?"

A sheen of sweat appeared on Deger's forehead. "Well, now, Wyatt, there is a little more involved than just that one law about playing music. There was the unwritten law, too. You know the one about not having whores . . ." His eyes widened as he looked from Wyatt to Katy. "My apologies, ma'am."

"Accepted," she said. "Perhaps you would like to use the term 'waitresses' to describe the ladies you are referring to?"

"An excellent idea," Deger said. He looked back at Wyatt. "Excellent idea, that. Luke had waitresses working at his saloon. That just isn't done north of the tracks, Wyatt. I can't prosecute Luke for it, and that's why he was asked to leave town. It was the only way to preserve Dodge City's reputation as a respectable, decent town."

289

Wyatt dropped his cigarette to the floor beside Deger's feet. "I'm glad you brought that up about the town's reputation, Mayor. As an officially deputized officer of the law here in Dodge . . . you did know that Deputy Morrow deputized me and four of my friends, didn't you? And as fully authorized officers of the law, we spent the afternoon observing just how respectable Dodge City is. We're disappointed, Mayor." Wyatt leveled the full impact of his gaze on Deger. *"I'm* disappointed."

Deger's upper lip was also starting to sweat. "Why is that, Wyatt?"

"Because I don't think my friend Luke Short was treated fairly. You say he had prostitutes, I mean, waitresses north of Front Street. Yet today I saw waitresses working in Hoover's saloon, the Lone Star, the Alhambra, the Old House and the Occident. All those are north of the tracks, but not one of them had their owners run out of town for breaking Dodge's unwritten law. That's not right."

Wyatt put his right hand on his raised knee and moved it up to where his holster thong was tied around his leg. The sweat on Deger's forehead started running like the Arkansas River.

"Then there's the official law that you say Luke broke," Wyatt said. "This afternoon I heard music coming from a dozen places that

290

weren't involved in literary or scientific purposes, including a church, but none of those people were being arrested. That's not right, either. What do you think, Katy?"

"Disgraceful," she said.

"I forgot to mention that Katy is a writer," Wyatt said. "Her uncle is R. T. Halliday, who publishes those popular paperback novels. There probably isn't a person in the whole country who hasn't read one of Halliday's books. Katy thinks this little affair in Dodge, this so-called war, might be worth writing about."

Katy gave Mayor Deger her most enthusiastic smile. "This could be our biggest seller ever. I'm thinking of calling it *Deger's Doings in Dodge; or, How the Mayor of Dodge City Put the Word "Wicked" Back in the West*. There's one thing I'd like to ask, Wyatt. These 'waitresses' you claim are working north of the tracks, can you prove it?"

He turned his gaze to the red-haired girl standing near Jack Vermilion. "I think maybe I can," Wyatt said. "What do you think, Mayor? Do you think that girl over there would turn a two-dollar trick with Texas Jack?"

"She's just a waitress," Deger said. Then he realized he'd been manipulated right into a corner. His face took on a pleading expression. "A real one, Wyatt, not like Luke's girls."

Wyatt cocked an eyebrow in an expression implying anything was possible. "That just may be true, but Katy's going to need proof. Maybe Rait Caldwell can convince that little redhead to change professions. He didn't take the oath of office at the depot today, which means she doesn't have to worry about having the cuffs slapped on her when she puts out her hand for his money. What do you say, Red?" Wyatt asked the girl. "Would you like to take a stroll down to the Dodge House with my friend here?"

Rait gave the redhead a lecherous leer that caused Katy to turn green with jealousy. Of all the men in the room, why did Wyatt have to choose Rait to tempt the seductress into sin? She was looking mighty tempted, too. Her beady little eyes were sparking like lightning bolts and her big buxom chest was heaving like she was having an asthma attack.

"I swear to you, Wyatt," Deger said in a quick defense of his disintegrating situation. "Spanish Sue is a real waitress."

Wyatt grinned at the name. "Spanish Sue," he repeated. He tipped his hat onto the back of his head and leaned forward to put his face at the same level as Deger's. Wyatt's golden hair fell in curls around his forehead, and his smile would have melted solid steel. "Do you think Spanish

Sue would turn me down?" He turned to Katy. "What do you think?"

She liked this suggestion better than his last one and put her whole heart into her role. She looked from the still-wheezing redhead to Wyatt's deliciously handsome face. Katy was even feeling tempted.

"I think she wouldn't even charge you the full two dollars, Wyatt."

Deger began to turn green now, but not from jealousy.

"I could add a subtitle to my book," Katy said. She was looking past Deger to the alley door. "Does this sound creative? *The Story of How Wyatt Earp and Bat Masterson Wooed the Waitress In the Alamo and Won the Dodge City War.*"

"Bat . . . Bat Masterson?" Deger squeaked.

"In the flesh," Bat said and everyone in the room followed the direction of Katy's smile. His Colt was in his hand and his reputation was in his eyes. "I thought I'd drop into town to see how my favorite dime novel writer is getting along."

"With both your name and Wyatt's on this book, Bat, I think it will sell 500,000 copies."

"Hear that, Deger?" Wyatt asked. "Half a million people are going to read all about how the reputation of Dodge is more important to

293

its mayor than the rights of its citizens."

Katy assumed a thoughtful expression. "We could sell even more if the subtitle was *The Story of How Wyatt Earp and Bat Masterson Fought A Blazing Gun Battle to Restore Law and Order to Ford County, Kansas.*"

Bat's answering grin was so quick and wicked, Katy had to bite her tongue to keep from laughing. "I like that one a whole lot better," he said, and Deger turned a nice, slimy shade of nauseous green.

Wyatt moved his hand onto the handle of his Colt. "You heard the lady, Mayor. My boys would just love to be famous. They've been chomping at the bit for the last few days waiting to show Katy their best stuff. You know how grown men like to show off for a pretty girl."

Katy glanced up at Rait, who took his attention off the room long enough to wink at her. It thrilled her so much, she blushed bright red.

"Why don't we just cut all this talk, Wyatt," he said, "and get on with the shooting? My trigger finger's been itching all afternoon. I'd love to give it a good scratch."

"I guess that's it then," Wyatt said and brought his right foot down off the chair with a quick move that startled Katy.

"No!" Deger gasped, startling everyone. Half

294

of his men pulled their guns and the other half were headed that way before they realized it was their boss who had shouted. "I think we can settle this without guns, Wyatt." Deger took out the biggest handkerchief Katy had ever seen and mopped his streaming brow. "Name your terms."

"Luke comes back to Dodge unmolested," Wyatt said.

Deger nodded.

"There will be no further interference with him or his business, and no repercussions against Prairie Dog for his part in this."

Deger nodded again.

"The law about music is either appealed or enforced fairly, which means in every bar in town, including this one."

Deger nodded a third time. "Its appeal will be the first thing on the city council's docket tomorrow. Anything else?"

Wyatt checked with Bat, who shrugged, and Rait, who shook his head.

"That's it," Wyatt said. He dropped his hand away from his Colt. "Why don't we have a drink, boys?"

"Up," Rait said to Katy.

Bat moved over to her and the three of them headed out of the Alamo. The men kept an eye on every corner of the saloon as they left. Katy kept her eye on the redhead. She was still heaving, but now it was in the direction of Johnny Green, who was peeling two dollars off his back pocket bankroll.

The long afternoon had deepened into a purple twilight. Front Street was ablaze with light spilling from the windows and doorways of the saloons, dance halls and gambling parlors lining the busy Plaza. The tinkling sound of a dozen pianos and the deep-throated shouts from a lot of whooping gave the night a feeling of intense excitement.

Katy, too, felt exhilarated. She also felt a little stunned. "Why don't we have a drink," seemed a little anticlimactic for the end of the last great showdown of the Wild West. She hadn't wanted anyone to die, but Bat was the only person to pull a gun and she hadn't even seen him draw it. He'd already had it out before he came through the back door of the Alamo.

"It's all over," she said, sounding as disappointed as she felt.

"Not yet," Rait said. "Deger's promises may not hold when Luke comes back."

"He'll be here tomorrow," Bat said. "I wired him to leave Topeka immediately in case Deger had any men moving in on him."

"Until then," Rait said, "we'll have to watch our backs every second. And you," he took hold of Katy's arm with a firm embrace, "are not go-

296

ing to step one foot out of the hotel room unless I'm with you."

"I think that's an excellent idea," she said. Anyway, she had too much writing to do to go anywhere.

Chapter Twenty-three

Katy sat at the desk in her hotel room and wrote as fast as possible for as long as she was able. While she filled page after page with notes and scenes and chapters, the men filled the two rooms in the Dodge House with noise and tension.

After Wyatt and the other men had a couple of drinks with Deger and his men, they'd returned to the hotel to begin their all-night watch. Luke wouldn't be arriving in Dodge until tomorrow evening. Until then, there was nothing to do but wait.

Prairie Dog and the four gunfighters took up residence in room 24, where they sipped whiskey and dealt cards. Occasionally, Katy heard a sharply spoken curse as a game ended. The curse was immediately followed by the slapping of cards being shuffled for the next game.

Rait, Wyatt, and Bat were in room 22 with Katy. Wyatt was seated on the table under the window. His attention was on the alley and street, his hand on his Colt. There were two chairs in the room. Katy had one, Bat the other, which he sat on backwards while he kept an eye on the door. Rait propped himself up against the iron headboard and stretched his legs out on the bed. He kept his eye on Katy.

The three men talked gambling while Katy wrote and overheard four hours of recitations covering every card game they'd ever played, watched being played, wished they'd played, planned to play, or lied about having played. The only time they stopped was when they were eating, during which they talked about Katy's excited reception of a meal that included fried bear meat, fried prairie chicken, and fried frog legs.

"Disgusting!" she proclaimed and ate some of everything.

There were also fried potatoes, refried beans, and a lettuce salad. The salad was the only thing served that wasn't fried. To preserve the skillet-prepared theme of the meal, however, the salad had a hot bacon fat dressing.

Katy didn't care. She ate it, too. "I'm going to get as big as a cow if we stay here very long," she said between bites of bear meat. It tasted exactly like she'd imagined bears would taste . . . big and brown.

"How long will we be here?" Texas Jack asked.

He was mopping up the drippings on his plate with a piece of fried cornbread.

"Until we're certain Deger means to keep his word," Wyatt said. "Definitely a week. Maybe two."

Texas Jack grunted a reply while helping himself to another serving of frog legs. "Did you know these things jump around in the skillet while they're being cooked?" he said to Katy.

She shuddered and ate another one. As far as she was concerned, nothing could be as sickening as snake eggs.

When the meal had been consumed down to the last bite of deep-fried gooseberry dessert tarts, the gunfighters went back to their card game, Katy to her writing, and Bat, Wyatt, and Rait to their talking.

It was well after midnight when Katy simply couldn't concentrate on her story one more second. She capped her ink, arranged the pages of poetic prose in a neat stack, and went over to curl up next to Rait on the bed.

He welcomed her into his embrace, provided his left shoulder as a pillow, and smiled at the little sigh she exhaled as she snuggled against him. The men were discussing the way they treated cheaters in a poker game.

"Have any of you ever cheated?" she asked.

Rait looked at Bat, who looked at Wyatt, who

was so startled that he stopped looking out the window to look at Rait.

"I guess that means yes," Katy said.

"Don't jump to conclusions," Rait said. "Cheating is an ugly business. We were just surprised that you thought we were capable of such a vile crime."

"I would rather shoot myself in the foot than cheat," Wyatt said.

"I'd rather shoot Wyatt in the foot than cheat, too," Bat said.

Katy hid a yawn behind her hand. "You're all liars. I can't believe that three of my four favorite heroes are liars."

Bat bristled like an offended porcupine. "You have a hero other than us? Who? I'm going to go out and shoot him right this minute."

She tried to smile, but it came out as another yawn. "My uncle, of course."

All three men tried not to look affected by the sentiment of a female silly enough to wear a bow where her bustle should be.

Fifteen minutes later, while the men were spinning yarns about how tough, unsentimental, and unemotional they were, Katy fell asleep in Rait's arms. He knew the second it happened, and stopped telling the biggest lie he'd ever concocted in his life to look down at the pretty face resting on his shoulder. *Dear God, I love her so much.*

"Is she asleep?" Wyatt asked. In response to Rait's acknowledging nod, he stopped sitting quite so heroically stiff. Even Bat relaxed his legend-worthy pose and assumed a more comfortable slump in the chair.

"I'm sorry for roping her into that business today, Rait," Wyatt said. "I couldn't believe it when I came out of the Lady Gay and saw her coming right at me. The only thing I could think of was to take her with us." He caressed Katy's face with a tender, smiling gaze. "She did a good job, though. I was proud of her."

"So was I, though I'd rather be gutshot than let her know it," Rait said. "There's no telling what mischief she'd get into next if she knew I wasn't furious about today. It was the luckiest day of my life when she hopped off the train in Durango and asked me if I was going to rob her."

Wyatt did a double take on that statement. "She did what?"

Rait chuckled. "She was riding the cattleguard and decked out from head to foot in the brightest yellow dress I've ever laid eyes on. She took one look at me, thought I was a criminal looking for a victim, and promptly volunteered. I decided right then she was more trouble than she was worth." He gently brushed a strand of hair off her sleep-flushed cheek. "I was wrong."

Bat hadn't said anything for so long, Wyatt looked at him. Bat's expression made it easy for Wyatt to guess what his old friend was feeling as he watched Rait holding Katy.

I'll be damned, Wyatt thought.

When Bat realized he was being observed, he stood abruptly and turned his gaze away from the sleeping girl. "I need some air."

"It's not safe out there," Wyatt said. "Go play poker with the boys."

After Bat left the room, Wyatt glanced back at Katy. Without exception, she was the most surprising woman he'd ever met. He turned his attention back to the dark streets outside the hotel and watched the shadows until dawn.

It was fresh and early, and Katy was wearing her new dress and hat. Actually, she was still pinning the hat on, but the new dress was in place and had been admired at length by Rait, Bat, and Wyatt.

The cardplayers had been thrown out of room 24 by Bat so Katy could use it for her morning toilet. He'd straightened and fussed and fumed over the mess the men had left before allowing her to enter. The room still smelled of whiskey and cigars, but Katy was wearing a new bonnet, so she didn't mind.

"Ready for breakfast?" Rait called to her from the other room.

"Ready." She skipped in to show him the new hat.

He stared at the ruffles peeking out from beneath the brim. The back of the dress had been delightful enough. The hat was an unexpected and almost overwhelming bonus. It was going to be a long day.

"Look at my stockings," she said. She lifted the hem of her dress to reveal white stockings with little yellow flowers stitched above the ankle. "They look like dandelions."

She'd also pinned a yellow bow on the collar of her dress to give her outfit a bright spot of color. Rait looked from the stockings to the bow to the rainbows in Katy's eyes. It was going to be an unbelievably long day.

While Katy was showing off her stockings, her hat had taken on a strange tilt that sent her running back to the mirror in room 24. "I'll be just a second," she told Rait, who began to look around for something to keep him occupied for the next twenty minutes.

Katy rearranged her hair to give the hat more support, set her bonnet on top of the tumbling curls, and instead of jabbing the hat with her hatpin, stabbed her finger instead. She muttered one of the most popular oaths from last night's card game before putting her finger in her mouth to stop the throbbing pain. She heard Rait chuckle in the other room, then break into a full-fledged laugh.

"What's so funny?"

He didn't answer, but kept laughing. She tried the hatpin again, this time with perfect success, and went to see what had Rait in such a good mood.

He was reading her book.

"It's not a comedy," she said.

Rait looked up from the page he was reading.

"Why were you laughing?" she asked.

Her voice was strained with the hurt that was reflected on her face. Rait would have traded his interest in the Hub Saloon to take back the last few minutes.

"I've never read anything written by someone I know before. It felt strange, so I laughed."

"You're lying, Rait. I want the truth."

He placed the page he was holding on top of the unread stack. "I didn't want to hurt your feelings, Katy. The truth is, I really thought it was supposed to be funny. If it's not, then I can see why your uncle hasn't published any of your manuscripts."

"Why?" she asked. The word sliced out of her like a sliver of sharp ice.

"Do you really want me to do this, Katy?"

"I want to know what's so terrible about those pages that you felt compelled to laugh at them."

"All right," Rait said. "First, the way you describe things, like here in the first chapter." He sorted through the pages he'd read. "You call the conversation of the men in the saloon, 'the feverish braggadocio of simmering masculinity.' That sounds ridiculous, Katy." He sorted through a few more pages. "And here where Wyatt is walking around Dodge with the gunfighters, you say he wanted it 'noised around town' he was 'ready to slap leather and draw blood.' I don't know which is worse, 'noised around town' or 'slap leather.' Nobody talks like that. As for the story itself, it's exaggerated and most of the scenes don't make sense. Some of them don't even have anything to do with the story."

Katy was fighting tears of humiliation. She tilted her chin up, determined not to let him see her cry. "I'm sorry my writing isn't up to your standards of quality, but it's the best I know how to do." Unable to delay her tears another second, she ran out of the room.

"That was the cruelest thing I've ever seen."

The comment came from Bat, who had come upstairs to see what was taking Rait and Katy so long to join everyone for breakfast. He'd been standing in the open door during their discussion of Katy's writing and had almost been knocked down by her sudden flight from the room. Now he faced Rait with his right hand gripping the butt of his Colt so hard, his knuckles were white.

"She wanted the truth," Rait said. He slammed the pages of her manuscript onto the desk. "People shouldn't ask a question if they don't want to hear the answer."

"And the only way you could answer her was to rip her heart out and shoot it full of holes? Before you offer any more words of wisdom about Katy's writing, try reading her competition. Those examples you quoted are just as good as anything in this."

He tossed to Rait the dime novel Katy had said was her favorite, *Deadwood Dick and the Danger in Dirtwater; or, Calamity Jane Rides to the Rescue.* On the cover was a picture of Calamity. She was wearing a fringed buckskin jacket and carried a shotgun in one hand, a Colt .45 in the other. The Colt had a barrel almost as long as the shotgun, and Calamity was brandishing it like a saber as she rode to the rescue on a white horse racing down the middle of a crowded city street.

The book was well-worn. A tear in the cover across Calamity's jacket had been lovingly mended with neat little stitches that carefully drew the paper together.

Under the picture was a description of Calamity's character: "A spark of the unforgettable, a flair for the spectacular, an urgency for action." The description fit Katy so well, Rait laughed.

"I'll go find her," Bat said, "and make certain she doesn't do anything crazy, like regret running away from you."

"I don't need you to lecture me about the way I treat Katy," Rait snapped.

Bat was right, though. He'd acted like a jackass.

First, Angie. Now Katy.

Rait picked up the paperback book and traced a finger across the little row of stitches in the cover. What he needed was a way to mend his mistake.

Chapter Twenty-four

Katy was amazed. Wright, Beverly and Company, located on the northeast corner of Front and Bridge Street, had to be the most incredible place on earth. She and Rait had been passing the store when suddenly he grabbed her hand and dragged her inside.

At first, she'd been as mad as a bee-stung steer (Bat had said that this morning and she'd immediately made note of it. The next time someone called her writing ridiculous, instead of crying and running away, she'd be able to stand her ground and prove that her prose and dialogue realistically depicted the way Westerners flapped their jaws.)

Now she forgave Rait entirely. Well, not entirely. She forgave him for the grabbing and dragging. This morning's criticism was still a festering sore that hadn't been lanced (Dan Tipton's description of the way his breakfast beefsteak had been cooked).

Katy and Rait had spent all day ignoring each other, even though except for breakfast, he hadn't left her side. They'd walked all over town, up to the cemetery and down by the river; Katy—because she wanted to see everything in Dodge, Rait—because he'd been looking for a way to apologize.

It was close to six o'clock now, an hour and a half before Luke Short's train was due into Dodge. They'd been headed for the hotel and Katy's all night lockup in her room when suddenly Rait dragged her into the store.

She'd been lagging behind him in order to look in the store window. It had a wonderful display of Western clothing, including Stetson hats, several styles of riding boots, blue denim pants, and a variety of plaid, plain, and fancy shirts any cowboy would have been proud to wear.

Once Katy was inside the store, she'd been shocked to discover it also sold food. Who would have thought a person could buy clothes in the same store they bought beans? And not just beans, either. Wright, Beverly and Company sold anything and everything from "a paper of pins to a portable house," a sign claimed over the front door.

The moment Katy stepped through that front door, she'd entered a world dominated by smell.

There was the warm smell of the wood floors and the sawdust used to sweep them clean every night, and which managed to fall into cracks and crevices so a little touch of it was always there to tantalize the nose. There was the delicious aroma of leather coming from the saddles, boots, and belts piled and stacked and hanging beside the dry goods counter.

Plug tobacco gave the store a rich, smoky smell, along with the cigars in wood boxes displayed inside a glass case on the grocery counter. A hoop of cheese added its flavor to the room, a sharp, tangy, mouth-watering scent that beckoned customers to lift the hinged knife and slice off a wedge. The cracker barrel stood nearby. Beside it was the pickle barrel with its vinegary smell. There was a potbellied stove, too, that smelled of long winter days when its heat held at bay the bitter cold outside.

There was a grocery counter, a dry goods counter, and at the back of the store, a hardware counter. Overhead hung bacon and hams and animal traps and cooking pots and skillets and bridles and umbrellas and a sign advertising Dr. Lyon's Tooth Tablets, a compressed tooth powder that thoroughly cleans the teeth and is convenient for travelers.

The contents of the grocery shelves were limitless. Katy recognized names she'd read on advertising broadsides in New York City. Quaker Oats, Baker's cocoa, Burpee's seeds, Ivory soap, Hire's root beer, Le Page's glue, Pillsbury's flour.

In the hardware section was a glass case filled with knives, another with razors, and still another containing a display of pearl-handled and intricately engraved Colt six-shooters that were so fancy they scarcely looked capable of firing.

The hardware section also had washtubs big enough to bathe in, wire baskets, metal buckets, and wooden bowls. Nutmeg graters, washboards, coffeepots, dustpans, kerosene lanterns and a fifty-gallon barrel of kerosene with a spigot for filling a customer's empty can, bucket or jug vied for attention.

On the wall in the dry goods section was a kaleidoscope of calico colors stacked in bolts reaching from the floor to the sky. There were also shelves of shoes, rows of ribbons, bolts of lace . . . and Rait.

"Get over here, Katy, and pick out a pair of pants."

"Pants?"

"Levi Strauss's denims. What size would you wear?" he asked, more to himself than to her.

"What do I need pants for?"

"You told me your first day in Colorado that you came west to do research for your writing.

312

So far, all you've done is try to rob a train and shoot a gun. I thought we could hire a couple of horses tomorrow and ride south to the state border. You can pretend you're on the run from the law and every breath you take might be your last because somewhere out there is a bullet with your name on it. You can't do that in ruffled petticoats and embroidered stockings."

He was right. The only place she was equipped to run from the law was down Fifth Avenue in New York.

She knew Rait was doing this to make up for this morning. It was a sweet gesture. She wasn't ready to forgive him yet, though. It would take more than a pair of denim pants to make up for having the best story she'd ever written massacred with a dull tomahawk (Wyatt Earp's description of the shave he got at the barbershop before breakfast this morning).

A salesclerk named Mr. Samuels volunteered to help outfit Katy for a life of crime. Soon there was a stack of clothing on the dry goods counter that made her cringe at the thought of having to wear all this realism. There was a pair of stiff denim pants that looked about as comfortable as unsanded wood. A flannel shirt without a single formfitting dart, tuck, or pleat. A pair of scratchy woolen underwear that looked and felt gruesome.

"I'm not wearing these." She pushed the underwear back across the counter at Mr. Samuels. "I don't care how many banks and stagecoaches have been robbed by men wearing those things, I'm not going to wear them."

"All right, no long underwear," Rait said. He preferred her lacy drawers, anyway. "You will need socks, though." He chose a pair thick enough to be called boots. "Boots," he said next and pulled a pair off the shelf that would withstand the weight of an entire locomotive without a crack in the leather. "Hat."

Now he was really going too far! Katy wouldn't use that thing he was buying, under the guise of it being a hat, for a chamber pot. It was brown and ugly and floppy and looked like it was made from matted animal hair.

"It is made from matted animal hair," Rait said. "What do you think felt is?"

"Gloves," he said, and Mr. Samuels produced from beneath the counter a pair of leather gloves so big and thick that they looked like grizzly bear feet.

"Now let's pick out a jacket," Rait said, but Katy had lost interest in the whole idea of wearing real Western clothes. She wandered off to investigate the scented soap display.

"Katy, come here and try this on."

She went back to where the buying spree was

still going on, turned her back to Rait, and held out her arms for him to put whatever fashion atrocity he'd chosen on her.

"Here." He pushed her in front of a mirror. "How do you like it?"

It was more comfortable than she'd expected, but that didn't change her preconceived opinion. "I don't like it at all," she said . . . then saw what she was wearing.

It was the prettiest shade of brown she'd ever seen.

It was made of buckskin so soft, it felt like silk.

And it had fringes. Across the front. Down the sleeves. All the way around the bottom.

She was wearing the exact same jacket Calamity Jane was wearing on the cover of *Deadwood Dick and the Danger in Dirtwater.*

"Oohh," Katy said and threw her arms around Rait's neck in a hug that made both of them breathless.

"Does this mean you do like it?" he asked.

"Yes," she said against the front of his shirt. "I love it. It's beautiful. It's just like I've always wanted."

"I'm sorry about this morning, Katy," he whispered into her hair.

"I know," she whispered back.

He held her against him so tightly, he could

315

feel her heart beating all the way through the leather jacket. He looked across the top of her head at Mr. Samuels.

"We'll take it," he said.

Chapter Twenty-five

Katy was wearing her Western duds. It was 7:15 P.M., five minutes before Luke Short's train was due. She wanted to be ready in case anything exciting happened. She hoped if it did, it wouldn't happen too fast. She might run right out of these pants.

"They'll shrink when they're washed," Rait had promised when he was helping her button herself into them. "Bat's going to have a fit when he sees you in these. He's turning into a mother hen where you're concerned."

"Everyone should have a fit now and then," Katy had remarked. "It keeps life interesting."

Rait almost had one when he finished fastening her pants and she twirled around to show him how she looked. Although they were a little too big, the denim pants were beguilingly attractive on her. If there hadn't been a gang of gunmen in the other room waiting to discuss strategy for protecting Luke, he would have taken those pants right back off her.

The pants caused a stir among the gunmen, too. Bat glared, Wyatt stared, Johnny Milsap fell off his chair. When the initial reaction was over, the strategy meeting finally got underway. No one, however, paid any attention to it, so Wyatt moved it down to the depot. His parting words to Katy had been, "Don't leave this room."

Bat's were, "You look adorable in that jacket, honey. I don't know about those pants, though. Don't leave this room."

Texas Jack said, "I'd rustle steers with you any day, Miss Halliday. Don't leave this room." His sentiment had been echoed by the other gunfighters.

Rait's parting words had been, "I can't wait until we get rid of these cutthroats and have this place to ourselves again. In the meantime, don't leave this room."

Katy had always been impressed by unanimous decisions. Too bad this wasn't one of them. Her vote, which no one bothered to solicit, was, "If you think I'm going to stay in this room, you must be daft."

With only five minutes left until Luke Short's arrival, she loaded the pockets of her new pants with the only weapon she had at hand to help defend her men. Firecrackers.

It was the two strings of blasters she and Bat had purchased in the Chinese store in Silverton. When she'd been packing to leave for Dodge, she'd thrown them into her carpetbag to keep Rait from finding them in her room at the Grand. At the time, she'd figured she was in enough trouble just running away. She didn't need a lecture on the dangers of gunpowder in the hands of amateurs.

Now, with her pants full of explosives, matches in her shirt pocket and the fringe on her Calamity Jane jacket swinging in the wind, Katy set out to once again do her part in the Dodge City War.

Luke's arrival in Dodge was as anticlimactic as Wyatt's closing statement at yesterday's big pow-wow (Johnny Green's description of anything having to do with talking).

Luke Short got off the train. Bat shook his hand. Wyatt told him what the mayor had promised. Then they all took off for the Long Branch to open the bar and have a drink.

There was no doubt, though, that everyone was a little tense. The men had their hands on their guns and they looked as jumpy as frog legs in a frying pan (Katy thought of that one herself).

319

The Long Branch Saloon was considered the best establishment of its kind in Dodge City. It drew the best bartenders, the best gamblers, and the best girls. Since that was how all this trouble got started, Luke decided not to decorate the room too much on his first night back. Even without the girls, within minutes of the Long Branch's reopening, it began to fill with cowboys and locals ready to fill its coffers.

While the party inside was getting underway, the party outside was still ripe for trouble. Deger's men were out in force. Bat's men didn't shy away from their duties, either. They stalked around like mad dogs with their haunches up waiting for a chance to pick a fight.

Katy lurked in what few shadows existed on the busy street, mostly inside the recessed doorways of closed stores, and waited for the trouble to start. Four hours later, she was really bored and terribly sleepy. So was everyone else involved in the standoff. Wyatt started dealing faro in the Long Branch. Rait went next door to the Alamo to make the mayor nervous, Prairie Dog Dave Morrow went off to patrol the south side of the tracks since it was his night on duty. The four famous gunfighters tried to outdrink Deger's men in the Long Branch.

Bat paced around the boardwalk for a while longer. Finally he gave up the fight, too, and went three doors down from the Long Branch to the Lone Star Saloon to play a hand of cards. When he was sheriff of Ford County, he'd owned an interest in the Lone Star and now was enjoying renewing old acquaintances.

He'd been in there two hours when the trouble started.

The gunfire caught Katy asleep in the doorway of Zimmerman's Hardware Store. She ran out onto the boardwalk to see what was happening. People were stampeding out the swinging doors of the Long Branch like a herd of buffalo being chased by a band of screeching Indians.

Katy went out into the street to see better. What she saw was a fantasy come true.

The one, the only, the legendary Bat Masterson charging out of the Lone Star Saloon with a pistol in both hands and vengeance in his eyes.

He looked like an avenging angel of God as he raced down the boardwalk to the Long Branch. With guns aloft, he battled through the frenzied crowd of departing customers. Katy fought her way through the crowd, too, and entered the saloon right on her hero's heels.

Just inside the door he came to such a sudden stop, she slammed right into his back. His guns were cocked, his fingers on the triggers, but he didn't fire. He just stared.

"Who is that?" he asked.

Katy peered around him at the source of the commotion.

In the middle of the room surrounded by overturned tables and tumbled chairs was a big-boned brute of a man holding the strangest-looking pistol Katy had ever seen. Flame spurted from one of its two barrels and the jarring crash of the gun's discharge thundered in the Long Branch as the big brute shot at the globe-shaped chandelier overhead. One of the lamps exploded. Shards of glass rained down from a cloud of gunsmoke onto the smattering of customers who instead of running out earlier had merely hit the floor and taken cover behind overturned tables.

"He wasn't in the Alamo yesterday," Katy said. "I don't think he's one of the men who met the train when they thought Wyatt was coming in two nights ago, either. What type of a pistol is that, Bat?"

"It's a sawed-off shotgun, honey. Do you know who he is?" Bat asked Johnny Milsap.

"He's not one of ours."

"I know that," Bat said. "Is he one of Deger's?"

Johnny shrugged. "I don't know."

The shotgun discharged a double-barreled attack on the chandelier. When the glass stopped showering down, Luke Short popped his head up from behind an overturned table. "Why isn't somebody doing something to stop him?"

Texas Jack Vermilion was doing something, he was running. He appeared suddenly from behind the bar with a bottle of whiskey under each arm.

Bat stopped him at the door. "Who is that, Tex?"

"It's not one of our boys."

Bat sighed. "I know that. What I don't know is whether he's one of Deger's men."

"If he was, wouldn't he be shooting at us instead of the lights?"

It made sense.

"Maybe it's a trick," Katy said. "Maybe he's firing at the chandelier in an attempt to draw you out, Bat. Then Deger can say you started the war up again by firing on one of his men without provocation."

"That makes sense, too," he said. Dan Tipton was pressed up against the far wall of the saloon. "Dan!" Bat shouted. "Who is that?"

"Don't know!" The man fired again and another glass globe exploded. "Crazy son-of-a-bitch!" Dan dove under a table.

"I wonder where Rait is?" Katy asked after the spray of glass settled.

"Probably checking to see that you're all right at the hotel," Johnny Milsap said.

Bat regarded Katy with a displeased expression. "Why aren't you at the hotel, honey?"

"I didn't want to miss anything."

He laughed. "I should have guessed. Now that you're here, stay behind me because I want everything to miss you."

Luke's face was a livid shade of red. "Will you stop flirting with that girl, Bat, and shoot that man?"

Katy liked that someone thought Bat was flirting with her. She didn't like having his flirting interrupted by Luke's complaining.

"Why don't *you* shoot him?" she asked Luke.

"Because Bat thought it would be too dangerous for me to go walking around Dodge with a gun right now," Luke said. "Who are you?"

"Katy Halliday. I helped convince Mayor Deger to let you come back to town."

"Thanks, I think."

The shotgun roared again and the big-boned brute began reloading.

"Now's your chance, Bat," Luke said. "Shoot him before he can reload."

"I want to know if he's one of Deger's men first. If he is and I shoot him, we'll all be fair game. I don't want to restart this war just to save your chandelier."

"Then don't shoot him, just stop him."

Too late. The shotgun was reloaded and the poor chandelier suffered another direct hit.

"Will somebody please do something?" Luke begged.

Katy was getting tired of his whining. "I'll do something." She took out her firecrackers, lit one on the end of each string and tossed the whole lot behind the bar.

"Get down!" Bat shouted when he saw what she'd done. He threw himself on top of her, knocking them both flat on the floor just as the first firecracker exploded, along with several bottles of liquor. Now glass was raining down from the ceiling and shooting up from behind the bar. The Long Branch was beginning to look like a real war had broken out.

"What did you do that for?" Bat yelled at Katy.

"It's a diversion," she said between attempts to breathe. He was a lot heavier than he looked.

He rolled off her and craned his head around the spittoon they were behind to see what was happening. The firecrackers were blasting away in a spectacular display. Sparks were flying; bottles were popping. There was so much noise that it sounded like the cavalry was on its way to save the settlers. The crazy brute with the sawed-off shotgun looked stunned and disoriented.

"Not bad," Bat said. "I'll have to remember that trick."

Katy was straightening the tangled fringe on

her sleeves. "My new jacket had better not get dirty down here on this floor, Bat Masterson, or you're going to be one sorry gambler."

Wyatt Earp came flying across the room to land belly-down beside her.

"Nice move with the firecrackers, Katy," he said. "Do you know who that is shooting up the place, Bat?"

"Can't figure it out. I thought maybe you knew who he was."

"I haven't a clue," Wyatt said.

"Who cares?" Luke wailed.

All three ignored him.

Wyatt poked his head up to watch the explosions behind the bar. "Do you think those firecrackers will set the liquor on fire back there?" Sparks were rocketing everywhere.

"Probably," Bat said.

"I wish I could reach one of the bottles before it goes," Wyatt said. "All the burnt gunpowder in the air is making me thirsty."

Texas Jack offered one of his bottles. "I got an extra."

Wyatt opened it, took a swig, and started coughing. "Why didn't you steal the good stuff instead of this rotgut, Vermilion?" He took a second swig before passing the bottle to Katy, who handed it to Bat.

"Damn," he said after he tried to tip the bottle

up for a drink. "It's hard to drink while you're lying facedown on the floor."

The big brute appeared to be pulling his few wits together. He was taking a bead on the chandelier again.

"Aren't either of you going to do anything about him?" Katy asked.

"How?" Wyatt asked. "We're being pinned down by firecrackers."

Bat thought that was funny.

"My heroes," Katy muttered. Not even in her wildest imaginings had she ever thought she'd be hiding behind a spittoon with Bat Masterson and Wyatt Earp while an unknown assailant murdered a chandelier.

"I wonder where Rait is?" she asked.

"Doing something to stop this madman, I hope," Luke moaned from behind his table.

The brute squeezed off another shot, a glass globe shattered; more firecrackers went off with a whine and a blast and a rocketing of sparks that rained down all over the saloon.

"Wow," Johnny Green said. "That was real pretty."

"My business is being destroyed and he's enjoying it," Luke said. "I can't wait to move out of this town." He sounded really disgusted.

"You're leaving?" Bat asked. "After all we went through to get you back into Dodge, you're leaving?" He looked so angry that Katy thought he was going to crack Luke over the head with the whiskey bottle.

"You didn't really think I'd stay, did you? I wouldn't last ten minutes without you and Wyatt here to protect me. As soon as I can sell this dump, I'm heading for Texas. If somebody doesn't stop this fool soon, though, I won't have anything to sell."

"I guess that makes sense," Wyatt said. "We can't stand guard over him forever, Bat. The best thing for Luke to do is move on."

"Now that you've approved my travel arrangements, will you stop that crazy bastard shooting up my saloon?"

Another shot was let loose by the brute. This time part of the ceiling came down with the chandelier.

"I think we should wait until he's out of bullets again," Wyatt said.

Bat agreed. "That's a good idea." He grinned at Katy. "Is this showdown everything you dreamed it would be, honey?"

She ducked the shower of plaster. "Are they always like this?"

"This one's a little unusual," Wyatt said. "Most of the time, one side or the other backs down before any gunplay can get started. When the bullets do start to fly, it usually takes only two or three before someone gets hit and the whole thing is over."

Fred Singer came flying across the room and landed headfirst on the floor beside Bat. When he'd recovered from the impact, he asked, "Do you fellas know who that is doing all the shooting?"

"We thought he was one of yours," Bat said.

"Never saw him before. Hartman's over there under the piano. He doesn't know him either."

"I wish I knew where Rait was," Katy said. "He should be back from the hotel by now. I don't want him sneaking up behind me and doing something crazy, like trying to strangle me. Oh, look! There he is!"

Rait wasn't hiding like everyone else in the room. He was walking across the middle of the floor right at the big-boned brute, who was taking fresh aim at what remained of the chandelier. When he saw Rait, his face grimaced into what looked like a snarl, and he drew down on his assailant.

For the last five years, Katy had prayed every night to see Dodge City in all its gunfighting glory. Now here she was up to her hair ribbons in gunfighters and glory . . . and she desperately wished she could take back every single one of those prayers to keep Rait from being hurt.

Before she could start listing the things she

would trade God for Rait's safety and before the big brute could fire, Rait pulled his Colt and rushed forward. He ran right up to the man and clubbed him over the head with his gun barrel.

The brute went down like a felled tree, and Katy almost fainted.

"Good job," Bat said. "Did you see that, honey? Rait buffaloed him."

To buffalo a man meant to outdo him in a game or in business. During Bat and Wyatt's reign as Dodge City lawmen, they'd added a new twist to the term's definition. Because a liquored-up cowboy was quick to go for his gun when faced with being arrested, and because they didn't want to shoot their way out of trouble every night, Bat and Wyatt had started outdoing troublemakers by knocking them over the head with the barrels of their guns.

Now the technique was widely used in what was known as the "knock 'em down and drag 'em out" method of law enforcement. It was also one of the main reasons Colt .45s were so popular with lawmen in the West. Smith and Wesson handguns weren't heavy enough to withstand the bruising blow of a buffaloing. A Colt could render a man unconscious and not even dent the barrel.

Rait was checking his victim for signs of life. Wyatt helped Katy up off the floor while Bat put his guns away. The one with the oversized front sight he put in his holster, the other he shoved under his belt.

"Is that my gun?" she asked him.

"Your gun?" It was Rait, of course. He had the best timing of any sneaky person she could imagine.

"I meant *the* gun, the one I learned on."

He didn't look very convinced by her lie.

"I thought Wyatt was the only man crazy enough to walk right up to his enemy," Bat said, demonstrating his own bravery by wading into the middle of Katy and Rait's showdown. "How did you know he wouldn't shoot you?"

"I was counting his shots. He was out of bullets."

Katy laughed. "If I'd written that, you would have said it was ridiculous."

Wyatt's men and Deger's were starting to get up from their hiding places on the floor. They were glancing at each other with embarrassed expressions and laughing at how ridiculous they all looked.

"I think the crisis is over," Bat said. He yawned. "I'm going back to the hotel and get some sleep."

Jack Bridges, the town marshal, was helping Fred Singer drag the unconscious brute out.

Bat held the swinging door open for them.

331

"Who is he, Jack?"

"Just a drunk cowpoke who wanted it noised around that he was the toughest hombre in town."

"Hah!" Katy cried. "Did you hear that, Rait? He wanted it 'noised around.' "

"That's it, honey," Bat said. "Don't let him get away with a thing." He winked at her before strolling off down the boardwalk.

"Clark!" Jack shouted at his deputy, who was standing in the street with the rest of the frightened flock. "Help Fred with this." He turned his half of the brute over to his deputy and turned back to Rait. "I'd like to talk to you a minute, Caldwell. Could you come down to my office?"

"I'll take Katy to the hotel," Wyatt said. He found his hat behind an overturned chair and slapped the dusty Stetson against his leg to clean it. Once it was back in place on his head, they left. It was a pretty night now that all the shooting was over. The breeze smelled of the river and the stars were bright. Not as bright as in Colorado, though, Katy decided.

When they got to the hotel, the room clerk motioned Wyatt over. "I have your room ready for you, Mr. Earp. Number 30, upstairs at the end of the hall. Mr. Masterson arranged it, along with rooms for the other men."

"Thank you," Wyatt said. "Looks like Bat decided to let you and Rait sleep alone tonight," he said to Katy.

Her face flushed. "What happens now, Wyatt? I mean, now the crisis is over?"

He scuffed his boot heel against the top step. "I'll stay until Luke's ready to leave. Maybe I'll send for Sadie to come out and join me. She's never been to Dodge."

"And Bat?"

"He'll stay awhile, too. By the time we're ready to leave Dodge, it'll be time for you to head back to New York."

It had been so long since she'd thought about going home, Katy was stunned. A week was all she had left.

Chapter Twenty-six

On the desk beside Katy's manuscript was the chemise Rait had cut off her. She hadn't seen it since Bat arrived. Its presence on the desk was a surprise. When she went to pick it up, her gun, a box of cartridges, and a note fell from between the folds.

Katy darling,
Keep this close in case you ever need to protect the little bit of you that belongs to me.
Don't carry it loaded, honey.

Bat

She smiled at his sweetness, then folded everything, including the note, back into the chemise and tucked it into the bottom of her carpetbag. Because of this morning's ransacking of the desk by Rait, she also put her manuscript in the bag, along with the photographs of her and Bat.

"Just to be safe," she told her reflection in the mirror. Rait would no doubt have a few choice words to say about her presence in the Long Branch tonight. She didn't want to add fuel to a fire that was most likely already out of control.

She flirted with her fringe-decorated mirror image before taking off her Calamity Jane jacket and carefully hanging it on a hook behind the door.

When Rait came back to the hotel a half hour later, she'd washed, brushed her hair, and was putting on her nightgown. He stormed into the room, threw a caustic glance at her, and said, "Get dressed. We're leaving."

She stopped trying to tie the ribbon closure on her gown. "We're what?"

He grabbed her carpetbag and began stuffing everything in sight into it. "Leaving," he said. "Checking out. Going back to Silverton."

"Now? In the middle of the night?"

"In fifteen minutes on the 2:50 A.M. train. Get dressed!" he ordered. The scattered items on top of the bureau were swept into the bag.

"Why?"

"Because I said so." He was going through the drawers now.

"But why? Are you angry with Bat again? Are you angry with me? Did Marshal Bridges throw you out of town?"

335

Rait's mad rush stalled. "Just this once," he said in a tight voice, "don't argue with me and don't ask questions, Katy. Just do as I ask."

"You didn't ask. You ordered."

He turned to face her. "Then I'll ask. Will you please stop stalling so we can catch that train?"

"Yes," she said, knowing if she refused, he would just throw her over his shoulder like an unwilling wench and carry her off into the night, anyway. It had taken a lot of years and effort to get to Dodge City. She didn't want to leave it like a sack of pirate loot.

While she put on the pantalettes and chemise she'd worn tonight, along with the petticoats and burgundy traveling dress she barely managed to save from being wadded into the carpetbag, Rait went into room 24 and stripped it of everything including the towel beside the washstand. Katy was surprised he didn't pack the washbowl and water pitcher, too.

"I want to leave Bat a note. He'll be worried when he gets up in the morning and we're gone."

The whistle of the approaching train split the silence.

"We don't have time for notes," Rait said.

He pushed her into the hall and was closing the door when she suddenly cried, "Wait!" and ran back inside.

"Katy, we don't have time!"

She came running out with her leather jacket cradled in her arms. "I almost forgot it."

Rait lifted his gaze from the jacket to the shadows clouding her eyes. He put his hand on the side of her face and brushed his thumb across her soft skin. "I'm glad you remembered it. Is there anything else I didn't pack?"

"The bed, but I don't want to overload my carpetbag, so maybe we'd better leave it." She pushed past him and down the steps. He closed the door to room 22 and followed her.

The train pulled slowly out of Dodge City, almost as though it was as reluctant to leave as Katy.

They were in a day car. There was only one other passenger, an old man in a sweat stained Stetson slumped in a seat near the front of the car. He snored softly as Dodge fell farther and farther behind.

Katy turned her face to the window and watched the nighttime landscape rush past. Trees. The river. A lonely house with a light in the front window.

"Why?" she asked Rait. He was sitting in the aisle seat beside her, arms crossed, hat pulled low across his eyes.

He didn't answer.

"I have a right to know," she said, and could almost feel the sigh her insistence forced out of him.

"Jack Bridges offered me a job."

Oh. Katy closed her eyes and tried not to hear Angie's whispery voice telling Rait to forget his schoolboy dreams.

"Jack's quitting and Deger told him to appoint his own replacement."

"I think telling him 'no' would have been sufficient. Running all the way back to Silverton isn't necessary."

"I'm not running."

"Yes, you are. You're running because you think it's your fault Angie went back to that woman. Not wearing a badge won't change what she was. It never could."

"I don't want to talk about Angie. She's not part of my life anymore."

"Then why are we on this train? Isn't it because you wanted to take the job Bridges offered you and the only way you could refuse was to get as far away from it as these tracks can take you?"

"Let it go, Katy."

"I can't do that, Rait. I can't let it go because you won't let her go. You're still trying to save her, still trying to hold on so you don't have to face the truth. Angie didn't go back to that woman because you wouldn't quit the law. She went back because she wanted to be with that woman instead of you. Your badge was her excuse, not her reason."

"My badge," he said, and his voice was like poison. "That's all you want, isn't it? A man with a star on his chest. I should have left you back in Dodge with Bat. You'd have a better chance of convincing him to pin a star on again than you'll ever have with me."

Katy's hands were shaking. She curled them into fists and willed herself not to cry.

"Is that why you think I made love with you, because you use to wear a badge or because I think you might wear one again someday? All the stars west of the Mississippi couldn't make me want the bad-tempered, disagreeable bully you act like most of the time. I wanted you because underneath all that ugliness I saw a man who was tender and patient and loving. A man who was willing to put up with me to repay a debt that allowed him to bury his father in a coffin. A man who used his own napkin to wipe meringue off my lips even though I'd embarrassed him by acting like a spoiled child. A man who wanted desperately to turn his back on a request for help from his friends so he'd have another chance to punish himself for his wife's desertion, but who followed his heart instead.

339

That's the man I made love to, the one who believes in tilting at windmills instead of drowning in guilt." She stood. "Let me by. I need some air."

The observation platform at the back of the train was shrouded in shadows. Katy stood against the back railing watching the tracks flow out from beneath her feet like the wake of a boat in dark water.

The rhythm of the wheels pounded at her. The wind caught at the fringe on her jacket and whipped it up against her face. And her heart. It ached.

The door to the observation platform opened and closed. He stood behind her. She could feel him there, could feel how much he wanted to reach out to her. She turned to look at him. There was pain on his face, sorrow and shadows.

"She begged me, Katy. I could have saved her, but I didn't."

"Now I'm begging you. Stop running away from what you want."

"All I want is you."

Three weeks ago, he'd been nothing more than a dream she was afraid would never come true. She lifted her hand to his face and touched the warm reality of him and told herself that he was all she wanted in the world.

But, it was a lie.

340

Katy wanted her dreams: Not fairytales with fantasy endings of "happily ever after." Not storybook heroes who never had problems. Not romantic imaginings where tomorrow never comes because there is only now, only today.

Katy wanted tomorrow. She wanted obstacles to overcome. She wanted to reach and strive and quest for everything she'd ever wanted and all that she could find. She wanted to live a life that fulfilled her, a life that was more than just today. She wanted a life that stretched out before her like a road waiting to be traveled to the horizon . . . and beyond.

That's what dreams were—believing in today and reaching for tomorrow.

He covered her hand with his. "We can make this work between us, Katy. If you want it half as much as I want you, we can make it work. We don't need a badge. We don't need anything except what we have right now."

"What do we have? What I feel when you touch me? What you feel when you want me? Is that enough for you, Rait? It's not for me. I want more. I want a home and children. I want you to know and share my dreams. And I want to know yours. I want to share them, not watch you run from them."

"I love you, Katy."

That almost stopped her. She wanted so desperately for it to be enough. It would take more than just words, though, to make her abandon the hope that she could have all of Rait, not just the part Angie didn't want.

"Right now what we feel is golden and beautiful," Katy said, "like the dandelions the day I arrived in Silverton. But just like you knew they would die, I know what we feel will die, too, and it will be Angie who kills it. Every time I look at you, Rait, I see her. She's there in your eyes now, refusing to let you live your life the way you want to. You don't deserve the hairshirt of guilt you're wearing. When I see how miserable it makes you, I resent it, and I resent you for not being able to let it go. Because of that resentment, one day we'd wake up and all that would be left of what we feel now is the memory of how it used to be. I don't want just memories. I want forever."

He was still holding her hand. He bent it behind her and pulled her full against him. He lowered his mouth to hers.

"I love you, Katy," he whispered against her lips. "Now. Tomorrow. Forever. I want you to be my wife. I want you to have my children. I want you."

And he kissed her, filling her with his heart and his soul and his need. He lifted her up and pressed her back against the railing of the observation car. Wrapping his arms around her, he held her there between him and the world, protecting her from everything except the reason they were on this train.

"Please," she whispered when he moved his kiss to her eyes, her face, her hair and throat.

Please let her go, Katy wanted to say. *Please stop running.* But those, too, were just words. She had only one chance to make her wish come true, and that was to risk losing him completely. But right now while his arms were around her and the time for decisions was still miles away, she could taste heaven once more.

"Please make love to me," she said, and he held his head against her breast as he warmed her with kisses and breathed fire into her heart.

In the wind and the darkness, standing at the rear of the car with the almost empty coach behind them and the rhythm of the train filling their heads with noise and madness, he put his hands on her skirt. Then he lifted the flowing folds of velvet and drew apart the split crotch of her pantalettes and touched her. His fingers touched her, felt her, stroked her. He made her ache, made her cry out, made her cry.

His mouth was on her breast, touching her dress, wetting her chemise, exciting the core of her soul.

His body, big and hard, pressed against her.

Holding her with his power, he possessed her with his passion.

He entered her, filled her, and lifted her. He had a burning purpose: Making her want him. Making her need him. Making her forever his with just his touch, and his love.

And when the heat was upon them, when the passion and the fire were consuming them, when all they should be thinking of was the splendor, Katy could not forget that this might be the last time.

When it was over and he was holding her warm and safe in his arms, she pressed her face against his shirt and touched a kiss to his heart so she could feel it beating against her lips.

"I love you, Rait," she whispered. Her words were so wet with tears, he could feel them against his skin.

Chapter Twenty-seven

They reached Pueblo at one o'clock in the afternoon and transferred to the narrow gauge line of the Denver and Rio Grande Railroad.

It was an hour and a half before the D&RG left for Silverton. Rait hadn't slept in three days and was numb with exhaustion. When the conductor refused to make up berths in the Pullman sleeper car for him and Katy because it would "disturb the other passengers, sir," Rait rented the whole car, ordered their berths made up, and went immediately to sleep.

Katy lay in her berth across the aisle and watched him. He was too tired to be restless. Still, his sleep was not peaceful. The agony of his flight from Dodge lay heavy across his features. And it lay heavy in her heart.

When their car was coupled onto the main D&RG train, the noise and fitful lurch of the Pullman brought Rait awake. Katy was standing in the aisle beside him.

"What is it?" he asked.

"We're switching tracks. The train will be leaving in a few minutes." She brushed the hair back from his forehead and smiled into his eyes. "I'm going out to buy a piece of chocolate from the trainboys before we leave the station. Do you want anything?"

"Just you."

She touched her lips to his, closed her eyes, and tried to memorize the way it felt to kiss him softly. When she started to turn away, he tangled his fingers in her hair and studied her face for a long moment.

"I love you, Katy."

She pressed her face against his neck so he wouldn't see her cry. "I know," she whispered.

Rait slept twelve straight hours. When he woke, the D&RG train was four and a half hours out of Durango and laboring up the side of one of the numerous mountains that made the trip from Pueblo to the San Juans so tediously long.

He got out of his berth to stretch his legs and check on Katy. Her berth was empty, her carpetbag gone.

For a long moment he just stared at the emptiness. Then he opened the door to the car and began his search. He found the conductor in the dining car drinking coffee with the brakeman. On the table between them lay a dandelion.

"Where is she?" Rait asked.

"The young lady left the train in Pueblo, sir. She said I was to give you this flower when you woke." He handed the dandelion to Rait.

It was wilted and its butter yellow brightness was beginning to fade.

"She said something else, too," the conductor said. "It was a bit strange, so I wrote it down." He pulled his ticket punch out of his pocket, a packet of Smith Brothers cough drops, and a scrap of paper. "Here it is. I said I'd put the flower in water until you woke and she said no, 'the only way to keep it alive is to stop running.' " The conductor looked from the paper to Rait. "I don't know what the young lady meant by that, sir."

"It means she was looking for a hero." His fingers closed around the dying flower. "And all she found was a weed."

Chapter Twenty-eight

The gentle swaying of the train kept threatening to put Katy to sleep. No matter how much she wanted it to succeed, though, she stayed steadfastly awake.

She was alone in the AT&SF railcar as it sped east across the rolling Kansas landscape. Just as Rait had refused to share his car to Silverton with strangers, so Katy had refused to share hers to New York. She needed to be alone while she came to terms with the possible consequences of the drastic action she'd taken in Pueblo.

Renting a whole Pullman sleeping car had been expensive. When Katy left Rait in Pueblo, she'd had $5.73.

She could have wired Basil Pellingham, but she'd only had an hour to catch the next eastbound train. It would have taken days to convince her uncle's secretary this really was an emergency and she really did need funds wired to her. By then, Rait might have found her. Because she would never have the strength to leave him twice, she'd been desperate to get out of Colorado as quickly as possible.

The reason she left Rait was because she believed it was the only way to make him understand how important it was to her that he live his life his way and not Angie's. Katy also needed to know that his pledge to love her forever included all of him, not just the part that wanted her in his bed.

Since watching his train roll away from her in Pueblo, she'd questioned her reasoning so many times, she was sick with worry. Despite her besieging doubt, though, Katy knew deep inside the only way she could ever be certain she had all of him was to risk losing him entirely.

Aside from Basil Pellingham, the only person she could have wired for help was Bat. Right now, though, she couldn't face even him.

A knock on the Pullman car's door was followed by the entrance of the conductor. "Dodge City is our next stop, Miss Halliday."

"You'll have the message I gave you delivered to the hotel?"

"Yes, and I'll see that you're not disturbed while we're at the station."

"Thank you," Katy said, and listened to the latch snap close as he left.

The whistle, the brakes, the squeal of metal wheels against dark metal tracks, then, a complete stop.

Katy didn't raise the shades on her windows. She sat in the semidarkness and listened to the people getting off the train, hearing their voices, and their laughter. Music was playing somewhere, a tinkling, tinny sound. It reminded her of the event which finally brought her to the city of her dreams, and had caused her to realize the only dream that mattered was the one she'd already found, and was now leaving behind.

She listened to the noise of the water tower beside the station emptying its reservoir into the engine, the thunder of a baggage car door being opened and closed. The time ticked slowly away until the train's whistle blew again and the wheels began to roll.

As the train pulled out of the station, Katy's letter to Bat was being delivered. She closed her eyes and tried to imagine his laughter when he read what she'd done instead of wire him for help when she was stranded in Pueblo.

The first thing she did was take inventory of her belongings. Rait had piled a strange assortment of debris into her carpetbag, including his Bowie knife. Selling it wouldn't have bought her a ticket to Dodge, though, much less fare to New York. Even selling her gun wouldn't get her past Kansas City.

The only other thing of value Katy possessed was an intimate knowledge of how deeply the American public loved the lore and legends of the Wild West.

It was one of those legends that paid her way home.

Dearest Bat,

I carved twenty-eight notches in the handle of my Colt and sold it to a fool in Pueblo who believes everything he reads. Now I'm on my way home. It wasn't Rait's rules that drove me away, though. It was his guilt.

Katy

p.s. Notches twenty-seven and twenty-eight are explained in the enclosed article.

The article came from the *Commonwealth*. It detailed the "gruesome killing of two men by the redoubtable Bat Masterson in the Long Branch Saloon in Dodge City. Hundreds of shots were fired during the blazing gun battle. 'It looked like the Fourth of July in there,' stated a reliable witness. When the shooting was over, Bat Masterson strolled away into the night while his victims were dragged out by their boot heels. With the former Dodge City lawman during his latest killing spree was a dance hall girl known locally as Lacy Katy. While blood was being spilled by the bucketful all around her, the mannishly dressed Katy swilled liquor and made eyes at her man. Last evening's tragic deaths offer further confirmation that Bat Masterson, whose body count now totals twenty-eight, is the most dangerous man in America."

As proof that Katy knew Bat, and therefore had access to his famous notched gun, she'd had only to display the Silverton photographs.

Immediately following his viewing of the photos, the buyer, who owned a gunshop in Pueblo and had Western memorabilia littering every inch of counter space in his store, had eagerly paid Katy the exorbitant price of $500 for the infamous notched Colt. As the money was counted into her hand, she'd gazed at the feathered warbonnets mounted on the wall beside her and wondered if any of them were real.

The train picked up speed, carrying Katy further away from not only the man she loved, but also the true friends and the real West which she'd come to know and cherish. For the thousandth time since she picked that dandelion beside the tracks in Pueblo, she wondered if she would ever see any of them again.

Chapter Twenty-nine

Katy lifted her Gypsy print scarf from her smallest travel trunk and pressed it against her face. It smelled of Colorado. It smelled of Blair Street dances and midnight walks beneath starry skies. It smelled of the "Shoo Fly" and "Skip to My Lou." It smelled of Rait; hair tumbled, eyes laughing and full of fun, his hand holding hers; she wanting so much for him to kiss her.

Before Katy left Pueblo two months ago, she'd wired the Grand Hotel in Silverton to express her luggage via Wells Fargo to New York. All her trunks, gripsacks, and hatboxes had arrived at her uncle's suite in the Astor House hotel a few days after she did. Until this morning, she'd been unable to look at the mountain of baggage, much less open it and begin putting away the things that reminded her of Rait.

This morning, though, she finally slipped the lock on the small trunk and began sorting through the memories. She'd been at it for over an hour. The Gypsy scarf was only the third item she'd unpacked.

"Katy Alice."

She lowered the scarf, turned, and threw her arms around her uncle's neck.

He smoothed the hair back from her face and kissed her forehead. "I thought you were doing better."

"So did I." She showed him the scarf. "It smells of Colorado. Here we have odors. In Silverton, there are scents. The wind, the river. Flowers and rocks and moonlight and evening dew and fresh cut wood and sun-warmed bark. Everything I unpack smells like that, Uncle Richard. Everything smells like heaven."

"Close the trunk, Katy. Close it up and we'll throw it away. We'll throw them all away and everything in them."

"We can't do that!"

"You can buy a whole new wardrobe. It's been what, almost four months since you bought this one? It's probably time for a new one anyway."

Katy hugged the Gypsy scarf to her. "I can't throw this away. I can't throw any of it away. My blue dress is in there, the one I wore my first night to dinner with him. And the pinafore I wore to the dance and the yellow suit I was wearing when we first met and the black lace . . ." Her voice broke.

Her uncle took her in his arms again and let her silent sobs shake them both.

"You have to stop doing this, Katy Alice. You can't keep torturing yourself by thinking of him. It's been two months. You have to face it, Rait's not coming after you."

She shook her head. "You're wrong. He'll come. I know he will. It's just taking longer than I thought, that's all."

"I have an idea. It's almost noon. Why don't you leave all this for now and we'll go downstairs to the rotunda restaurant for lunch? Francois can open us some fresh oysters. That always used to cheer you up."

Katy sniffed. "Lunch is a good idea, but not the oysters. I want frog legs instead."

Because Richard Halliday believed in using his legs instead of the Astor House elevator, when he and Katy went downstairs — they went down the stairs!

She grew up in this hotel and everyday since she'd learned to walk had either skipped down the staircase, dashed headlong down it, or, when she was really in a hurry, slid down the banister. Since returning from the West, she'd sedately walked.

356

Her demeanor was having an unnerving effect on the staff, who worried that she was either sick or growing up. Both were equally calamitous. Katy had provided more enjoyment to the hotel employees than any guest the Astor House had ever known.

Now, as she walked quietly at her uncle's side, she didn't notice the worried glances from her friends who worked for the hotel. She barely even noticed her uncle. Her gaze was on the people checking in at the registry desk and wandering around the lobby and heading to the rotunda for lunch. A search of their faces didn't reveal the one person she was hoping to see.

There was another person who caught her attention. A redoubtable sort of person who carried a gold-headed cane and wore an elegantly cut suit with a diamond stickpin, a perfectly coiffured moustache, and a pearl-gray bowler.

"Bat!" Katy cried. Her demure demeanor disappeared as she threw herself down the remaining stairs, raced across the lobby, and flung herself into his arms. "Oh, Bat, I can't believe it!" She hugged him so hard, she could feel his laughter tickling the top of her head.

"I missed you, too, honey." He smiled down into her sparkling face while everyone in the

357

lobby stared at them first in astonishment at their brazen behavior, then in disbelief as recognition slowly dawned.

"My God, that's really him!"

"I can't believe it, he's a real person."

"Do you think he's wearing a gun?"

"What's he doing here? Who's that girl with him?"

Katy's excitement suddenly waned. "What are you doing here? Is Rait all right?" Her heart stopped beating. "Is he with you?"

"No, honey, but he is all right, or was when I left Silverton five days ago. You haven't heard from him?"

She had to fight her tears while she shook her head. "I'm glad you're here." She pressed her face against the front of his suit coat. "I thought I'd never see you again."

"What a silly notion. I told you once, the trains go everywhere and I like to go with them. New York's a little farther east than I usually go, but I'm not about to let a few miles stand in the way of seeing my favorite dime novel writer again. Honey, could you come up for air for a minute and introduce me to this man glaring at us?"

"Oh!" She gave her uncle a guilty smile. "I forgot all about you. This is my uncle Richard Halliday. And this, dear uncle, is the man you didn't really believe I met, even though I had photographs to prove it; the one, the only, the infamous Bat Masterson."

"Be careful with those superlatives, honey. Someone here might ask me to live up to them and then I'd have to spend the rest of my stay in New York in the hoosegow." Bat put out his hand to shake Richard's. "Did you really doubt Katy meeting me? You should be ashamed. She's the most honest person I've ever known."

Richard Halliday looked almost as incredulous as the rest of the people in the lobby. "Katy runs a bit on the warm side of extreme with her stories sometimes. It wasn't that I actually doubted her, I just didn't completely believe her."

"Good Lord," Bat said. "You sound like her."

"It's in the water," Katy said.

"Then I'll stick to whiskey while I'm here."

"We were just on our way to lunch," Richard said. "Come join us."

"Let me guess," Bat said. "Grizzly bear steaks."

Katy laughed. "Unfortunately, no. I asked Francois to order some, but he refused. He won't cook anything bigger than he is."

When Bat met the chef a few minutes later, he roared out a laugh that shook the plates on the table. "Not even a grizzly is that big," he said and let go another laugh.

The parlor in Richard Halliday's suite in the Astor House was so quiet Katy could hear the clock ticking on the table in her bedroom.

"How was Clayton Ogsbury killed?" she asked in response to Bat's unbelievable news about Silverton's marshal.

After the Fourth of July celebration while the hoopla and wild doings inspired by the holiday were still running hot in the blood of some of the attenders, a few men with calloused gun hands who had come to Silverton for the gala events started making trouble. Marshal Ogsbury doubled his patrols and, while walking one of those patrols himself, was murdered by a pair of toughs.

The citizens of Silverton were so enraged by the cold-blooded killing of their valiant marshal, a mob tried to extract justice from the end of a rope and lynched an innocent man. The town council had to wrest control of Silverton from the mob by brute force. Rait Caldwell had played a major role in subduing the vigilante madness gripping Silverton. Immediately after peace was restored, the town council offered him the job of marshal.

"He accepted," Bat said.

Katy wasn't certain she'd understood him correctly. She stood and walked to the fireplace. With one hand gripping the mantel, she turned to Bat for confirmation of what her heart couldn't believe. The gentleness in his gaze, and his regret at having to be the bearer of the news, told her that it was indeed true. Rait was finally wearing a badge again, but it wasn't hope that she should feel. It was horror.

"How long ago?" she asked, the question whispering its way past the ache in her throat and chest.

"Two weeks, honey."

It was a nightmare. She'd wanted this so much. She'd wanted it for Rait. Only now it had come true, she wasn't happy that he was finally free from his guilt. All she felt was a loss unlike anything she'd ever imagined.

"When he didn't immediately leave for New York, I expected to see you arriving in Silverton a week later," Bat said. "When you didn't show, I asked him what happened. He said he didn't wire you. I caught the next train out of town and headed straight here. I was afraid you might have subscribed to one of the Silverton newspapers and would read about his taking the job. I couldn't bear to have you find out that way, honey."

"He didn't come after me," she said, still not believing it. She looked at her uncle. His love

361

for her and the pain he felt for her was so obvious on his face that she couldn't bear to breathe. "I really believed he'd come, Uncle Richard."

He held out his arms to her, but Bat reached her first and caught her as she started to sink to the floor. He pulled her to him and held her close, cradling her while her body shook with sobs, and her tears spilled onto his shirt like a rainshower.

"I'm sorry, honey."

"No," she said. "You don't have to be sorry. I took a chance. It didn't work, at least not for me. I'm glad Rait's doing what he wanted. That's more important to me than anything, his happiness, that he's finally free of Angie. I'm just surprised, that's all. I really thought he loved me, Bat."

As she said the words, she heard again, as she had a million times in the last two months, the insistent knocking on the door of Lilly Gold's crib the night Katy went looking for Doc Holliday.

Rait had called Lilly's name while he knocked. He'd known it was her door. And Lilly had known it was Rait calling to her. "It's the marshal," she'd said. But if it had been Clayton Ogsbury, there would have been no reason to warn Katy to stay out of sight.

362

She closed her eyes tight, trying to shut out the memory of the hazy light in Lilly's crib, her narrow bed, the seductive clothing in Lilly's back room.

"Cry it out, honey," Bat said as he rubbed her back. "When you're through, I'll go back to Silverton and shoot him."

Katy tried to smile as she looked up at him through wet lashes and puddled tears.

"Finished already?" he asked in surprise. "I thought this might take hours."

"Your stickpin hurts."

He laughed.

Her uncle gave her a handkerchief. She used it to try to staunch her flow of tears, but she was beginning to think she'd sprung a permanent leak. It was hard to believe there were this many tears left in her after all the ones she'd shed in the last two months.

Bat put his arm around her shoulders. He pulled her with him to the sofa, where he sat and drew her down into his arms again. "Feel better?" he asked after she went through both her uncle's handkerchief and his.

She nodded yes, then shook her head no.

"Tell me something," he said. "Did you really carve twenty-eight notches in the handle of your gun?"

Katy started to laugh. She laid her head on

Bat's shoulder and let the laughter and tears spill out together. "I had a blister the size of a quarter on the palm of my hand from wedging Rait's knife into that hard rubber. I thought Uncle Richard was going to give me a few blisters someplace else when I told him what I did."

"I couldn't believe it," Richard said. "I sent the man his money back with an apology."

"You probably broke his heart," Katy said. "Imagine thinking you owned the most famous gun in the world, only to find out you've been hornswoggled. He probably shot himself in the head with it."

Bat laughed. "That would make a great book, honey. You could call it *Lacy Katy and the Twenty-Eight Notches, or, The Gullible Gun Dealer and the Good-Looking Girl.*"

"There aren't going to be any more books. Rait was right, Bat. I'm a terrible writer. I realized it on that long trip home when I didn't have anything to read except my own manuscripts. My scenes are choppy and the stories aren't great, either, although the ones I wrote out West are infinitely better than the ones I used to write."

"You can't give up writing, honey. It's your dream. Don't let Rait Caldwell spoil it for you,

364

Katy."

"I haven't given it up, Bat. I'd never do that, but I'm not trying to awe the world with my talent anymore." She smiled. "At least, not for awhile. I'm going to learn how to do it right first. Instead of just reading dime novels, now I'm studying them, learning what works and what doesn't. When I'm ready to try one again, not even Rait will be able to find fault with it."

Her heart broke when she realized that when she was ready to try again, Rait wouldn't be there to share the moment with her.

A knock on the door to the suite drew Richard Halliday out of the room. Katy drew a shaky breath and let it out in an even shakier sigh before pulling away from Bat's comforting embrace so she could face him. She wanted to see his answer to what she was planning to ask, not just hear it.

"Will Rait be safe, Bat? I mean, will what happened to Clayton Ogsbury happen to him?"

Bat scowled. "Rait deserves to be shot for treating you like this, honey. He's not good enough for you. He never was. I should have shot him that first day on the train right after he rescued you, then carried you off for myself."

"Can you imagine the two of us together?" Katy laughed. "We'd drive everyone around us crazy. We'd wear each other out."

He gave her the most deliciously devilish grin she'd ever seen. "I don't know about that, honey. I have a lot of stamina. Whores charge me triple rates for taking up so much of their time."

She blushed so suddenly, she could feel her face burning. "Oh, you," she said and punched him in the shoulder to stop herself from giggling in embarrassment.

Richard Halliday came back in the room carrying a basket. He took one look at Katy and Bat, and frowned. "What are you two doing?"

"Bat's being silly. What's that?"

"The bellboy just delivered it. It's for you."

She took the basket. It was big enough to hold a picnic lunch. A piece of beautiful, delicate lace covered its contents. When she lifted the lace, she saw dandelions. Hundreds of them. Each as bright and beautiful as a droplet of yellow sunshine, and as fresh as if they'd been picked only moments ago.

"The boy who delivered them said there was a message, too, Katy Alice. You're to look out the window at Broadway and Park Row." Those were the major streets on whose intersecting corner the Astor House stood.

The dandelions blurred in Katy's vision as she tried to come to terms with what they meant.

366

She looked up at her uncle, then Bat. "Does this mean . . . is he here?"

"I'm in the dark, honey," Bat said. "Rait was still in Silverton when I left."

Katy set the basket down and ran to a window. She threw it open and leaned out so far her uncle had to grab her to keep her from falling.

The street below was normally frantic with traffic. It was used as a terminal in lower Manhattan for the horsecar lines that spanned the city. Dozens of tracks were set into the pavement in large loops to allow the cars to be turned in the broad intersection.

Every other mode of transportation in New York passed through here, too, for not only was the Astor House one of the most popular hotels in town, but right across a small side street from it was historic St. Paul's Church. The small shops fronting the Astor also drew a lot of business, plus the corner was located in New York's busy printing district.

But the street outside the Astor wasn't buzzing with traffic today. In the middle of the broad intersection stood a bedraggled white horse that looked as though it had spent too many years dragging a milk wagon around the city. Its head hung almost to the pavement, its tail was limp and yellow with age, and the poor creature appeared to be trying to stand with all its weight on one leg so it could rest the other three.

Sitting astride this pitiful beast's back was the strangest apparition Katy had ever beheld. A knight-errant in dented and mismatched armor who was holding a lance so big, the front of it drooped onto the street like a bedraggled banner.

She started to cry again, this time with joy.

"Is that Rait?" her uncle asked. He was still holding onto her while he tried to see through the window above her. She was crying and laughing too hard to answer, so she nodded.

"What's he supposed to be?" Bat asked. He was trying to get the other parlor window open.

"Don Quixote," Katy said.

Rait was trying to raise his visor. The sound of Katy's laughter drifting down to him renewed his determination to unhinge the rusty thing. Seconds later, he was looking up unencumbered at her beautiful face. All his carefully prepared words were lost in that moment of complete happiness. He just sat on his unsteady steed and gazed into that beloved face smiling at him from the third floor of the Astor House.

"You look ridiculous!" she shouted down at him.

"Do you have any idea how long it took me

to find this armor?"

"Two weeks," she said and he was so surprised, he almost dropped his lance.

"I sent telegraphs to every museum in the country trying to borrow a complete suit. All I could come up with were spare parts from a half dozen places. I'll never remember which part came from where when I try to return them."

Katy leaned her elbows on the windowsill and gazed down at his wonderful face. "We'll figure it out on our honeymoon."

He cocked an eyebrow at her. "You're presuming a lot, aren't you?"

"For the last two months, I've been presuming a lot. Now I'm only presuming one thing."

He grinned. "And what might that be, pretty lady?"

Even from three stories below, he could see the twinkle of delight in her eyes as she pointed behind him. "You're about to be arrested by that officer for obstructing traffic and making a public nuisance of yourself."

"Not a chance. I have a special permit from city hall to block traffic at this intersection, to carry a lance inside the city limits, and to shout certain statements at a certain rich girl hanging out of a fancy hotel room window like an upstairs girl in a Blair Street brothel."

She laughed. "And what, Sir Knight of the Mournful Countenance, is it that you are permitted to shout at this brazen girl?"

"I'm not running anymore, Katy. Somewhere underneath this metal plating is a badge. My badge."

He looked so proud. There was something more, though. He looked at rest, as though he finally had his soul back.

"I love you, Katy, and I want to marry you."

She could barely see him for the tears that filled her eyes.

"And I wish there was a windmill around here so I could tilt at it for you."

"My hero," she said.

His smile made her heart ache with happiness. Her own smile suddenly faltered. "I thought you weren't coming."

His gaze was tender and loving. "It just took a little longer than we both expected."

"Did it take this long for you to run after Angie?"

He looked puzzled. "Who?"

Katy smiled. "That, Rait Caldwell, is the nicest thing you've ever said to me. And yes, I will marry you, and I wish there was a windmill around here, too, because I've always wondered what tilting looked like. But since there's not, you'll have to do something else heroic to prove yourself worthy of me."

"Like what?"

She grinned. "Court me."

"Court you? Isn't this getup enough?"

She shook her head. "You have to quote poetry, or sing love songs, or kiss the back of my hand."

He hoisted the sagging lance a little higher under his arm while he considered his options. "I can't reach your hand and I can't sing. What poetry do I know?"

"What's he doing?" Bat had stopped trying to open the other window and was trying to see out Katy's.

She pulled part of the way back into the parlor so he could hear her. "He's trying to think of some poetry to quote."

Richard Halliday sighed in disgust. "I never should have trusted you with that man, Katy Alice. He's obviously crazy."

"I know," she said with a smile. "I've known that ever since he told me I was eating snake eggs. I think I fell in love with him while I was throwing up. He'd been acting like such a glowering, unpleasant, bad-tempered beast, but he held me while I was sick, then told me he'd lied about the eggs just to irritate me. It was such a silly thing for a man dressed like a desperado to do, I couldn't help falling in love with him."

371

"Ridiculous," Bat said. "What's he saying now?"

"It's Shakespeare." She turned her attention back to Rait.

"I want to hear this," Bat said. He pushed her over so he could lean out the window beside her. Richard Halliday stayed where he was, holding onto Katy and looking out the top glass.

". . . through yonder window breaks?"

"Not very imaginative, is he?" Bat said to Katy.

She blushed. "He has his moments."

". . . It is the east, and . . . Bat?" Rait jerked so hard on the reins, his poor horse almost toppled over in surprise. "What the hell are you doing up there, Masterson?"

"I didn't think you wanted Katy, so I came to console her."

"You mean you came to seduce her."

Katy looked at Bat. "Did you?"

He pretended to be offended by the idea. "It never crossed my mind."

"Too bad." She gave an excellent imitation of his earlier devilish grin. "It crossed mine."

He laughed. "Are you really in love with that jackass down there, honey?"

Katy turned her smile to Rait. "I really am. Hey, you down there! Are you going to climb up the side of the Astor House and kiss me now?"

Rait was pushing at his helmet again. His ears were sweating. "No, I'm going to come inside, pry myself out of this tin can, take the elevator upstairs and kiss you, as soon as I can figure out how to get off Rosinante without killing both of us with this lance."

One of the officers who had been holding back traffic for Rait came to assist. The horse should have looked relieved when freed of his burden, but the beast had fallen asleep and didn't seem to even notice. While Rait clanked his way inside the Astor's lobby, Katy and Bat pulled their heads inside.

"I'll go downstairs to be certain Andrew doesn't try to chuck him out," Richard said. "I'm happy for you, Katy Alice. I'm also worried about you."

She hugged him. "You've been worrying about me for nineteen years, Uncle Richard, and I love you for it."

When she and Bat were alone, she turned to him. All trace of her earlier lightheartedness was gone. "I asked you a question that you never answered. I want an answer now, Bat. Will Rait be safe?"

"No," he said and her heart fell. She wanted sweet lies, not the pale, stark truth. "But he does have a better chance of staying alive than most men with a badge, honey. Rait's smart and he's good with a gun. Those are the two most important factors for a lawman's survival."

"I've never been afraid of anything in my life," she said, "but I'm afraid now, Bat. He'll be out there every day and every night risking his life. I don't know what I'd do if I lost him."

Bat brushed away a tear glowing like a pearl on her soft cheek. "He'll be all right, Katy."

She tried to smile. "Do you promise?"

"Yes, honey. I promise." He let his hand fall away from her face. "I've been thinking of staying in Silverton for awhile. If anyone starts trouble, I'll just join in the fight and see that Rait makes it out all right."

She threw her arms around him. "Thank you."

He accepted her embrace a little stiffly. "Shouldn't you be saving all this hugging for Rait?"

"I'll always have enough for you, too." She looked up at him, and Bat almost laughed at the devilish light in her pretty eyes.

"What?" he asked.

"Before I go out that door and into the arms of the man I'm going to spend the rest of my life with, there's something I'd like to do first." Katy stretched up onto her toes and kissed him right on the lips. When she drew back, she laughed at his shocked expression. "Imagine what my grandchildren will say when I tell them I kissed Bat Masterson."

"Here's an even better one to tell them, sweet Katy," he said softly.

He took her in his arms, lowered his mouth to hers, and kissed her. Not a chaste kiss like she'd given him, but a full, deep, lingering, breathtakingly wonderful kiss that turned up the temperature in the room several degrees and threatened to melt the elastic in Katy's pantalettes. When he released her, she was physically and morally staggered.

He crossed his arms over his chest. "Now you can tell your grandchildren that Bat Masterson kissed you."

She blinked through the haze fogging her mind. "You . . . you do that rather well," she managed to say.

Bat's intentional hard-eyed expression faltered a little. "Katy, honey, it's not too late . . ." He was reaching for her again when the sound of Rait calling her name came through the open parlor door.

Katy's whole body seemed to come instantly alive. Her face glowed, the light in her eyes softened, and there would have been no doubt in anyone's mind who saw her at that moment, she was in love. But not with Bat.

He took a step back from her. "Go to him, honey."

She looked up at his dear, beloved face. "You're the best friend I've ever had," she said. Then, with her heart in her eyes and her happiness in her smile, she turned from him and ran out the door toward her future.

Richard Halliday left Rait alone in the hall to meet Katy. Young love was a personal thing. Their reunion belonged to them, not to stray relatives who didn't have the sense to get out of the way. Besides, Rait looked so much like his father, George Caldwell, Richard couldn't help remembering how he'd lost his one true love to George so many years ago.

Though Katy's happiness was Richard's primary concern, he couldn't help feeling a bit of resentment toward these Caldwell men who kept stealing his women.

When Richard entered the side door to the parlor, Bat Masterson was standing alone and looking like a man who had just lost a dream.

When he saw Richard, he assumed an immediate jaunty air as he picked up his hat and perched it on his head.

"Where are you off to now?" Richard asked.

"There must be a lot of opportunities for a man like you, both behind a badge and at a card table. It must be exciting to live the way you do, a new town every few days, adventures, excitement."

Bat adjusted his diamond stickpin and retrieved his gold-headed cane from the table beside the sofa. "I'll be settling in Silverton for awhile."

Richard was surprised. He would have bet money Bat would want to put as much distance as possible between him and Katy now that she would be marrying Rait.

"Any reason?" Richard asked.

Bat glanced at the doorway Katy had run through to go to Rait. "I have a promise to keep." He gave Richard Halliday a martyred smile. "It seems I've just volunteered to be Rait Caldwell's guardian angel. In a year or so, once those two have started a family, he'll most likely turn in his badge for a seat on the city council, or some equally boring, but safe, job. Then I'll move on." Bat turned to gaze out the window at the New York skyline. "It's a big world," he said quietly. "Surely somewhere out there is another girl with blue-gray eyes looking for a hero."

* * *

All Katy's fear, all her doubt, all her night-mares were over. The only thing she felt now was love and hope and, as she met Rait in the hall outside her uncle's suite, perfect joy.

He pulled her into his arms, brought her full against him, and wrapped himself in her touch and her love.

"Now I know what God was doing when He thought up the name for heaven," Rait said. "He was holding you."

Katy couldn't say anything. She just held onto him and let his embrace heal the heart she thought would be broken forever.

"I thought I'd die when I woke up on that train and realized you'd left me, Katy."

"I thought I'd die when I left you."

"Don't ever do it again," he whispered as he buried his face in her hair.

"I love you, Rait."

He held her tighter.

"You smell like rusty armor," she said and he laughed, lifted her up, and swung her around like a merry-go-round. Her ruffled skirts danced about her and her hair ribbons flew while her eyes sparkled with rainbows, and his heart overflowed with love.

Katy knew that there were no perfect "happily ever after" endings in real life. The only way to keep the love they felt now always fresh and beautiful was to work hard at it every day of their lives, and even that wasn't a guarantee.

But right this moment, with Rait holding her so close she could actually feel his heart beating against her own, Katy couldn't help but believe that fairy tales really do come true, and the two of them really would live happily ever after.

CATCH A RISING STAR!

ROBIN ST. THOMAS

FORTUNE'S SISTERS (2616, $3.95)

It was Pia's destiny to be a Hollywood star. She had complete self-confidence, breathtaking beauty, and the help of her domineering mother. But her younger sister Jeanne began to steal the spotlight meant for Pia, diverting attention away from the ruthlessly ambitious star. When her mother Mathilde started to return the advances of dashing director Wes Guest, Pia's jealousy surfaced. Her passion for Guest and desire to be the brightest star in Hollywood pitted Pia against her own family—sister against sister, mother against daughter. Pia was determined to be the only survivor in the arenas of love and fame. But neither Mathilde nor Jeanne would surrender without a fight. . . .

LOVER'S MASQUERADE (2886, $4.50)

New Orleans. A city of secrets, shrouded in mystery and magic. A city where dreams become obsessions and memories once again become reality. A city where even one trip, like a stop on Claudia Gage's book promotion tour, can lead to a perilous fall. For New Orleans is also the home of Armand Dantine, who knows the secrets that Claudia would conceal and the past she cannot remember. And he will stop at nothing to make her love him, and will not let her go again . . .

SENSATION (3228, $4.95)

They'd dreamed of stardom, and their dreams came true. Now they had fame and the power that comes with it. In Hollywood, in New York, and around the world, the names of Aurora Styles, Rachel Allenby, and Pia Decameron commanded immediate attention—and lust and envy as well. They were stars, idols on pedestals. And there was always someone waiting in the wings to bring them crashing down . . .

Available wherever paperbacks are sold, or order direct from the Publisher. Send cover price plus 50¢ per copy for mailing and handling to Zebra Books, Dept. 4028, 475 Park Avenue South, New York, N.Y. 10016. Residents of New York and Tennessee must include sales tax. DO NOT SEND CASH. For a free Zebra/ Pinnacle catalog please write to the above address.